I DON'T
EXPECT ANYONE
TO BELIEVE ME

I DON'T
EXPECT ANYONE
TO BELIEVE ME

Juan Pablo Villalobos

Translated by Daniel Hahn

SHEFFIELD – LONDON – NEW YORK

This edition first published in 2020 by And Other Stories
Sheffield – London – New York
www.andotherstories.org

First published as *No voy a pedirle a nadie que me crea* by Editorial Anagrama in 2016
Copyright © Juan Pablo Villalobos and Editorial Anagrama, 2016
English-language translation © Daniel Hahn, 2020
Translator's afterword © Daniel Hahn, 2020

9 8 7 6 5 4 3 2 1

ISBN: 9781911508489
eBook ISBN: 9781911508496

Editor: Bill Swainson; Copy-editor: Gesche Ipsen; Proofreader: Sarah Terry; Typesetter: Tetragon, London; Typefaces: Linotype Neue Swift and Verlag; Cover design: Elisa Von Randow. Printed and bound by CPI Group (UK) Ltd, Croydon, CRO 4YY.

And Other Stories gratefully acknowledge that our work is supported using public funding by Arts Council England.

CONTENTS

ONE

TWO

THREE

EPILOGUE

I DON'T
EXPECT ANYONE
TO BELIEVE ME

Humorousness is realism taken to its logical conclusion. With the exception of most humorous literature, everything man does is laughable or humorous.

AUGUSTO MONTERROSO

This city is so sad that, around here, when a person laughs, they do it badly.

NACHO VEGAS

Barcelona is home to a number of Mexicans, proper and discreet people, who, as we have seen, cause no trouble. It would never occur to me to expect them to have to affirm in their letters home or in their newspapers or magazines that Tibidabo fascinates them, or that we Catalans are amazing people.

PERE CALDERS

ONE

My cousin calls me up and says: I want to introduce you to my business partners. We agree to meet at five-thirty on Saturday at the Plaza México shopping center, outside the multiplex. When I arrive, there are three of them there, plus my cousin. All with dark fuzz on their upper lips (we're sixteen at this point, maybe seventeen), faces covered in spots oozing a viscous yellowish liquid, with four enormous noses (one apiece). They're in high school with the Jesuits. We shake hands. They ask me where I'm from, just assuming I can't be from Guadalajara, maybe because when we shook hands I kept my thumb pointed skyward. From Lagos, I say, I lived there till I was twelve. They don't know where that is. In Los Altos, I explain, three hours' drive away. My cousin says that's where his father's family is from, and that his father and my father are brothers. Ah, they say. We're fair-haired people from up in Los Altos, my cousin explains – as if we were some subspecies of the Mexican breed: *Blondus altensis* – and his business partners exchange glances, each in turn, with a sarcastic little glint in their upper-middle-class Guadalajaran eyes, or possibly lower-upper-class eyes, or possibly even aristocracy-come-down-in-the-world eyes.

So what's this business you guys are doing? I ask, before my cousin gets a chance to start detailing the genetic havoc wreaked by French soldiers during the Intervention, the nineteenth-century bastard origins of our eyes that are blue, and our hair that is blond, or at least light brown. A golf course, says my cousin. Over in Tenacatita, says one of the others. A piece of land that belongs to my friend's brother's father-in-law, says another. We're having lunch with him next week at the Industrialists' Club to present the project, says the one who hasn't spoken yet. They explain that the only problem's water, you need a huge amount of water to keep the greens green. But my cousin's neighbor's brother-in-law runs the public waterworks for the state, says another. That'll get fixed with a quick backhander, says another. Everybody nods, pimples bobbing up and down, totally certain. All we need is a capitalist partner, says my cousin finally, we got to raise two million dollars. I ask them how much they've managed to get hold of so far. They say thirty-five thousand new pesos. I do the calculation in my head, and it comes to something like fifteen thousand dollars (this is all happening in 1989). Thirty-seven, another corrects him, I've just gotten hold of another two thousand from my sister's friend's sister. They exchange congratulatory hugs for the two thousand new pesos. So, are we going to a movie or not? I ask, because my cousin and I usually go to the six o'clock screening on Saturdays. We discuss what's on the bill: there's an action movie with Bruce Willis and another with Chuck Norris. The two-thousand-new-pesos guy says there's nobody back at his place, his family's gone to spend the weekend in Tapalpa and he knows where his dad hides his stash of porn movies. And his house is nearby. Just behind the square. In Monraz. Why don't we check it out? Some pimples pop from the excitement, like purulent premature ejaculations.

Our host picks the movie. It's called *Hot Shrinks and Wild Kinks*. We draw lots for our turn to masturbate (every man for himself, one at a time). My cousin gets to go first, and though there's a limit of ten minutes per guy, he takes ages. While we wait for him, all excited, drinking Cokes, his business partners quiz me, as we sit together in the living room of a house decorated like a colonial ranch, totally fake, with these incredibly uncomfortable armchairs, because it apparently didn't occur to anybody that the neo-Mexican style is no use unless you're doing the set design for a telenovela. They ask me if we have cars in Lagos. If electricity and telephones have made it there yet. If we brush our teeth. If my father carried my mother off on a horse. I answer yes, yes, of course. And where did you leave your big sombrero? they ask. I forgot it in your sister's bedroom, I say to the one who asked, who as it happens is the host, the one whose parents think if you paint a ranch house in a wash of bright colors it's going to look a picture of elegance. My sister's six years old, he says, suddenly angry, and he gets up to hit me. I'm kind of amazed that the sister of a friend of his sister's, who is six years old, is in a position to invest two thousand new pesos in this proposed golf course. If her friend is a friend from school, in year one of primary, and she's also six, how old can her sister be? Eight? Ten? And that's assuming it's her older sister. What if she's her younger sister? But I don't have time for financial speculation because the sister's brother is up with all his pimples and his fists ready to lay into me. I leap to my feet, knocking a ceramic watermelon off a little side table – though, whatever people say about the fragility of Tlaquepaque handicrafts, it doesn't actually break – and run across the front garden, out into the street, slam the gate behind me, cross over and run very fast down the median, really incredibly fast, just like the hero of one of those action movies we didn't watch, except with a great ache in my testicles (I never got my turn to masturbate).

Fifteen years later, we're in 2004 now, another call from my cousin: I want to introduce you to my business partners, he says again. I tell him I'm really busy, I'm going off to do my doctorate in Barcelona. I know, he says, your dad told me, that's why I'm calling. I don't see what one thing has to do with the other, I say. I'll explain when I see you, he says. Honestly, I can't, I insist, I've got this long list of errands that need doing, this is my only week in Guadalajara, I've got to go to Mexico City to process my visa and then back to Xalapa to finish packing and pick up Valentina. You owe it to me, he says, for old times' sake. Anybody's guess what he could be referring to. In the old days all we ever did was go to the movies at six o'clock on Saturdays. And those old times didn't last even a year, exactly up to the afternoon I had to run away from the house of one of his business partners who wanted to lynch me. That same night, my cousin called to say my behavior was damaging his business prospects. I told him he could stick his project up his ass, though I used a paraphrase that didn't involve the word 'ass'. We stopped seeing each other. When I finished high school I went off to live in Xalapa, to study Spanish literature at the University of Veracruz. He went off to do International Business at the ITESO university, being a good follower of those Jesuits, but he never graduated. He went to live in the US for a bit, in some town near San Diego, where a sister of our fathers' lives. He said he was going to do a postgrad, an MBA, that's what he told my dad, ignoring the minor detail that in order to do this he'd need to have completed his degree. One of my aunt's kids, one of the cousins who live in America, that is, told me our cousin had settled in their parents' house, where he did nothing but watch TV, supposedly to learn English though he actually only watched Univision. Then he came back to Guadalajara and went over to Cabo San Lucas. According to my mom, my aunt told her he bought a small motorboat to take tourists out whale-watching. But he didn't have a license and the union of whale guides made his life hell, until one day they sank his boat, which he'd kept docked at a secret jetty. He came back to Guadalajara. He set up a surfboard store in Chapalita, which never caught on, and he had to close it within a few months. He set up a stand selling Ensenada-style fish tacos on Avenida Patria, but within two weeks the health inspectors from the Zapopan district council had shut it down. They're really out to get me, that's what my dad said my cousin told him at my grandfather's ninetieth birthday party, which I didn't go to because I was in Xalapa. He says he's been the victim of a bureaucratic plot. That it's impossible to do business in Mexico. He left again, for Cozumel this time, where for years nobody really knew what he was up to. My uncle told my sister he was waiting tables in a little thatched palapa hut where they made pescado zarandeado, except that's a Pacific-coast fish recipe, not a Caribbean one. My aunt told my mom he was taking care of some projects for a group of foreign investors. She couldn't say what projects, or where the alleged foreign investors were from. Assuming they even existed, these alleged investors. One of the few times we were together again, at the wedding of another cousin, he shouted in my ear, amid the din of a small brass band (the bride's family was from Sinaloa), that he was living off his rental income. I thought I'd misheard, not least because at that time we can't have been older than twenty-seven or twenty-eight. You have property on the Caribbean? I asked him, with the utmost suspicion. Yeah, he said, ten sunbeds plus their shades. He had recently returned to Guadalajara, supposedly as a project manager for an investment fund. Someone in the family told me, I can't remember who, that it was money from American retirees living in Chapala.

As for me, the only thing I'd done in all those years was complete my degree, write a thesis on the short stories of Jorge Ibargüengoitia, win a scholarship from the Institute of Literary-Linguistic Research and teach Spanish to the very occasional foreign students who showed up in Xalapa.

I swear you won't regret it, says my cousin, bringing me out of the long silence that followed his demand for totally unearned loyalty, and of which I'd taken advantage to cast my mind back over the fifteen years that separated the old days from the new. I won't take up more than half an hour of your time, he says, if you're not interested you've only wasted half an hour, but I totally know you're gonna be interested. Specially 'cause that scholarship you got isn't going to get you very far. Your dad told me. Life in Europe's seriously expensive.

And now, instead of describing how I eventually ended up agreeing to meet my cousin, instead of dwelling on the swiftness with which I came to the conclusion that this was the only way of getting him off my back, instead of acknowledging that I did go, voluntarily, on my own two feet, to throw myself off the precipice, I'd rather, as the bad poets say, draw a dark veil over this fragment of the story, or more precisely, choose this place and this moment to make use of an effective and moderately dignified ellipsis.

My naivete in business matters was so great that I didn't know investor meetings were held in the basements of lap-dancing clubs and with one partner tied to a chair, classic kidnapping-style. My cousin greeted me with a raise of his eyebrows: the rest of his body was roped down. Though his mouth was taped over, he did try to give me a smile, albeit unsuccessfully. There were two people here, besides my cousin. They were very squat and dumpy, as my mom would say, and sported bellies pregnant with beer and a lot of gel on hairdos so baroque they were almost Churrigueresque, but with a couple of guns (one apiece) that instantly gave them the ferocious appearance their genes had denied them (unarmed they would have looked like a pair of jolly, chubby little guys, the type that are always kidding around to disguise their homoerotic urges). The basement was full of boxes, and there was a red bulb hanging from the ceiling that to be frank was mostly pointless.

Anyone see you come down? asked the one waiting for us in the basement, the one who seemed to be the boss of the one who had come to fetch me at the Gandhi bookstore on Avenida Chapultepec where I'd agreed to meet my cousin, apparently for him to introduce me to his business partners, figuring if I was going to waste my time I might as well at least make the most of this chance to buy a few books I needed. Negative, said the other, the one who'd found me skulking around the Mexican literature section, alone as a rapist in an alley, and who'd asked me, showing me the gun stuck into his waistband, if I was my cousin's cousin. Are you your dickhead cousin's cousin? is what he'd said, to be exact, and when I said no, I didn't even know who my cousin was, he pulled out a cell phone which I saw had my photo on it. Quite pixelated, but not so badly that I couldn't be recognized. Ah, you must be Projects' partner, it's so great to meet you, I said, incredibly unconvincingly. (Though my cousin's name was Lorenzo, everyone called him Projects.) Let's go, he said. Where? I asked. To see your dickhead cousin, he said. I asked if I might please just pay for a collection of the aphorisms of Francisco Tario that would perhaps be useful for my doctoral thesis. I imagined that if I behaved normally, the threat from the gun would evaporate. He looked at me with some surprise (he didn't agree with my theory) and made as if to pull out the all-too-concrete gun. It won't take a minute, I insisted, only it's a really hard book to find. Do it quick then, asshole, he said, and he stood behind me in the line for the cashier, his gun tickling me down below, as my mom liked to call it.

The line was unusually long, because if you bought twenty pesos' worth of books they were giving you a discount on the sandwiches at the place round the corner.

We got into a pickup truck with tinted windows and no plates, which was double-parked with the impunity that reigns over the country as a whole, and after a brief loop we were soon on Avenida Vallarta. The guy drove impeccably, the way I imagine crooks do drive in real life, or the way they should, so as not to attract attention. I looked at him out the corner of my eye and the only thing I managed to register, before he reprimanded me, was that he had a cold sore on his upper lip. What you looking at? he said, with an accent from someplace in the north, Monterrey or maybe Saltillo. I pulled the book from the yellow shopping bag and started to leaf through it, entirely out of nerves, and because I didn't know where to direct my hands or my eyes. When we reached the Minerva statue intersection, we hit a red light.

So, like, you're really interested in that, then? he asked when he saw me pretending to read, though anyone who knows me will be well aware I can't read in the car because it makes me feel sick. I said yes. Let's see, then, he said. See what? I asked. Just read something, asshole, he said. I glanced randomly at page 46 and read: However, the way things are, man does not truly take possession of the earth until he has died. The light turned green. What else? he said. That's it, I said, it's an aphorism. A thought, I added, not assuming much when it comes to the rhetorical knowledge of criminals in general, and the one driving this pickup in particular. And this author, he's a communist? he asked. Was, I say, he's dead now. But was he or wasn't he? he insisted. I couldn't say, I answered, I don't think so, he owned a movie theater. And people who own movie theaters can't be communists? he asked. What if they only show communist movies? Yeah, but this movie theater was in Acapulco, I replied. So? he said. And then So? again, to make it clear his question was not a rhetorical one and that it required an answer. He scratched his belly with his right hand and when the T-shirt rose I once again saw that insolent gun. Could there be anyplace less communist than Acapulco? I asked. Acapulco's in Guerrero, he said, it's a nest of guerrillas, vermin and poisonous snakes. But this was in the fifties, when Miguel Alemán Valdés was president, I explained. So? he said again. Could there be anything less communist than the Alemán family? I asked. But that doesn't change the fact that what you were reading was a communist thought, he said. It's really a joke, I said. But I didn't think it was funny, he pointed out firmly. Am I laughing? So I closed the book and put it back into the shopping bag, concluding that the best thing would be to devote the remainder of the journey to the innocuous pastime of staring intently at the vehicle's windshield.

Sixty-eight gnats, assorted butterflies and mosquitoes had lost their lives on the right-hand side of the windshield, as if the pickup had just driven across a vast stretch of the Republic and as if, what was more, its driver had committed himself, systematically, to not clean it, and that nobody, none of the thousands of beggars at crossroads, at parking lots and gas stations, should clean it either. Finally, we arrived at our destination, a lap-dancing club on Avenida Vallarta, before you get to Ciudad Granja.

You this dickhead's cousin? asks the one who's acting like he's the boss, gesturing toward my cousin with his chin. Beneath the knots of the rope, I can see my cousin's put on some weight (our family's genes make it hard for us to put on weight), and that he's gotten a tan, though it's possible the color of his skin is due to a combination of the red bulb and the tightness of the rope. I say yes, and take this chance to say: So, I'm sorry to ask, but how come you got him tied up?

'Cause the fucking dickhead won't sit still, says the one who came shopping with me in the bookstore. Don't ask dickhead questions, says the other one, the one who looks like he's the boss, then straightaway he adds: Juan Pablo, right? I nod. Juan or Pablo? he says. Both, I say, Juan Pablo. Your cousin tells us you're going to live in Europe, *Juan Pablo*, says the one who looks like the boss. If you aren't going to live in Europe, if your cousin was being such a titanic fucking dickhead that he's lied to us, tell us now so then that'll be both of you fucked instead of just one. My cousin twists on his chair, trying to wriggle out of the rope, he manages to get his right arm free and the one who looks like the boss gives him a whack around the head. Christ, which dick tied this fucker up? he asks. Though this one seems like a rhetorical question (that's how it seemed to me), the other answers: It was Chucky, boss, confirming my hypothesis that the one who looked like the boss was the boss. And the dick was never in the Boy Scouts, I guess? asks the boss. Blood starts trickling from my cousin's head and into his eyes. My cousin blinks as if he's trying to see stars, the tape muffling his moans. The boss walks over, pulls an unlikely handkerchief from his shirt pocket (here's when I notice he's wearing a dark suit and this was why I'd thought all along that he was the boss, because the other guy is in a T-shirt and jeans), unfolds it unhurriedly and cleans my cousin's eyes with care, almost affection, a real Mary Magdalene. You look like one of those little Tlaquepaque ceramic jugs, he says to him, then to me: Well? Well what? I say, slightly disoriented, because the truth is, action always has that effect on my speech. What do you mean well what? he says. Jesus, seriously, if being a dickhead is genetic that's all I fucking need, well is it true you're going to live in Europe? I say yes. He seems relieved, as if the fact of the European Union having given me a grant to do a doctorate in Spain will spare him the bother of executing me. Then he says: So this motherfucking cousin of yours has come up with a very, very, *total* gold-plated motherfucker of a plan, seriously such a motherfucker of a plan that if you aren't as much of a dick as he is, you might even come in useful. He pauses to scratch his nuts with the barrel of his gun, and I come to the conclusion that ever since Cicero the human race has done nothing but de-evolve *ad nauseam*. So look, I say, first you untie Lorenzo, if you don't let him go, no deal. Your name's Lorenzo, fucking Projects? says the one who thinks Francisco Tario is a communist. What deal? asks the boss. I bet this guy's watched a lot of movies, boss, says the other. It was true, some free association of ideas, or rather of people, meant that what I'd said was the same thing Harrison Ford said to some terrorists in a movie I watched with my cousin in 1989. And why was I suddenly starting to act the martyr to defend my cousin now, anyfuckin'way!

When do you go? the boss asks, tightening the rope around my cousin's belly, obeying my instruction except in reverse. Where? I say. Europe, asshole! says the boss. Where else? In three weeks, I say, last week in October. Barcelona, right? he says. Affirmative, I say, without even realizing, out of pure nervous imitation. And what are you going to do? he asks. Study for a doctorate, I say. Which university? he says. So, like, I say, at Barcelona's Autónoma Uni. Sure it's the Autónoma? he asks. Yes, I'm sure, I say. What's it about, the doctorate? says the other. I'm still not sure they know what a doctorate really is. Answer, motherfucker! says the boss. So like, um, literary theory and comparative literature, I say. Your cousin told us that already, asshole, what we need to know is what your thesis is on. Oh, I say, my research project? A project? says the boss. You mean you aren't actually going to do it? You'd best take care with those projects, people who just do project after project end up tied to a chair. It's about the limits of humor in Latin

American literature of the twentieth century, I say, blushing. Explain, says the boss. Well, I say, so, like I'll try to explore the way notions of political correctness, or Christian morality, work as repressive forces that imbue laughter – which is by definition spontaneous – with feelings of guilt. The two thugs do in fact suppress a laugh at this point. Ultimately, I add, this ends up authorizing what it's acceptable to laugh about and what isn't. Ah yeah, fuck, says the one who'd rather have a dirty windshield than give people a bit of charity, so like if it's acceptable to be making jokes about the fact that we're fucking your cousin up? Something like that, I say. And what do you think? says the boss. So like, well, it depends, I say. On what? he asks. On who's telling the joke, I say. If my cousin tells it, it might be a good laugh. Your cousin only tells totally dickhead jokes, says the other. The three of us look at my cousin, who moans something, probably some useless defense of his comic abilities, useless because the tape muffles his arguments and because my cousin honestly is just terrible at telling jokes. That was one theory, I say, it's not the same when the joke's told by the victim as when it's told by the killer. Don't talk shit, says the boss, dead men don't tell jokes. Is that a threat? I say, without thinking, as if the guns and the sight of my cousin tied up and bleeding weren't enough. The thugs burst out laughing.

So to write a thesis about Latin America, then, a dick like you's got to go to Europe? asks the boss when he's done laughing. So, like, I want to include the work of this Catalan writer, who lived in exile in Mexico for more than twenty years, I say. He's not a Latin American writer, but he has two books about Mexico that I argue should be considered a part of the canon of twentieth-century Mexican literature. His work has been read poorly in Mexico, I go on, read very little and poorly interpreted, misinterpreted, even in his own day he got accused of being a racist. OK, enough, just stop, the boss interrupts me, that's not my concern, I just got to be sure you aren't such an asshole that you think you can lie to us. Negative, I say. Are you trying to be funny? asks the one in the T-shirt and jeans, getting ready to raise his gun. I'm sorry, I say, it's just I'm so nervous, I'm not used to it. What aren't you used to? says the boss. So, I say, well, to the guns, to being threatened, I've never even seen a gun before, only in the movies, I say. Well you'd better get used to it, says the boss. Do you speak Catalan? he asks. The change of subject dizzies me. Answer, for fuck's sake, says the boss. I say no, but that I was thinking about enrolling in some Catalan lessons when I arrived. And that I can't do a doctoral thesis reading translations into Spanish, I've got to analyze the Catalan originals. Well you'd better put your fucking back into it, says the boss. Into what? I ask. Into Catalan, dickhead! says the boss. What else the ungodly motherfuck are we talking about? Who gives a fuck if you speak it, what matters is that you understand it, he says, otherwise your fucking Catalan business partners will think we're all a bunch of total weapons-grade fucks. Get it? he asks. I tell him yes. Then he changes the subject again, without any kind of transition, without a paragraph break, I presume that's just what the syntax of organized crime is like: Your dickhead cousin told us you're taking your girlfriend, he says. I remain silent. You met her at university, right? he insists. Totally silent and even totally still, completely motionless. Don't say anything if you don't want to, he says, we've already tracked her down anyway, and then he says to the other guy: Take him to the lawyer. I'm still not moving, not speaking, not following the one who's going to take me to the lawyer, who's starting to climb the flight of stairs, which are shining like someone's spilled a bottle of glitter on the steps. What? says the boss when he sees me just standing there. So, I say, my cousin, persisting with my newfound vocation of martyr or suicide. I really ought to learn how to be nervous. You're right, I'd forgotten about him, he says. Then he shouts out to the one going upstairs: Call Chucky! Next thing I know he's reaching out his right arm with the gun in his hand and holding it to my cousin's head. My cousin whimpers and shakes, pulling his head away from the barrel of the gun. Quiet, for fuck's sake! says the boss, and puts the gun once again to my cousin's temple. He fires and when the echo of the bang dies down, when the pieces of my cousin's brain stop scattering all over the room, he asks me: And how about if I'm the one telling the joke, huh? Do you know what San Lorenzo the martyr said when he was being roasted on a grill? You don't? I'm already nicely toasted on the back, he said, you can turn me over now.

What about Valentina? says Rolando when he sees me dragging my bags over to his car on my own. So like, Valentina's not coming, I say. What do you mean she's not coming? he says. We broke up, I say. No shit, he says. When? Today, just now, half an hour ago. No shit, he says, did you break up with her or did she do it? I did, I say. How come? he says. I want to go to Barcelona on my own, I say, I want to make a new life for myself, I need a new life plan. What the fuck are you talking about? he says, with the same anguished expression on his face he had that day in 1991 when I told him I was off to Xalapa to study literature (You're going to starve to death, was what he said that time). The thing with my cousin really hit me hard, I say. What does your cousin having gotten himself run over have to do with you dumping Valentina? he says. He's holding the car keys in his hand and he isn't opening the trunk. It's just like one day you're alive and the next you're dead, I say, so it's like, I don't know if I love Valentina enough to want to go live in Barcelona with her. No shit, he says. And this only just occurred to you now? Before leaving for the airport? Man, you're harsh. We'd talked about it before, I say, but she was determined, and I've only just managed to convince her. Convince her? About what? he asks. Not to come, I say, that it was best for both of us. No shit, he says. You're going to regret it. It's normal you'd be confused right now. Maybe, I say, but what's done's done. Let's get going. It's getting late. And what's supposed to happen now? he asks. What do you mean? I say. What do you mean what do I mean? he says, I mean what happens to her! Nothing, I say, she's going back to Xalapa. No shit, he says. Finally he opens the trunk of the car and as I'm putting my suitcases inside his cell phone rings. It's for you, he says, surprised, handing me the device. Some friend wants to say goodbye.

Yeah? I say. So what about your girlfriend, buddy? says a voice with an accent from the north. Who's this? I say, stepping away from the car and Rolando so he can't hear me. It's Chucky, dickhead, he says. Look over at the corner. No, buddy, other side. See me? So, where's Valentina? So, I say, she's not coming, we broke up. Go get her, he says. I can't, I say. Why not? he says. Because she won't want to, I say. Oh I get it, buddy, was it you told her to fuck off? he asks. You wanted to protect her? Oh boy, you really are such a dick. If you want to protect her what you need to do right now is convince her to get on that plane. She won't want to, I say, I was pretty cruel. You know what cruelty is, dickhead? he says. Cruelty is those stupid fucking microbus drivers, you seen how they just drive straight over your head? Stupid fucking heads, don't make them like they used to, buddy, they smash like watermelons, like pieces of Tlaquepaque ceramics. But there's no time, I say, our flight's going to leave. So what the fuck are you doing wasting time talking to me? he says, and hangs up.

The lawyer phones me on the cell I've just bought and says: Find a call shop and call me back. A what? I say. A call shop, he says again, don't you know what call shops are? Jesus, it's like you're not even a real immigrant. So, look, I say, I just got here yesterday. Last night. Call me, he says, and hangs up. I look around, at the signs for all the stores that line up, one after another, all the way down Avenida del Paralelo. I go back to the store where I bought the cell phone. Do you know where I might find a call shop? I ask the Pakistani man who served me and who is now leafing through a phone catalog. The Pakistani man looks up, deep in contemplation, or consulting an imaginary map of the neighborhood on the ceiling. There is a customer looking at the cell phones, a Chinese man wearing a black leather jacket, possibly not real leather. He's smoking, inside the store. He takes a drag on his cigarette and turns to look at the Pakistani man, who's still silent but is now, to improve matters, stroking his chin. Just round the corner, the Chinese guy says, and he explains how to get there.

In the call shop there is an Ecuadorian or a Paraguayan (I can never distinguish between the accents) who tells me to go into booth number two. In my wallet I find the piece of paper on which I've written down the endless sequence of digits that looks less like a phone number than a secret code. I dial. One moment please, says the operator in English, and then the lawyer says, without a greeting: Pay attention. Every day. Between 10 a.m. and 2 p.m. Mexico time. You're going to call me. Every day. Always from a call shop. Always a different one. Understand? I answer um yes, and then I ask, so like, how'd you get hold of the number for my cell which I've only just bought? Don't ask me fucking idiot questions, he says, it's four in the morning. There's a pause, I look at the clock on the call-shop wall. It's a quarter past eleven.

And what about Valentina? says the lawyer. I left her at the hostel, I say, she's sleeping. Has she forgiven you yet? he asks. So, I say, like, more or less. Work on it, asshole, he says, we're going to need her. Make the most of the fact she's asleep for the Chinaman to take you to the apartment. What? I say. The Chinaman, he's going to take you to the apartment. I don't understand, I say. You don't need to, he says, there's nothing to understand. The only thing you have to do is whatever the Chinaman tells you. Get it? he says. So, I say, well, I, and he hangs up.

I head out of the booth toward the cashier in order to pay and I notice there's a Chinese guy leaning up against the window display, next to the Peruvian or Bolivian or whatever he is. He's wearing a black leather jacket, possibly not real leather, jeans and a pair of sneakers, Nikes, which are probably Wikes. If all Chinese guys didn't look the same to me, if reality wasn't feeling like a dream, or more precisely a nightmare, thanks to my jet lag, I'd say it was the same Chinese guy who gave me directions for the call shop back at the cell phone store. What's up, man? he says to me when I ask the South American cashier how much I've got to pay. So um, hi, I say. One twenty, says the cashier. I take out my wallet and a twenty-euro bill. We don't give change, says the cashier, and he points at a small poster notifying customers that they must pay the exact or approximate amounts. Maximum change five euro, says the sign. I put my hand in my trouser pocket to show him I haven't got any coins. Forget it, says the Chinese guy, I'll pay. He hands the cashier two coins, pushes open the door then stands to one side to allow me to step out.

You're going to need five hundred euro, says the Chinese guy when we're out on the sidewalk. Two hundred and fifty deposit. Two fifty for the first month's rent. I take a good look at his almond-shaped eyes, the slicked-down hair, the badly shaved stubble dotting his round cheeks. He can't be much over thirty. So, I say, are you this Chinaman guy? The Chinese man laughs. What do you think? he says. I mean, the lawyer's

Chinaman? Come on, he says, without answering me, they're waiting for us, and he makes as if to start walking. I don't move. Hey, man, move your ass, he says. Where are we going? I say. Where do you think? he says. Don't make me lose my patience, 'cause the lawyer said if I need to kick the crap out of you I absolutely should kick the crap out of you. We start walking, reversing the route that brought me from the cell phone store to the call shop. Two hundred and fifty's expensive, I say, trying to keep up with the Chinese guy. I was thinking of spending two hundred at most, I say. Lawyer's orders, says the Chinese guy. I need someplace cheaper, I say. The Chinese guy stops. He takes a pack of cigarettes from his pocket. Man, he says, don't you know what orders are? Orders get obeyed and that's that. You think the rent's expensive because the Chinaman here is trying to screw you over? The lawyer said he was going to set you up in a neighborhood where there aren't a lot of police, and that costs money, man. He pauses a moment to light his cigarette. The apartment I'm taking you to is uptown, man, he says. San Gervasio. You'll see, two fifty isn't a lot, in that part of the city you can't get a room for less than three hundred, they haven't got Africans or gypsies there, and the police never go in except when some old guy croaks and they need somebody to smash the door down to carry the carcass out. Those old snobs are real loners, he says, you'll see. He draws on his cigarette a second time: with two drags half of it has already gone up in smoke. The Chinese guy resumes his walking. So, look, I say, I can't make this decision on my own. I should talk to my girlfriend about it. For fuck's sake, man, says the Chinese guy, your girlfriend isn't going to complain, I've seen the place already, it's a fucking awesome apartment, seriously it's got these views to make you shit yourself. Yeah, but the thing is, I start to speak again, but the Chinese guy interrupts me and says, as he crushes the cigarette butt underfoot: You really don't know what orders are, man? So how in the name of holy fuck are you working for the lawyer? We go down into the metro station, the Chinese guy explains what kind of ticket it would be best for me to buy, and we continue the rest of the journey in silence until we are standing at the door to apartment 6D of a building in a minuscule street called Julio Verne.

What's up, Chinaman, how's it going? asks the guy who opens the door, in an Argentine accent. So, this shithead, this is him? says the Argentinian now, and he holds out his hand in greeting. I'm Facundo, he says, and he shakes my hand vigorously, too vigorously, almost manically. How're you doing? he says. So you're Mexican, yeah? I say yes, yes I am. We walk across the hall into the living room and the big window takes my breath away. No, not the window: the city that spills out down below, all roofs and towers, and, on the horizon, the blue fringe of the Mediterranean. Beautiful, isn't it? says Facundo, who doesn't stop talking as he shows me the kitchen, the laundry area, the two bathrooms and the bedroom at the back, the one that's for rent, truly very spacious, albeit shapeless (it has seven walls). A window overlooking the well of the internal courtyard lets a little light in, though not enough to rescue the space from the gloom. Besides the bed, there's a closet for keeping clothes and a foldable table bolted to one of the walls.

We return to the living room along the corridor where there are two other bedrooms. I live here in the apartment along with this other shithead, says Facundo, Cristian, Argentinian too. I got a daughter, she's six, she comes to spend the night two or three times a week. Alejandra. She's a great kid, you won't even notice she's here. I work all day and Cristian's usually only around in the morning, he does shifts in a restaurant at nights. If you've come to study, it's ideal, it's real quiet here, there's a lot of light in the living room and it's a mega fucking peaceful neighborhood. Hey, weren't you coming with your girlfriend? he asks. I say yes. Perfect, he says, there was a Colombian couple living here till last month, you'll be all fucking set here with your girlfriend. You can even come today, if you want. Where are you staying? In a hotel? You shouldn't spend any more money, you should come here right away.

The Chinese guy claps him on the back. Man, he says, you're totally wired, what are you on? What are you saying, Chinaman? says Facundo. It's the máte, shithead, and the two of them crack up. Well, there we are, then, says Facundo, you going to come today, shithead? I look at the Chinese guy. This evening, I say. Awesome, says Facundo. Listen, Chinaman, I work at a hotel on Plaza España, let me give you a card in case you have any customers needing a short stay. He takes the little rectangular piece of card out of his wallet and hands it over. The Chinese guy puts it away without looking at it. Say, did you actually have a name, Chinaman? asks Facundo, I don't remember, I'm sorry, it's just Chinese names all sound the same to me. I'm called the Chinaman, the Chinese guy says, and he walks over to the apartment door in order to cut short the valedictory ceremonial verbiage of Facundo who's now telling me that the nearest metro station is the one on Plaza Lesseps but that there's also a train station on Calle Pàdua and there's a supermarket only just round the corner and a Pakistani on Calle Zaragoza who's open at night and on Sundays.

We walk out onto the landing and step into the elevator. I told you this place was the shit, says the Chinese guy. He takes out a cigarette and lights it. The journey down those six floors, really seven including the basement, is enough for the elevator to fill with smoke. I start coughing. The Chinese guy waves it aside to try and see my eyes. You don't smoke? he says. I say no. We cross the garage and when we get out into the street the Chinese guy tells me he's leaving. And now what? I say. Now what, what? he says. What do I do now? I ask. Man, how the holy fuck do I know? he says. Go take a fucking stroll down the Ramblas? No, I'm talking about, I begin, but the Chinese guy interrupts me: The lawyer will tell you, he says, and he's gone.

My dear son, your mother hopes this message finds you settled and recovered from your tiring journey. Now you're not to go thinking your mother's gone crazy and is going to make a habit of writing you every day while you're living in Europe, the truth is, your mother has already gotten used to being far from you in all the years you've been living away from home. Your mother only wanted to tell you a few things she'd have liked to chat about before you left, but what with all the hurry and all the arrangements and the business with your cousin we didn't get a moment's peace.

Which reminds me, do talk to your uncle and aunt when you get a chance, they were so offended you didn't go to the wake. Your mother explained you had an appointment at the Spanish embassy to apply for a visa, and that you couldn't change it, but there was just no way to make them understand. Your aunt came out with something about how you were the last person who should have missed it given how close you were, you and your cousin. This seemed a bit of an exaggeration to your mother, who didn't think the two of you ever really spent all that much time together, but your mother wasn't going to start arguing with your aunt in those circumstances.

Very sad, that wake, very lackluster, like it always is whenever a young person dies. Your mother has never understood why mourners act so ashamed of the dead person, as if he didn't deserve a funeral as God intended because of having died before his time, as if the death was a weakness that needed hiding. In cases like these people think the best thing is to be discreet, and then discretion always just ends up looking like a poor, unimportant, stingy sort of death. Appearances matter even at times like those, son, this is your mother telling you now, appearances matter at times like those more than ever. Your mother wants, when the time comes, for her wake to be held in a room that's airy and cool (if it's summer) or cozy and warm (if it's winter). There should be good coffee, from Coatepec, your mother is making you responsible for getting hold of some high-grown coffee, put all those years you wasted in Xalapa to some use for once. These things matter, Juan, otherwise on the day after the wake you'll get people going around with heartburn and speaking ill of the dead person at the burial. And wreaths, your mother wants wreaths of exotic flowers that are brightly colored and happy, your mother's death should be a hymn to life, bird-of-paradise flowers, tulips flown in from Holland, Brazilian orchids, sunflowers!, sunflowers aren't expensive and they fill a room with light, like little pieces of sun. Look, your mom's made a metaphor!, you must be proud of your mother, son, has your mother ever told you that when she was young she used to write poems? That all stopped when your mother married your father, but your mother's digressing now, and your mother doesn't want you thinking she's only writing so as to complain about your father, to tell you about her sufferings and her frustrations, you know perfectly well that's not the kind of mother she is.

Anyway, there weren't many wreaths at your cousin's wake, and they were small, of rather ordinary flowers, the cheapest kind. Your uncle's work colleagues sent a wreath of pink carnations, there was some sort of confusion and they thought your cousin was a girl, they went around the entire blessed night apologizing to your uncle for the mistake, they blamed a secretary who spent the whole time in a corner crying with shame. As if that wasn't enough, the coffin was kept closed for the whole thing and nobody was allowed to approach it, they put a rope around it like it was a crime scene. Your uncle told your father that your cousin's head had gotten totally smashed up, he said it was like someone had thrown a pumpkin from the roof of a tall building. He was very upset, your uncle, he didn't know what he was saying, your father had to prescribe him sedatives, an extra-strong tranquilizer, one of those ones they keep in the safe at the pharmacy so they won't get stolen by drug addicts. And you can imagine what it was like for your poor father, giving free consultations the whole night, people really are so selfish, they'd come up to him quite casually then start telling him about how, well, they've got this pain beneath their ribs, or what should they be taking for their reflux, or their kid's had this cough, or a rash has broken out on their buttocks. You know how your father's unable to say no, he sees himself as a bit of a Samaritan, we'd all be living the high life today if he'd figured out soon enough that people's health is a business, a very good business, actually, your father must be the only dermatologist in the city who hasn't made millions. By the way, let your mother tell you about how your aunt Norma came over to tell your father that she had a sore throat and your father sounded her chest and told her to go to the doctor's surgery the following day, and then your father told your mother that your aunt Norma had signs of thyroid cancer. That cancer is horrific, your father says, and your aunt Norma is so fickle, such a hypocrite, like butter wouldn't melt. Let's just hope your father is wrong, your mother begs you to keep this to yourself, you're not to go telling anybody before the diagnosis has been confirmed.

Oh my son, do forgive your mother for telling you these dreadful things right now, just as you're starting a new life, I guess your mother probably needs to get it off her chest, your mother still hasn't recovered from the bad impression left by the wake. You should have seen your cousin's friends, his former schoolmates, who spent the whole time on a patio smoking and drinking whiskey and talking business. Your sister told your mother they spent the whole night arguing about what name they were going to give some new roast chicken franchise. That some of them wanted to call it The Flying Chicken, and others Chick-Out, I guess to sound like Take-Out, because it was going to be chicken to go. And then they started trying to explain to your uncle why their franchise was going to be more successful even than Pete's Chicken! They talked about branches in the US and Central America. They said the rate of chicken consumption in Honduras and Guatemala was the highest in the world. Can you believe that? Must be because the chicken's cheaper.

People started to leave at about one and when your aunt Concha realized the wake was going to empty out she gathered all her friends from the church choir to liven things up a bit, as it really was actually getting kind of depressing. So there they all were, all singing away. Church songs. Country songs, and boleros. Then your aunt sang a song by Maná she said was your cousin's favorite. The sobbing really did start then.

So listen, Juan, and let your mother tell you about how the famous Karla showed up, remember her, the supposed girlfriend from Cozumel your cousin was always talking about? Eventually your mother actually got to believing your cousin had made her up, since he never brought her over, and you know how your cousin was given to lying. Well, she shows up, this Karla, goodness knows who could have told her. Real short, big head, swarthy, pure Maya. With these little tiny feet perfect for running up pyramids. There wasn't much to her, it almost would have been better if she really had been made-up after all. Some friends from Cozumel showed up too, they looked like they were going to set up a hammock stall in the middle of the wake. They came by bus all the way, just imagine, and went straight to the wake from the central bus station (well, they came by bus from the coast, they must have taken a boat to get off the island). They just washed their faces in the bathroom, they smelled like rumpled-up old bedsheets. Your uncle was absolutely mortified, he didn't know where to hide them.

When it got to the delirium of 4 a.m. your aunt Concha asked for silence from those who were still there and announced very solemnly that she and your uncle, with the support of the Jesuits, were going to set up a foundation in your cousin's name. The Lorenzo Villalobos Foundation. Apparently, the foundation will be devoted to teaching traffic safety, so that children learn to cross roads, and teaching them to take footbridges over the top instead of crossing down below like your cousin did. People clapped. The husband of one of your aunt's friends, from the church choir, well, it turns out he's a congressman and he promised the full support of the state congress. He even launched himself into a speech, but it didn't come out great because at one point it sounded like he was criticizing your cousin for being careless or distracted. Or plain dumb. It was apparently an accident, but the truth is, your mother can't help wondering what your cousin did to get his head smashed up, did he just lie down on the road for them to drive their tires right over him?

But your mother is not writing to tell you this, but to tell you that your mother wants you to know she is so proud of you. At the wake, even though you didn't go, you were still the star of the show. Everybody was talking about you. Your cousins asking away, they're dying of jealousy now you live in

Europe. Just think, how much they all used to tease you, how insignificant you seemed to them. Your mother remembers this one Christmas, when your grandpa was still alive and you were in Xalapa at the time, and when your mother told them you couldn't come because you were finishing writing your thesis, they all started making up titles. Like hemorrhoids in the work of Octavio Paz. Like apocalyptic gay urban post-revolutionary narrative. Like the gerund as a tool of Yankee imperialism. Clowning around, that's all. Now they'll have to eat their words. They've stayed behind in this dilapidated old country, managing their car washes and their motels (sounds like your cousin Esteban's gone bankrupt, by the way), and there you are living it up in Europe.

Son, you know you are your mother's favorite child, but don't tell your sister, and your mother will deny it if you do. I've just found the photo albums from when you and your sister were little and I remembered the house up in Lagos, how your mother used to sit in the living room and look out the window and see the highest branches of the fig tree, the towers of the parish church down in the center, and it's like it was yesterday when your mother would be sitting there and see you and your sister hunting wood lice in the garden or throwing stones at the neighbor's window.

Ah now, son, there you go, your mother's ended up writing a very long message, do forgive her, and with you probably so busy just now. Say hello from your mother to Valentina, your mother would have liked to have spent more time with her, but it's obvious she's a nice girl. Besides, your mother trusts your good judgment. And of course, if you meet a beautiful Spanish girl, your mother would be delighted to improve the breed with some European grandchildren. Write your mother when you can, and don't forget that your mother is thinking about you and sending you a hug from far away.

THE JULIO VERNE DIARY

Tuesday, November 2nd, 2004

I'm sure there can't be anything phonier than a woman who's spent the last few years studying diaries, memoirs, autobiographies and all kinds of private writings, suddenly starting to write a diary herself. Especially if her interest up until this point has been academic rather than creative. But I don't want to make literature, I'm sure of that. Two certainties in the first paragraph, that's not bad. Though they are, as always, only theoretical certainties.

Private writing is so deceitful that I'm already justifying myself as though these pages might one day be read by someone. Or worse, as though they were going to be published. If the impulse that made me buy this notebook were genuine I'd just get on and write about something, directly, no preamble. How it didn't rain today. How I'm on page 92 of *The Savage Detectives*. A transcript of the ludicrous conversation I had this morning at the stationer's (so much trouble just to buy a pen, the pen I'm writing with now and which here in Spain they call a 'bolígrafo'). A record of the fact that today I ate a tangerine and two apples. That a week has passed since I arrived in Barcelona and I still haven't spoken to Juan Pablo and he hasn't made enough of an effort for me to respond. And after these two or three banalities, I would now, as at the start of any confession, offer an emphatic assurance that everything I'm going to write will be the truth. All of it. Rousseau-style. The promise of veracity. The autobiographical pact. As if anybody was going to believe me, anyway. I don't expect anyone to believe me.

Fine, so I've written two lies. I didn't eat a tangerine. Or two apples. It was a manner of speaking, I could just as easily have said I'd eaten a pear. Or a slice of pineapple. It was actually a bit of plagiarism, taken from the diaries of Sylvia Plath, who was a great eater of tangerines. I had spaghetti with tomato sauce for lunch. I had spaghetti with tomato sauce for dinner. Just like yesterday and the day before yesterday and also tomorrow, I'm guessing. Juan Pablo made chicken and salad for dinner. He offered me some. I said no and lay down with Bolaño in the bedroom as soon as I was done stuffing myself with the spaghetti standing in the kitchen next to the microwave. I could make out Juan Pablo's chatter with the two Argentinians in the living room, they were having dinner with the TV on, watching a football game (I should write somewhere that we live in an apartment with two Argentinians, Facundo and Cristian, both from Buenos Aires, both from the La Boca neighborhood).

When Juan Pablo came back to the bedroom he also lay down and started reading. I don't know what he was reading: I turned my back on him. I wanted to hit him over the head with my hefty Bolaño tome (I know it's only the pocket paperback, but I bet if I got enough momentum behind it I could give him a decent bruise). We carried on reading. Since nobody said anything, not even good night, the lamp stayed on until morning.

Wednesday 3rd

11 a.m. Juan Pablo went off to university. I went out to take a wander around the neighborhood, on a sort of reconnaissance mission. Out the back of the building there's a very wide highway (the Ring, they call it), incredibly noisy, one of those monstrous urban borders. In front there is a tangle of little streets. The Ring that's always crammed with cars, plus the slope of the city, always pushes me downward (I've not yet crossed the highway to see what's further up).

The only people in the neighborhood around this time of day are old people. All very stiff. Wearing overcoats that are too thick for the cold (it isn't very) and pulling little carts into which they put the vegetables, bread, meat or wine they buy. The oldest of them don't pull anything: they get pushed. They travel in wheelchairs pushed by Latin American women. Their faces make me feel at home, sometimes. Until they speak and I hear those accents so different from mine (these women are Peruvian, Ecuadorian or Bolivian, mostly). On Calle Pàdua there's a butcher's and a baker's that look like designer boutiques. A charcuterie where a hundred grams of jamón serrano costs what I spend on three days of spaghetti and tomato sauce.

I think I've figured out why it is that Juan Pablo made up his mind to live in this neighborhood, even though there were cheaper options. Two hundred and fifty euro is insane, a stupid extravagance. I've seen advertisements for even a hundred and fifty, or one eighty, and most of them are around two hundred. Of course, that was for places in Paralelo, or in El Raval, but the location wasn't an issue, either way Juan Pablo still has to take the train to go to his university in Bellaterra. Unless . . . Unless what Juan Pablo wanted was to avoid the streets filled with Moroccans and Ecuadoreans, with Dominican mulattos and women in veils. Those halal butchers and Afro hairdressers. What Juan Pablo wanted was to live in a neighborhood of respectable people. He's brought all his family's prejudices over with him, packed up in his suitcase. If you ask me, from what I see on the streets and the way other people look at me, those stares that pierce me like thorns, it seems to me we've placed ourselves bang in the middle of a neighborhood of one-time Francoists.

Thursday 4th

Tonight I ran down to the supermarket before it closed to restock on spaghetti and tomato sauce. I was squatting in front of the shelf of canned food when a woman asked me for two jars of asparagus. I held them out to her, stretching out my arm but not getting up, and she signaled with her eyes that I was to put them into her shopping cart. Then she told me to go with her to get the milk, as she couldn't carry the containers because they were too heavy. I gave her a puzzled look. Only then did she notice what I was wearing.

'I'm sorry,' she said, 'I'm sorry, I thought you worked in the store.'

With her right hand she made a gesture encompassing her face to indicate, metaphorically, my features and the color of my skin, to explain how she'd made a mistake on account of my appearance.

'But you're very pretty,' she said.

I shouldn't pay any mind to that, but.

I shouldn't write about this, but.

But.

But.

Saturday 6th

It was beautiful out today, not one cloud in the sky and you could hardly feel the cold. I went down to the street to find myself some sun, like a cat. Or like a little old granny: just the other side of the Ring I found a very lovely park that acts as public solarium for people of the third age. Rows of wheelchairs turned to face the sun, the benches filled with those elderly folk still in control of their own mobility.

I found a spot next to a lady who was dozing peacefully. When I sat down she woke with a start. She had beautiful blue eyes, even lighter than Juan Pablo's. Her face was covered in tiny little stains which in her youth might have been freckles. I guessed she couldn't have been more than seventy. I apologized for waking her.

'Oh, don't worry yourself, my dear,' she said. 'I shouldn't really sleep, or I can't get to sleep at night.'

I turned my face up toward the sun and closed my eyes.

'Where are you from?' said the woman. 'You can't be from here, we don't have people as pretty as you around here.'

I laughed happily. I told her I was from Mexico.

'Beautiful country,' she said.

'You've been?' I asked.

'One of my kids is living in the capital,' she said, 'working for a Spanish company, a construction firm. I went to visit him in the summer and we took the grandchildren out to the Caribbean coast for a few days, to see the pyramids. It's all very lovely. The only shame about your country is that the people in charge are so terrible. My son says it's impossible to do business there unless you're corrupt, and you're always having to give money to some politician or other.'

I would have liked to tell her that wasn't true, but since it was true I didn't say anything. I kept quiet. Then I thought about how a lot of the blame was also down to the company where her son worked, who paid the bribes instead of reporting this extortion or refusing the deal.

'What's the company called, where your son works?' I asked her.

She burst out laughing.

'It's all right to name the sin, dear,' she said, 'but not the sinner.'

Sunday 7th

'I'm going to take a walk,' Juan Pablo said, midmorning. 'You should get outside a bit, too.'

I was stretched out in bed, in my pajamas, on page 235 of *The Savage Detectives*. I don't know what I found more hurtful: the fact that his comment excluded me from his own walk (that he hadn't only not invited me, but he'd made it impossible for me to go with him without humiliating myself) or that he believed he was in any position to offer me advice.

'I don't know who Juan Pablo thinks he is to offer me advice,' I said, and went back to focusing on my book.

What was I expected to do? Go for a walk along the beach or a stroll through the Barrio Gótico? What for? To confirm that Barcelona is indeed an attractive city? That Barcelona is 'stunning', as the city council's advertisement claims?

I'd rather stay behind with the wretched Barcelona of Fray Servando's memoirs, that Barcelona of the poor where 'the man who isn't constantly on the go doesn't eat', that Barcelona of pigsties inside houses, of courtyards overflowing with garbage and excrement, that insurgent Barcelona where, following a mandate by the Bourbons, a bread knife needed to be kept chained to a table and it was necessary to ask permission and pay a fee to obtain a rifle for hunting rabbits.

Later I interrupted my reading because I was hungry. I found Facundo in the living room with his daughter Alejandra, who had just turned six and had come to spend the weekend with him (he's separated from her mother).

'Ále, do a picture for Vale,' Facundo said to her, taking advantage of the opportunity to go to the bathroom.

I stood watching as the girl drew a sun, a princess, a flower, a mountain. She was absolutely terrible at drawing.

'The princess is you,' she said, and she painted her face black.

When Facundo returned, I went off to the microwave to reheat the spaghetti I had left over from dinner and I heard him scolding her.

'But Vale isn't black, Ále, the little thing's going to be all sad now.'

'She is black, Pápa, look at her properly and you'll see she's black.' (The way she said 'Pápa', stressing the first syllable instead of the second, meant she was actually calling Facundo the Pope, or a potato.)

'Stop being silly now, Ále, you look at her properly, you'll see she's just dark-skinned. Go on, do her another picture.'

Monday 8th

I woke late and there was nobody in the apartment (Juan Pablo had gone off to the university). I thought I might make the most of this solitude to stretch out and read in the living room, where there's natural light. I made myself a coffee and reread the last few pages of *The Savage Detectives* I'd read last night before falling asleep, while the milk was warming in the microwave. I'm terrible when I read novels, I forget things and I'm always having to go back, I fret about losing the thread of the plot. Reading a diary is completely different: knowing that what gives the narrative its logic is a life rather than a strategy, that is, an artifice, is something I find soothing.

The living room was chaos: colored pencils, dolls, drawings, little balls of plasticine, tiny fake gemstones scattered everywhere. The wreckage of Hurricane Alejandra, as Facundo calls it when he's telling her off. I picked up only what was strictly essential to be able to make myself comfortable, piling things up on one of the little side tables. Among the drawings I found a piece of paper on which the girl had written several times:

> i will go without staying
> i will go like somebody going

I couldn't settle down to my book for the feeling of alarm. I remembered a Korean horror movie and a story they used to tell in Coatepec when I was little, about a girl who'd said goodbye to everybody before dying in an accident. I'm going now, the girl would say, or that's what people said she'd say. In the Korean movie, two little twin sisters filled one wall of their house with apocalyptic messages, which turned out to be death sentences on the people they'd pass on the street, over the course of the movie. Just as well it wasn't long before Facundo got home.

'Have you seen this?' I asked him as he was opening the door, blocking his way.

'Oh, yeah,' he said as he took off his jacket – 'they're lines from a poem, Alejandra's shithead mother has it tattooed on her back – don't you know it, didn't you study literature? It's by Alejandra Pizarnik, the shithead got it tattooed in Buenos Aires when she was eighteen and couldn't wait to scram, she said Argentina wasn't a country, it was an incurable disease, you can see what a shithead that shithead is.'

Tuesday 9th

Two-thirty in the morning. I woke with a start. Juan Pablo was groaning. Sobbing. I didn't know if he was having a nightmare or if he was awake. I rolled over to face him. The light had been left on again.

'What's up?' I said when I saw he was shivering, his eyes lost on the wall to the left, hands pressing down over his breastbone.

'Gastritis,' he said. 'I can't bear it.'

'Have you taken anything?' I asked.

He said he had. He got up and went to the bathroom and when he came back he said he was going to the ER. While he got dressed I couldn't decide whether or not I should go with him. I came to the conclusion that he could ask me to. Make me feel like he needed me. He went without saying goodbye. I started reading *The Savage Detectives*, unable to recover my sleep.

When he arrived back it was after four. They'd prescribed him the same medicine he was taking already.

In the morning, Juan Pablo insisted we go to the Fundación Miró and I accepted because I wanted to believe that he was finally beginning to react in some way. That the gastritis emergency might have meant he'd hit rock bottom. I thought some simulacrum of normality would do us good. But no such thing. All the good intentions (if he actually had any) evaporated along the way. We wandered the museum in silence and he didn't even look moved by the Calder mobiles, which he apparently liked so much (and which he'd only seen previously in photographs and videos).

To cap it all, that night Juan Pablo started getting these rashes all over. He went back to the hospital. They said it was an allergy. According to Juan Pablo, he'd had it before and it had gone away in Xalapa. I told him that, as far as I knew, it was the opposite that happened: people got allergies from Xalapa's damp and its mushrooms.

'What Juan Pablo's got looks like dermatitis nervosa to me,' I said.

'I'm sure you know better than the doctor,' he said. 'I had these rashes when I was little and my dad treated them. Don't forget my dad's a dermatologist.'

He put on a cream which I'm sure is for dermatitis. At least we didn't fight.

Thursday 11th

This afternoon I went to Pompeu Fabra University to ask for information about the doctorate in humanities and it turned out there was a lecture at seven on auto-fiction, by Manuel Alberca. I took refuge in the library to kill time and then I looked for the classroom and crashed the talk uninvited, or rather, I thought I was crashing, because I ended up discovering it was actually a public event.

I loved the experience of a bibliography being transformed into a person of flesh and bone. I told Dr Alberca this at the end, I went up to thank him, for the lecture and for his writing, which had helped me so much in my undergrad thesis. I think I must have exaggerated my enthusiasm, because he even blushed, and I started telling him about my thesis on Fray Servando, I told him I was thinking of taking advantage of my stay in Spain to get more deeply into those fragments that can be read as travel writing, the most fun part of his memoirs, where he says outrageous things about Madrid and Barcelona, and that the following year I was going to matriculate in the doctoral program at Barcelona Uni, because I wanted to work with Nora Catelli (all half-truths, prompted by the euphoria of the moment). He told me he was at Málaga (I knew this already), in case there was anything he could help with. The university people were trying to hurry him along, with a certain amount of impatience that irritated me. He said they were going to have dinner somewhere nearby, and I should go with them. A big group headed out, saying they were going to a tapas bar, with everybody trying to attract Dr Alberca's attention, talking about their research projects and what they were reading. As the group stretched out, I found myself increasingly lagging behind, shy and indecisive, invisible, until I was no longer a part of the group. It looked more like I was pursuing them. I saw the entrance to the metro in the distance and headed for that as though this had been my intention all along.

When I reached Julio Verne I found Juan Pablo at the entrance to our building. He was just going out to meet some friends from his doctoral program and his hair was all slicked up with gel. He asked if I wanted to come too, and since I imagined he thought I'd say no (and he wanted me to say no), I said yes. He didn't seem especially annoyed that I'd accepted, as if he had much more important problems than his problems with me.

We walked down to a bar in Gràcia, crossing a couple of squares full of dogs and squatters, in silence the whole way. The squatters are a mystery to me, an astonishing phenomenon, one of those things I'd only ever seen in movies. In the bar, a cramped, dark, red-colored room in which it was almost impossible to breathe for the cigarette smoke, I was finally able to witness for myself what I'd been trying to imagine all this time: Juan Pablo's new life. There were two guys from Mexico City, two Peruvian girls from Lima, a Colombian guy from Medellín, a Brazilian girl from São Paulo and a guy from Bahia. A Catalan guy from Tarragona. A Catalan girl from a town in Lleida. They had met at a Jungian mythology class.

God knows what Juan Pablo was doing registered for that class, God knows what Jung has got to do with humor in Latin American literature.

We were at one end of the table, next to Iván, the Catalan from Tarragona, who immediately got talking to Juan Pablo about parody, with no prologue and no introduction, as though he were resuming a conversation that had been interrupted.

'The problem with parody,' he said to him, 'is that for it to be intelligent it needs to be ideological, and if it's ideological it stops being fun, or it's only fun if you share the ideology yourself, and deep down that's a real pain in the ass.'

I imagined they must be talking about Ibargüengoitia, from Juan Pablo's undergrad thesis, or about his doctoral thesis project. Juan Pablo did indeed say he didn't believe there was any ideological predisposition to Ibargüengoitia's work.

'If it has no ideological predisposition, it's an empty parody, an idiotic one,' said Iván. 'You're laughing at something, ridiculing it, but what for? For no reason? Just because you feel like showing that the thing you're mocking is a piece of shit? And then what? Man, that's just cynicism, it's what Sloterdijk called wicked realism.'

He started to explain what Sloterdijk said in *Critique of Cynical Reason* about the 'cynicism of a new age', interspersing it with something from Freud's *Civilization and Its Discontents* and an example from Thoreau's *Walden*, and for a few minutes, while Iván delved deeper into this chatter, I had the cheering sensation that nothing had changed and it was just any old night in Chiva, the bar in Xalapa where we used to go up until a few weeks ago. When Iván argued that the person parodying is implicitly attacking one ideology and defending another that he believes superior to it, Juan Pablo introduced Baudelaire into the argument, I say introduced not because he wasn't relevant, on the contrary, he presented him as you might a gleaming collectible figurine or an academic totem.

'Baudelaire says that laughter arises from the idea of the superiority of the person who's laughing. The person who's laughing is laughing at somebody else, at the other person who's tripped and fallen over, for example, and the laugher is laughing because, deep down, he knows that he's out of danger, that he's not the one who's falling.'

'Baudelaire said that?' asked Iván.

'More or less,' answered Juan Pablo. 'Baudelaire said it more crudely. Baudelaire said that laughter is satanic because it arises from the idea of one's own superiority. He says that the only person able to laugh at his own falling-over is a philosopher, who is in the habit of splitting himself in two and of, open quote, witnessing in a disinterested fashion the phenomenon of his ego.'

From that point, Juan Pablo predictably began to talk about a project he always talks about when he's a little drunk, though without his usual vehemence: setting up a reading group for foreigners reading and talking about Ibargüengoitia's stories, a project of literary sociology, really, which according to him would be seeking to confirm his hypothesis about the primacy of the reader's prejudices over the text's contents in the production of meanings, a project which would show how readers can appropriate a text and distort it to make it confirm their prejudices, in this case against Mexicans.

'The fact that Mexicans are lazy, corrupt, a sort of degenerate race,' said Juan Pablo.

'But it's not the readers who wrote the text,' answered Iván, 'however foreign they are. That thing you're talking about is in the stories themselves, it was Ibargüengoitia who portrayed the Mexicans in that way.'

'Fine,' said Juan Pablo, 'but you can't compare the effect on a Mexican reader of a process of self-recognition, which could even be cathartic, with the effect on a foreign reader of a process of generalization of the other, which just confirms prejudices that lead to xenophobic attitudes.'

They went on in this way for a while longer, for a couple of beers longer, until Juan Pablo moved over to the other end of the table, to chat with the Peruvian girls. Iván forgot about the earlier conversation, in which I hadn't said a peep, he changed the tape and started talking to me about medieval swords (his thesis is on an archaizing poet). I was so focused on keeping an eye on Juan Pablo (he didn't exactly look very happy, more absent than anything else) that it took me a while to realize that Iván was coming on to me. They were subtle comments, which could be interpreted as jokes if I didn't let him go any further, allowing him to withdraw with dignity in case I called a halt to his advances, but which were also the preface to a strategy of seduction if I reciprocated.

My puzzlement wasn't because he was coming on to me, that might even have been flattering (in other circumstances), but because I realized now that Juan Pablo hadn't introduced me as his girlfriend. And that he hadn't mentioned me to them before. I interrupted Iván's disquisition on Gothic crosses, I told him to wait for me, and escaped to the basement of the bar where there was a line to get into the women's bathroom. I saw the half-open door of the men's, I went in, it was a tiny room with a toilet, it was unoccupied, and I shut myself inside before anyone could object.

I cleaned the spatterings off the toilet seat and sat down to pee. I'd drunk three or four beers, and was starting to feel drunk. Fucking asshole, I thought, what a fucking asshole. Jerk. Motherfucker. Shiteater, as a Medellín Colombian would say. Dickhead, as Iván would say – Iván who wanted to pick me up, or rather to fuck me. I looked up and saw the door scratched from top to bottom. 'We want Cataluña free from Latinos, Moors and Spaniards.' 'We're all Catalans: we Latinos, Moors and Spaniards are more Catalans than this hick who's just come down from the mountains.' 'Yes to Moors and Latinos, no to Spaniards.' 'Fascist scum.' I took out the apartment keys and scratched in uppercase a line from Fray Servando that I thought would be a perfect way to conclude the decoration of this door: 'YOU CAN'T TELL THE TRUTH ABOUT SPAIN WITHOUT OFFENDING THE SPANIARDS.' It took me a while (there was impatient knocking on the door, twice).

I left the bathroom. I went back up to the bar. Juan Pablo and his friends were no longer there.

Saturday 13th

'Know what I like most about you, shithead? You ain't like all those shitheads who come live in Barcelona and spend their time open-mouthed like cretins, arrive here and go to the Ramblas every day or to look at the Sagrada Familia until one day some gypsy swipes their wallet, for being shitheads. But you're different, shithead, you do your own thing, you know what you want, you don't let yourself get impressed by the flashiness of this phony city. You get what I'm saying, shithead?'

I was going to say something, but Facundo carried right on, the price I had to pay for accepting his empanadas for dinner.

'Honestly, shithead, it's a deadly combination, on the one hand those shitheads who come live here and they think it's more beautiful than Disneyland, and on the other those *mega*-shitheads the Catalans, who since they don't know anything they say Cataluña's got everything, seas and mountains, and think they live in paradise.'

Facundo filled his mouth with the half empanada which for several minutes had been waiting, hopelessly, for him to finish eating it. I took advantage of the pause to horn my way in:

'That's exactly what Fray Servando was saying at the start of the nineteenth century,' I said. 'That since Spanish people don't travel they have no way of making a comparison, which is why they think Spain is the best thing in the world, the garden of the Hesperides.'

'Right, shithead, exactly,' and Facundo was off again, still chewing the empanada, I could even see the olives crushed between his molars. 'They think Barcelona's hot shit because they don't know London or New York, seriously shithead, they don't even know Paris.'

I went on eating empanadas, which were actually really delicious by comparison: after so many days eating spaghetti, the empanadas seemed a delicacy of the gods. I let Facundo prattle away to his heart's delight, dropping in an 'ah' from time to time, swigging from the bottle of beer after every three or four bites. We were almost alone in the apartment, Juan Pablo hadn't yet come back (he'd gone out in the afternoon 'to go for a walk'), Cristian was on the night shift at the restaurant and Alejandra had been asleep in Facundo's bedroom since nine-thirty. Facundo had unexpectedly felt obligated to invite me for dinner, which he said was to thank me for having spent the whole afternoon drawing with Alejandra, making bracelets, combing her hair, though in fact this exact same thing always happens whenever the girl comes over.

'Before you there were a couple of Colombians living here, shithead,' Facundo went on, 'in the room where you now live with your shithead boyfriend. Incidentally, I got to tell you what a shithead your boyfriend is, the other day we were riding the elevator down together and I asked him where he was going. And you know what the shithead answered?

Only that he was going to his Catalan class! Taking Catalan classes! You must be shitting me, shithead, the Catalans don't want anybody else learning Catalan, what they want is to feel superior, or at the very least different, but your shithead boyfriend will discover that soon enough when he wants to talk Catalan in the street and nobody will even notice he exists. But I was going to tell you about the Colombians, a couple of shitheads the size of the Barça stadium, saying these totally shitheadish things the whole time about how beautiful Barcelona was, the shitheads used to make themselves sandwiches and sit in front of Gaudí houses to eat them, seriously such total shitheads those shitheads. They were always coming to me with these stories about museums and parks and did I know such and such a restaurant where they made the best pan con tomate anywhere in Cataluña, but seriously, shithead, I fucking live here! I don't do the tourism thing unless it's for a job, Lonely Planet can hire me and they can pay me a shitload of money and maybe then I'd put up with Gaudí and all his dicking around, shithead. And then the shitheads argued, the chick got together with a Catalan and left the shithead, obviously, the girl liked Barcelona so much she said nobody's ever going to make me leave, and this shithead guy instead of putting a brave face on it, instead of making the most of the breakup to go around the world in eighty chicks, because that's something Barcelona does have, shithead, here you can go around putting little flags on the map, there are such gorgeous chicks in Barcelona, oh man, Scandinavian ones, Black ones, Latin ones, Asian ones, whatever you feel like, shithead, but the shithead ups and goes back to Colombia! Such shitheads, those Colombians, they don't deserve all the blessings God's given them! Hey, listen, do you want a do a quick line? Would you mind if I did one?'

Best for me to stop writing now, to quit this exercise in the cheap picturesque to ridicule Facundo, my sad revenge for his having wanted to feel me up after doing three lines, and because he'd wanted to charge me ten euro for the empanadas after I'd indignantly rejected him, after I'd shouted that in case he hadn't noticed I was Juan Pablo's girlfriend and Juan Pablo might be arriving at any moment.

'You're such a shithead you haven't even noticed, shithead?' he said. 'That shithead and you are heading in opposite directions, you're a classic case of a couple broken up by Barcelona. Textbook case. *Divorce a la catalana*. People who arrive here together never make it, shithead. Barcelona's a real bitch. I'm telling you this as someone who's separated. You really are a shithead, it's two in the morning, at this moment your shithead boyfriend must be fucking some shithead chick like you, a shithead he picked up in some bar in Gràcia or El Born, a shithead just like you, shithead, but more attractive. Who do you think you are, so dignified all of a sudden, Humble Maria from that fucking telenovela?'

3:45 a.m. I've finished reading *The Savage Detectives*. Juan Pablo's not back yet.

Dr Elizondo grabbed the bunch of keys from her desk and said, 'Let's go get a coffee.' At the next desk, Dr Valls, whose anthology of contemporary Spanish stories published by Anagrama I'd read, pretended to have no idea what was going on, behind the pile of books surrounding him. Maybe he had no idea what was going on. Although, however distracted or self-absorbed he was, it was unlikely he hadn't heard the words I'd just said: I want to change adviser, I'd said, in a tone of voice that was unnecessarily assertive.

We walk out into the hallway, and Dr Elizondo stops in front of the machine that dispenses coffee. You wouldn't rather go to the cafeteria, professor? I say. She presses the button for a cortado and gives me a half-second scornful glance, with the exact same amount of fury and disappointment in it as the looks I've been getting from Valentina ever since we arrived in Barcelona (with the same mixture, I mean). Dr Elizondo does at least still acknowledge my existence, unlike Valentina, who refers to me in the third person as if I wasn't present and she's talking to an imaginary friend (an imaginary girlfriend, to be precise, judging by the rhetoric and content of her comments). What annoys me most about Juan Pablo is that he wants to act like nothing happened, she says. I don't know if a day will come when I'll be able to forget all the terrible things Juan Pablo said to me, she says. And even – just last week, standing in front of one of the Alexander Calder mobiles at the Fundación Miró: Juan Pablo would have loved this, she said, as we watched the almost imperceptible movement of one of the little colored balls, as if I was dead.

I ask the machine for an espresso, wait for the little cup to finish receiving the liquid and go out into the November cold and walk toward the flower bed where Dr Elizondo is sitting, waiting for me. What's the problem? she says. So like, there's no problem, I say (the itching starts at the back of my neck and runs down my spine). Well then? she says, and so I get tangled up explaining things to her that she already knows I already knew when I asked her, by email, to be my adviser and would she do me the favor of signing the papers for my application for a scholarship. That she's a specialist in Andean narrative. That my research project is mostly focused on Rio de la Plata, Cuba and Mexico. That she works with mythology. That she's a Greimasian. That while I admire Greimas's work very much, especially his concept of the semiotics of passions, it doesn't seem the most suitable methodology for my research. That humor and semiotics don't go together. I say everything scrambled together and without a break as if instead of talking I am scratching or as if it had been scientifically proved that verbal diarrhea cures itching (my whole body is prickling now). I close my mouth when I realize that I'm babbling: Comedy is an effect and semiotics are a cause, I've just said, but it's the effect of a different cause, comedy and semiotics are parallel discourses that never meet, so like, not like semiotics and tragedy, or semiotics and mythology, which are perpendicular. Behind the glasses that lend a certain turtlishness to her appearance, like the wise tortoises of the Galapagos Islands to be precise, the look in Dr Elizondo's eyes is so expressive that she doesn't need to say a word for me to understand that what she's thinking is that I'm a moron. Or a cretin. Or that my face is covered in rashes. I squeeze the little cup I'm holding between my right thumb and index finger. The coffee goes down, immediately portending gastritis. I don't know why I'm doing it, I would tell her if I was telling the truth, if I could tell her the truth I'd say I was only obeying orders, that I've found myself caught in the net of a criminal organization that is compelling me, under pain of death, to change my adviser and the subject of my doctoral thesis. I don't expect anyone to believe me.

Have you been to the doctor to get that dermatitis looked at? says Dr Elizondo. I tell her it's an allergy, my father's a dermatologist. It looks like a case of dermatitis nervosa, she says, and I suspect her concern for my health isn't altogether disinterested (a diagnosis of nervous breakdown due to the change in country or stress of the doctorate would allow her to accept what I'm asking for without this wounding her amour propre). It's a multifactorial allergy, I insist, I've had it since I was very little, I lie, stealing this possibility away from her, more worried – thanks to some narcissistic reflex – about protecting my own amour propre than hers. I ought to do a bit more work on my sense of self-preservation (I'm going to need it). Dr Elizondo puffs, annoyed. Who have you been thinking of to take my place? she says, with evident hurt, as if academics could be the singers of country songs too. Who? I repeat, momentarily deferring the revelation of the name that the lawyer spelled out to me in the last of our calls, which this time I made from a call shop in Sants. Write this down, said the lawyer. I haven't got a pen, I said. Then ask for one, fuck's sake, said the lawyer, get a move on. I opened the door of the booth and three people immediately rushed at me, thinking I'd finished, a woman in a veil, a guy who looked Bolivian or Peruvian and a sub-Saharan, as if it was the start of a joke:

there's a Muslim woman, a Black man and a Latino man in a call shop. I gestured that it was still being used and did anyone have a pen, a *bolígrafo*, I said, a *boli*, I said again, looking at the people who were standing in the line, until the Bolivian or Peruvian took a Bic out of some pocket in his paint-stained overalls and handed it to me. I went back into the booth, closed the door, scratched my neck and my stomach, took a little piece of paper out of my wallet and said: Ready, and the lawyer spelled out the name that Dr Elizondo is waiting for.

Fernando? says Dr Elizondo, referring to Dr Valls, at the next desk. So, like, no, I say. Well then? she says. I take another sip of gastritis. She sighs, exasperated. Dr Ripoll, I say finally. Though I actually say *Ripol*, because I still can't pronounce the double-l at the end of the name the way the Catalans do it. Meritxell? she says, pronouncing the double-l at the end perfectly well, and she almost jumps to her feet, and when she realizes her reaction was exaggerated and that it could be misinterpreted, as if there were something personal between them, she says: Well, maybe you can explain to me what your project has to do with gender studies. I'm not going to lift a finger to process the change of adviser for your thesis, she adds. You do it yourself, and bring me the papers to sign when they're ready. And she leaves at too speedy a pace for her tortoise-like wisdom, thereby saving me the shame of having to confess that I'm changing not only adviser but also research project, and that the topic of my thesis is now going to be misogynistic and homophobic humor in Latin American literature of the twentieth century. Immediately afterward, I start scratching all over my body as though the topic of my thesis has brought me out in hives.

The cell phone in my pants pocket is also shaking, to the rhythm of the itching, and it takes me a while to realize that's where the vibration is coming from. Number unknown. Hello,

I say, and an English voice says: One moment, please. Two or three seconds go by. How'd it go? says the lawyer. So, like, fine, I say. Any problem changing? he asks. No, I say, but I've got to go through the process. When do you have your class with Dr Ripoll? pronouncing the final double-l perfectly. There's a seminar next week, I say. Fine, he says. Pay attention. Find out everything you can about Laia Carbonell. She's a doctoral student working with Dr Ripoll, I'm sure she'll be in the seminar. Laia Carbonell, he says again, spelling it out with the final double-l. Get close to her, I need you to make contact with her. You're not going to screw this up, learn all the gender studies chitchat, you're going to need it. From now on, no more jokes. Mess this up and you're fucked. Get it?

The seminar attracts a handful of lost souls like me, though 90 percent are composed of a compact group of doctoral students who are working on research projects in the field headed up by Dr Ripoll, entitled 'Textual Bodies and Bodily Texts'. Most are Catalan women, with the exception of a subgroup of four Colombian women, they all seem to have known one another for some time, they demonstrate that rigid complicity of those who went to progressive elementary schools, guerrilla warriors of the Waldorf method, or Montessori at the very least.

The Colombians do a presentation on the progress they've made in their project on the masculinization of the female body, showing a video in which they are disguised in dark suits, black ties, false moustaches and top hats, wandering down the Ramblas. The video lasts about ten minutes, during which time they do nothing but dodge tourists, talk in phony voices, smoke cigars, grab their genitals the way Javier Bardem does in the *Golden Balls* poster and complain about how people are laughing at them. Back in reality, meanwhile, maybe to hide the embarrassment at seeing themselves on the screen, the Colombians all start interrupting one another, chattering away confusedly about transvestism and transsexuality. When the projection comes to an end, Dr Ripoll asks them what the greatest challenge was that they faced in embodying the male. The Colombian women say the hardest part was not laughing. Or smiling. How so? asks Dr Ripoll, who I guess was imagining, as I was, that they were referring to how hard it was to take their performance seriously and not make a joke out of it. But that wasn't it, one of the Colombians explains, it's that since men don't smile or laugh, the thing they found trickiest was not to smile or laugh. Men don't laugh? asks Dr Ripoll. The Colombians all say no, in unison, and I laugh, I let a burst of laughter out and instantly everybody discovers that I exist, that I'm there, at the back of the class. Sorry, I say, that made me laugh.

Dr Ripoll asks me to take this opportunity to introduce myself. I talk briefly about my CV, about my research project on machista and homophobic humor, I tell them that I've already analyzed Jorge Ibargüengoitia's stories in my undergrad thesis, and in one of these, for example, there's a character who considers it the greatest humiliation possible that a doctor stuck his finger in his ass. I actually use the words 'inserted' and 'anus', which sound more academic. And I say it all in a sort of appalled tone, though the truth is I think it's an awesome story. The Catalan women forgive me. The Colombians not so much. The professor says we're going to take a ten-minute break while we wait for the guest lecturer from the University of Santiago de Compostela to arrive.

During the break I go to the gastritis vending machine, I stand in line behind the Catalans, alert to what I can hear of their conversations, which is almost nothing. The problem is, it looks like there are two or three Laias, apparently being called Laia in Barcelona is as common as being called Claudia in Mexico or Jennifer in Honduras. The break ends without my having made any progress, the Catalan classes I'm taking are a disaster, almost a month going twice a week and I still don't understand a thing.

The Galician professor heads up a research group at Santiago de Compostela on the oppression and repression of phallic discourse. After a brief institutional speech celebrating the collaboration between his university and the Autónoma, he sets about showing us some slides in which we see him with his boyfriend, inserting monstrous latex penises in the most varied positions. Missionary. Doggy. Spoons. Advanced Cow. Beautiful, says one of the Catalans. Lovely, agrees one of the Colombians. In the gloom (the lights have been turned off to allow us to appreciate the photos better), I look at the faces of the research students illuminated by the dazzle of the screen. There are three or four of them who look more or less attractive, I think. One very much so. All of them watching hardcore homosexual porn together, spellbound. In normal conditions, as Valentina might have put it, Juan Pablo would have loved this.

Very interesting, says Dr Ripoll, when the lights come back on, following a huge close-up of the visiting professor's anus. The phallus as subversion, she says, or the subversion of the phallus. The *mise en abyme* of the phallus. And then she declares the class over and tells us we're expected back before the holidays, on December 10.

I dawdle, as my mother would say, in the classroom, until the Catalan girls have finished chatting to the visiting lecturer, probably asking him what cream he uses for his piles or something. When they finally leave, I follow them discreetly through the maze of corridors leading from the Philology classrooms to the train station. There are eight girls in total, two of them split off to go to the library, another heads for the cafeteria (the most attractive one), another says goodbye when they pass the computer room, and though there's a chance that one of them's Laia, the Laia I'm looking for, I go by probability and decide to stick with the four who are still together headed for the underpass that leads into the station, I hurry to reach the train platform at the same time as them, I stand next to them as if we were together and I look at them blatantly, making it very hard for them to ignore me. Hi, I say, when I realize that, despite everything, they're really trying their utmost to do just that. Hi, they answer, somewhat reluctantly. I tell them I thought the Galician professor's presentation was really interesting, really stimulating, I say, and then to counteract any misunderstanding that my enthusiasm might have provoked, or to prevent the four Catalan girls from thinking I'm talking utter crap, I say that the photographs reminded me of an article by Gayle Rubin and Judith Butler that interprets the history of sexuality through the history of materials and technology, the urbanism that led to red-light districts, the darkness of the public space before the invention of electricity, perfect for clandestine encounters, I say it's impossible to understand fetishism or sadomasochism without considering the history of rubber production, the exploitation of the Amazonian Indians by English companies in the nineteenth century, and that we must always think about the political and social aspect of the erotic practices of post-modernity, because the Galician professor and his boyfriend's being able to reach orgasm required the creation of a market in sexual prostheses that goes back to the enslavement of the Putumayo Indians, who were tortured and mistreated like criminals.

So, what, we're supposed to feel guilty every time we come? asks one of the Catalan girls, when my hysterical verbal diarrhea finally subsides, the exact moment when a screen notifies us that it's four minutes till the Barcelona train. Ha ha ha, I laugh, totally faking it, laughing at her bad joke, because she's one of the kind-of-attractive Catalans, which improves her joke. I guess it'd be enough if you apologized for your colonialist attitude before putting on your panties, I say. What was your name again, Mexicano? she asks, laughing condescendingly, her upper canines are pushed slightly forward, or the four incisors slightly back. I'm Laia, she adds. I tell her my name and look at the other three, who say they're called Ona, Ana, with two n's, she says, Anna, and Laia, an ordinary Laia with milky skin who's wearing a Levi's denim jacket from prehistoric times. I look back and forth between the two Laias, waiting for one of them to offer the clarification that anybody might think appropriate (and to me was urgent, a matter of life and death), and finally the one with the pushed-back teeth says she's Laia Carbonell, *Carbonei*, she says, or that's what my pre-Catalan ears hear, and then she says the surname of the other Laia, another Catalan surname, but I don't care about that.

Truth is, Mexicano, says Laia, skipping over the introductions, it's also impossible to talk about fetishism without analyzing the history of misogyny, because even some of the 'noble savages' you defend were crazy fucking misogynists, and she starts illustrating her argument with a story about a Polynesian tribe. I take advantage of the three minutes left till the train comes, two minutes fifty-eight seconds, to compose a mental portrait of Laia, as if the lawyer's orders were really prompts for an exercise in a writing workshop. She has golden hair, almost red, trimmed up to the back of her neck, her earlobes adorned with two tiny little pearls, her nose turned up and leaning slightly toward the right (chasing after the trace of some succulent aroma), her cheekbones and forehead are healthy, ruddy, with no trace of adolescent acne, no greasiness, her small thin lips slightly blue with the cold (she doesn't use lipstick).

The train arrives and the three friends manage to get seats and Laia and I have to settle for leaning against one of the doors, at the exact moment Laia concludes her argument saying that ultimately totems were the first inflatable (she doesn't say blow-up) toys. I say that as far as Mexico is concerned, the Aztecs and the Mayas were more disposed toward annihilation than to eroticism or reproduction, and that their conception of eroticism, if anything, was pretty grim, necrophiliac, and Laia Carbonell laughs as if I'd told a joke and the position of her teeth starts giving me a tingly feeling between my legs. Before we find ourselves with one of those silences installing itself between us as heavy as a backpack full of sand, I ask her if she knows the Pygmalion myth, she pouts which means obviously she does (she unbuttons her coat, revealing her slender shape – her two breasts, which aren't big even when bulked up by the bra and blouse and sweater, must be smaller than plums), and then I up the level of sophistication and talk about Oskar Kokoschka, the painter, who when he came back from the First World War found that his lover had married another man, and instead of attempting to win her back, he did something simpler: he commissioned the production of a doll identical to her, and also, as if that wasn't enough, both the painter's ex-lover and his doll were called Alma, meaning soul, irony of ironies. Kokoschka would take his doll to the opera, to parties hosted in his honor, and after one crazy night the doll showed up decapitated in the garden of his house. Truth is, I say, as if it was a moral to the story, you can't talk about the history of misogyny without considering mental illness. You've hit the nail on the head there, Mexicano, guys are all total wack jobs, all of you, says Laia, opening her mouth wider as she hoots with laughter, showing the whole arch of her teeth.

I take advantage of the fact that she seems to have softened up to carry out the usual questioning, where she was born, how old she is, etc. She says she's from Barcelona. That she's twenty-nine, nearly thirty. That she studied Catalan philology at the Autónoma. I ask if she's always lived in Barcelona. She says she lived in Brussels for a year when she was finishing high school, because of her father's work, and she did an Erasmus study-abroad program for six months in Berlin. Do you speak German? I say. No, she says. Well, I say, six months isn't much to learn German if you're not very smart. You're such a cretin, she says, and goes back to laughing, and I go back to looking at her teeth. I didn't go to learn German, she adds, I went to the Institute of Romance Languages at the Humboldt. The train goes through Peu del Funicular station and she says: Next one's me, Mexicano. She gestures to her friends to stay sitting, they promise to call one another, and when she comes closer to give me a pair of goodbye kisses, not bothering to avoid contact with the rashes on my face, on which she hasn't commented either, I say maybe we could meet up for a coffee, or a beer. Or to study German. Maybe, she says, laughing, and I see her teeth again. And then, when the carriage door opens, she says: But don't get your hopes up, Mexicano, I like girls.

That evening I phone the lawyer from a call shop in El Poble Sec. I tell him the things I found out about Laia Carbonell. What else? says the lawyer. He doesn't seem to be taking notes. When I tell him that's all, that was all I've managed to discover so far, he says: Now you bang her, he says. What?! I say, and I press the speaker closer to my left ear as if suddenly all the waves and winds of the Atlantic Ocean had engineered some interference, and I even change the phone quickly to my right ear because I sense I'll hear better with the right. I said you're going to fuck her, says the lawyer, you've already forgotten the way we talk back home? and my right ear is apparently also unable to translate the message into anything remotely plausible (if he'd asked me to kill her, or to kidnap her, or to torture her, or to extort her, or to blackmail her, say, that would have more diegetic coherence, bearing in mind what had come before). Hello?! I shout, Yes?! Hello?! I say again, trying to buy a bit of time to see whether reality, which is so generally omnipresent, or realism, its common lieutenant, might finally make an appearance. You're going to B-A-N-G her! says the lawyer again. To F-U-C-K her! he repeats, as though the criminal organization's orders were a sublimation of the collective libido.

I smack the phone hard to cut off communications and race out of the booth and almost run right out into the street, but the Paraguayan at the cash register stops me with a hysterical yell: Where d'you think you're going without paying, asshole?! And my middle-class prejudices (my values, as my mother would say) are stronger than my eagerness to flee, and so I stop to wait for the Paraguayan to print out my bill, it's two euro eighty, while he tells me that a customer receiving a piece of terrible news and skipping off without paying is a con he's seen many times, that he's not such an idiot to believe it, that there was a Cuban woman in the neighborhood who would come out of the booth crying and shouting that her little children had died in Havana, or in Morón, she'd change the city depending on the call shop, and nobody dared to stop her when she left, until the word got around the neighborhood. Her reputation was her downfall, the Paraguayan is telling me, when the cell phone in my pants pocket starts to ring, number unknown, and I answer without thinking, just to get the Paraguayan off my back, as he wants to show me this Cuban woman's photo (he has it printed out on a sign stuck up next to the cash register), and I hear the operator saying, in English, One moment, please, and then there's the lawyer shouting: You do not ever hang up on me, asshole! You do not hang up on me! And I'm about to hang up when he adds: Your dad will be first, it's a shame, given how much I kind of liked your dad, so decent, such a hard worker. The other day I went to his office for him to check out a mark on my arm. A good doctor, your dad, he wanted to send me to get my circulation checked out, he was real concerned, but the mark was only a bruise that some dickhead had given me when he escaped Chucky when he cut one of his ears off, fucking Chucky can't tie proper knots, seriously, and the guy's supposed to have been in the Boy Scouts. Dial me again right now, he says, and he hangs up. I need another booth, I tell the Paraguayan, the itching running from my little toe up to the top of my head. The Paraguayan tells me to find someplace else, that over his dead fucking body is he going to let me back into his call shop, that I'm an idiot if I think I'm going to be able to swindle him just by insisting. I'll pay you up front, I say. Oh shit, says the Paraguayan, what's up with you, man? Your face is all covered in rashes. It's an allergy, I say, and I pull out my wallet and hand him a ten-euro bill. It's a matter of life and death, I say, and the Paraguayan grabs hold of the bill and tells me not to imagine for a moment he's going to swallow the con about being allergic, that when I've used up the ten euro he's going to come into the booth and kick me out with his own two feet. Number three, says the Paraguayan, and I run over to booth three.

That's what I like to see, says the lawyer when he answers. I'm going to the police, I say. Seriously? he says. Which one are you going to? If you go to the municipal police, ask for Gimeno, he's in charge in Barcelona. Tell him I'm sending him a hug. If you go to the Mossos d'Esquadra, that's the Catalan police, say hi from me to Captain Riquer. I say nothing: instead of answering, I scratch (my arm, my neck, my stomach, my lower back). And might I know what you're planning to tell them? the lawyer continues. That you're being blackmailed to fuck a girl who is also undoubtedly very rich? The Chinaman sent me some photos. Nice-looking, this Laia. Kind of skinny, the way I like them. Get her teeth fixed she'd be a stunner. I'm going to tell them, I say, that you people killed my cousin, that I witnessed it all. Your cousin got run over by a city truck, don't be an asshole, he says, if you want I can send you a copy of the death certificate. Your uncle and aunt made such a fuss they even put the driver in prison, hadn't you heard? Stop with saying these assholeish things, or jerkish things if you prefer, I think your dad would like to go on living, he strikes me as the kind of guy who's very attached to his life. Laia's a lesbian, I say, in case this small detail had escaped him, though my repeating it now marks the beginning of my capitulation. We knew that already, asshole, says the lawyer. What you're going to do is a threesome, that's why we needed Valentina. Now's when we're going to use Valentina. What?! I say, stunned, not so much at his explanation as at its effect: an unexpected erection. In reality, the lawyer continues, what we need is to get into Laia's inner circle, and the quickest and simplest way is through sex. And wouldn't it be easier for me to befriend her? To gain her trust? I say, unconvinced, but still stunned, all the more so at the recollection of Laia's teeth, the four upper incisors pushed slightly back, at the fantasy of sucking on them, the anthill between my legs competing with the generalized itching, the promise of a threesome and a death threat, Eros and Thanatos, I'm sure you could explain it with Bataille, I don't expect anyone to believe me. It's so obvious you have no fucking clue where you've gone to live, says the lawyer. It's easier for a camel to pass through the eye of a needle than for you to befriend a Catalan. Pay attention, jot down the phone number I'm going to give you. You just call this asshole for me, you're calling for the lawyer, you tell him, he'll give you what you need to set up the orgy, don't think I'm such an asshole that I'd rely on your gifts as a Don Juan. You brought a pen this time, asshole? Write this down.

The guy was wearing sweats and a green military jacket with a hood. He was walking around in circles, nervously, hands in his pockets, at the entrance to Artigues station. By his appearance and attitude you'd have thought he was a common delinquent, someone who doesn't even bother to hide it, or who is just very bad at hiding it. I approached him, hesitantly. You're from the lawyer, babe, he says, stepping forward. You're Babe? I say. You're late, babe, he says. I made a mistake changing lines at Sagrada Família, I say. We're going to that bar, he says, not taking his hands out of his pockets, gesturing toward the corner with his chin.

At the bar there's a Chinese guy serving. There are two slot machines, both occupied by Chinese guys. Six or seven tables with local people reading the paper, chatting noisily, watching the TV that's up on the back wall. We sit at a table next to the counter. I'll have a beer, just a half, Babe shouts to the Chinese guy. I'd estimate he's between twenty-five and thirty. His skin is pockmarked. Brown hair, I'd guess, to judge by the locks sticking out from under the hood which he doesn't take off even inside the bar. Eyes that are blue like mine. I ask for my usual dose of gastritis. Under the table, Babe touches my knee. I jerk back. Your hand, babe, Babe says nice and quiet, your hand under the table. I obey. I receive a little plastic bag which I hide in my jacket pocket without looking at it. Now he sits back, relaxed.

Which bit of Mexico you from, babe? says Babe, after taking his first sip of the beer. Like, from the capital, I lie. Oof, says Babe, that's got to be rough, babe, all those people squashed together, the mile-long traffic jams, and on top of all that it shakes, babe, one day you wake up in your undies and the whole fucking city's been destroyed. You did well to come here, babe, he says. What are those rashes on your face? It's an allergy, I say. See, babe? he says. I bet it's from the pollution, hey, do you know the joke about the Jewish leper? Are you Jewish? I ask, uncomfortable, looking around to see if anyone is listening to us. What are you saying, babe? says Babe, in Catalan now. Babe's from Badalona, babe, what made you think I'm Jewish? I don't know, I say. I guess I wouldn't tell a Jewish joke if I wasn't Jewish. Shit, babe, says Babe, so I can't tell a joke about Blacks or fags or Mexican immigrants? It's only a joke, babe. If I tell you a Jewish joke doesn't mean I'm a Nazi, babe. I wouldn't be sure, I say, you know the old saying: A man is known by the company he keeps. Or a man is known by the company he laughs with. Christ Almighty, babe, says Babe, I don't have any Nazi pals, I have a lot of nutty pals but no Nazi ones. It's an assumption, I say, imagine who'd laugh at your joke and I'm sure you'd come up with a Nazi, doesn't matter if he actually exists, it's an imaginary Nazi who'd be laughing at your joke. If you've got imaginary Nazis for your pals they lock you up in Sant Boi, babe, says Babe, ha ha ha. Fuck, babe, the things you Mexicans get worked up about, if you don't want me to tell you the joke I won't. The noise of a cascade of coins interrupts what he's saying. Man, those Chinese are motherfuckers on the slots, says Babe, looking at the Chinese guy who's collecting up the coins. Go into any bar in Barcelona and you'll see them, playing on the slots. You know what one pal told me, babe? That that's how the Chinese are funded, babe, with the cash they get from the slots, that's how they buy up the neighborhood stores, the bars, have you noticed? There are Chinese shops everywhere these days, it's a plan for global domination, babe, all of it with the cash from the slots, he says. He finishes his beer in one swig and makes as if to stand up. You pay for the drink, babe, the pills are paid for already. Then he moves closer to whisper to me, glancing one way and then the other, paranoid-looking: Those pills are the best of the best, he says, there's nothing purer, best aspirins in Barcelona. People kill for them. And you get given them for free. Who are you, babe? Are you Luis Miguel's dealer? Paulina Rubio's?

Whassup, my dumbass little cuz, and how are those Catalans treating you, asshole?, and have you already learned to spread your own pan con tomate?, and have you already been out to get mugged on the Ramblas?

I'm guessing if you're reading this letter it means it reached you, so you call me right-a-fucking-way on the number I'll give you at the end so I know communication channels are open. Also tell me if it's safe for me to write you there at the university if I need to write you again, I got the address off the internet, so did this letter reach you, asshole, or didn't it?

You got to be thinking it's weird I'm sending a letter by mail instead of email, but you'll soon see why, cause I'm certain my email account is being hacked. So I'm going to give the letter to the maid for her to take to the post office, she writes to her family in Oaxaca every week. Sometimes she sends them a letter with twenty pesos in it, I swear, little cuz, and she sends them postcards of Guadalajara like she lives in Paris, Jesus it's depressing. What a fucking country, I swear. But anyway, like this I can be sure my letter reaches you, and if it gets to you at the university that's got to be a safe place too, right?, tell me as soon as you can that the letter's gotten to you, man, and it did, OK, didn't it?

I bet you're thinking I must have gotten you into some weird shit, into something illegal, well that comes from you studying literature and living in a fantasy world and not knowing how fucking hard things are out here, in real life. In real life the blows we receive are some heavy shit, man, when you want to do real high-level deals, real heavy shit, you have to put yourself on that level too, little cuz. By now, if you're reading this letter you already know more or less what I'm talking about, the people who might intercept our communications are seriously heavy people, there's a reason they do deals at the highest level, don't think just anyfucker can get access to those kind of projects. And if they intercept our emails or our calls or spy on us it's not because they're fucking us over, little cuz, for real, these people just know how to look after their business interests, they know that for business to succeed at that level they got to take care of every detail, do some really shit-hot 'follow-up' like the Americans say, not leave a single tiny damn thread loose.

But what matters is you and me we're on the same page, little cuz, specially at just this minute when we're going to be in the start-up stage, seriously, it's a real bastard stage, most businesses don't make it two years, that's why we got to work together you and me, my dumbass little cuz, in both our interests. I'm not saying we play dirty with these fuckers here, no, there's a reason they're my partners, asshole, our partners, asshole, what I'm saying is we should keep our eyes open, we should look after our interests and you'll see how if we bring the project home we're going to mega-stuff ourselves with cash. Real heavy, these assholes, seriously, you must have noticed already, people who run projects it's almost impossible to get access to, these people sit down to eat with presidents, these people pick up the phone and the whole world starts shifting their ass to carry out their orders, these are mega-serious motherfuckers and I'm hooking you up with them just because you're my cousin, little cuz, I talked to them about you and told them you were fucking awesome, you'll thank me one day.

And if you're still thinking what the fuck do you have to do with all this, you who's just this fucking loser who wants to be a literature professor, that all you want is to write books about the immortality of statues, having your twice-monthly salary of seven and a half thousand pesos guaranteed, well you should stop being so selfish and think about Valentina too, you know what these old ladies are like, you've been with her how long now? Five years? More? Trust me, she's really really soon going to be saying how she wants kiddies, that fucking biological clock old ladies have is a total world-class asshole, asshole, you know what these old ladies are like. And with your fucking professor's salary you're not going to get anywhere, my dumbass little cuz, it won't be enough to keep you in diapers, seriously, but you're lucky because I haven't forgotten you, asshole, and even though you've always been an ungrateful little shit and even boycotted my business projects I've always kept on thinking of you as my favorite cousin, little cuz, the partner I want to do business with for us to stuff ourselves with cash together, pal. What's fucking family for otherwise, right? That's what family's for, little cuz, to fuck around together, to share contacts, to do big-B Business with total confidence, or otherwise how'd you think the Azcárragas did it, the Slims? I haven't forgotten what your dad did for mine, you think I don't know how your father supported mine so he could go to college? You don't forget these things, dumbass, I don't forget them, and now I've got this chance to pay you back, I'm opening up an opportunity for you you can't imagine, if you put some work into it you'll be shitting dough, my dumbass little cuz, we'll be shitting dough together, you and me, cousin. I've got pals who'd kill for me to make them an offer like this, on this level, but you're my cousin, little cuz, and I'm probably just kind of sentimental, I haven't forgotten everything we've been through together. Damn, I hope this fucking letter did get to you, call me right this minute, right-a-fucking-way, so's I know, get on with it, asshole, I can't hear the phone ringing.

I'm going to explain how the shit goes down so you and me will be on the same page, working together, don't go deciding you're going to go it alone, little cuz. I'm sending you this letter so you know where you stand, you're on solid ground thanks to me, asshole, don't go thinking I've gotten you into some fucking project with no future, into some totally *outta control* assfuckery or other, this business is solid and these dicks won't be able to get us out too easily, because I've got the info and you're the contact in Barcelona.

So I'll tell you now, read this very carefully and don't get distracted, if you got the TV on I want you to turn it off, or if you're listening to music get rid of it, and quit those fucking books you've always got in your hands. About two years ago, bro, I met these two Catalan girls in Cancún who were backpacking along the Ribera Maya. At first I wanted to pick one of them up who was kind of attractive, blonde, green eyes, nice and skinny, though her teeth were sort of crooked. You can't imagine how many European girls I went through on the Caribbean, little cuz, and me with the disadvantage of being light, with blue eyes. What the European girls are after is dark-skin fuckers, half-Indians, I swear, bro, they've got plenty of light-skinned blonds in Europe already, if you go to pick people up in the clubs on the Caribbean you'll find the fucking world back to front. Long story short I was busy trying to pick up this girl, except turns out she was a lesbian, and the other one was her girlfriend. But I really kind of liked them, they were supercool, actually, and you know I'm not prejudiced, little cuz, an open mind like the Americans say, each to his own, and besides, man, we've got to stay on the alert, when all the fags and the dykes come out of the closet it's going to be a serious fucking market. So I hooked them up with a few friends so they could have a wander round the eco parks and recommended a few beaches that no tourists ever get to, whoa, you have no idea what that's like. The fucking sea in the most motherfucking awesome colors, white sand, but motherfucking *serious* white, I don't know why you didn't take advantage of all those years I was living there to come visit me, the whole thing would have been free for you, seriously you're an ungrateful little shit for not visiting me. You totally missed out, my dumbass little cuz.

So anyway these girls ended up mega-grateful and told me to call them if I ever went to Barcelona. So far so normal, but this is where your cousin's business vision comes into it, because anyfucker else would have thrown away the bit of paper where they wrote down their names and email addresses and phone numbers, and would have forgotten all about them since after all there was zero possibility I was going to get to fuck them. But not your cousin, bro, because your cousin knows this globalized world we're living in, and I've got this fucking sixth sense for totally heavy business, I can sniff out opportunities from ten kilometers away, I can tell you when a hardware store's going to be a big hit in the center of Kathmandu and that there's no future in freezing tuna in Alaska. I had a shit-hot hunch, dipshit, I don't know why, no word of a lie, some people call it business instinct though that sounds like supernatural bull.

I started researching online to see who these girls were, and holy shit, guess what I found out? That one of them, the one I kind of liked, the one with the crooked teeth, was the daughter of a mega-heavy Catalan politician, an asshole who used to be in the European parliament and who now works in some big-shot public company, and the son of a bitch was on the board of fuck knows how many international companies, phone companies and gas companies, oil companies, banks. This bastard is *loaded*. And he comes from one of those families who's been loaded since back when they were living in caves, since the middle ages or the renaissance, since Neanderthal times. Nobody so much as farts in Cataluña without asking this bastard permission, for real.

So I start gathering info about this fucker in my free time, I put together this really heavy file with all his political and business connections, who his business partners and friends were, the projects he'd been involved in, and the fucker's political enemies too. I knew this would come in handy some-day, that I had to stay alert, wait for an opportunity to show up. I can tell you honestly I didn't know why exactly, it was just a kind of intuition, this might change my life one day, I thought, this might change my life for ever, and so you see it is doing, little cuz.

So anyhow time goes by but I never lost this bastard's trail, and then this year two things happened at the same time: a few partners I'd done some heavy business with came to me to see if I had any good business for them to sink some money into and your dad told me you were going to live in Barcelona to study for a doctorate. I started looking into your doctorate, my dumbass little cuz, and for real, I learned you were going to study at the same school where this girl works as a doc-toral student, the daughter of the Catalan politician, the one with the crooked teeth, you get me?, you're paying attention, right?, seriously put down that motherfucking book, dick-head!, I know you very well, I'm sure you've picked up some fucking book to read. I'm telling you this girl, little cuz, she works as a doctoral student in the same school where you're going to do your doctorate! Utter motherfucking total fucking coincidence, whoa, suddenly everything just clicked, little cuz, like in those telenovelas where it turns out the servant is really the long-lost daughter of a millionaire, I don't know if anything like this has ever happened in your life before, the planets align, you get all the aces in the pack just when all the money's on the table.

All the rest you must more or less know by now. I passed a copy of the file to those fuckers, our partners, I told them about you, I said you were fucking awesome and right-a-fucking-way they seemed to get interested. They asked me to set up a meeting before you go off to Barcelona, which is the meeting we're having tomorrow, that is, tomorrow from the day when I'm writing you this letter, don't get confused, not tomorrow from when you read it, don't be a dipshit, how the fuck am I supposed to know when you're going to read the letter, my dumbass little cuz?, for real! Oh shit, I hope this letter does get to you, let me know if it does get to you, seriously, do it, and quick.

If you've understood me you must have met those fuckers, our partners, tomorrow of today, which might be a month or two ago when you read this letter, I don't know how long it'll take to reach you, you know the Mexican mail service is slower than a fucking one-legged snail. But I'm sure you've met them, tomorrow, and you must have figured out by now these are some heavy people, bro, you don't get to that level in business if you're not a serious fucker, real heavy, you do what they say and you and I will stick together. And don't go wanting to be clever, little cuz, I'm telling you again these guys have no time to screw around, that's the only way of doing business at that level, if you want to get to that top level you got to be ready to deal with these people, with real heavy people, from a totally nother level.

Hey, little cuz, these opportunities only show up once in a lifetime, don't screw it up, and if for some reason they cut me out don't you go forgetting who opened this door for you, who gave you these contacts, don't fucking bail on me now. I'd do the same for you, we're together in this thing, cousin. Most important right this minute is that we do proper follow-up like the Americans call it and you let me have confirmation you've received this letter, and you did, right? Let me know right-a-fucking-way. Call me on the phone number I'm putting at the bottom of this letter, which is the corporate HQ of a roast chicken franchise some friends are opening, they're renting me an office for my business. If when you call I'm not there you leave me a message, OK?, you tell them to say my cousin called, that way I'll know you received this letter, don't say your dumbass name, little cuz, just that my cousin called. You must have noticed I haven't put any names in this letter, in case some fucking busybody secretary intercepts the letter. If it's you who's reading it, cousin, call me right this minute, right now, you're already taking too long, I'm not hearing my phone ring, asshole.

If you're some fucking secretary who's reading this letter, you know what? Fuck you, bitch. Or like they say in Spanish movies, just so you definitely understand me: go screw yourself, *man*.

If literature has taught me anything, it's that in order to attain something that seems impossible (or fantastic, absurd, marvelous, magical) you need only fulfill a series of requirements that are not themselves, deep down, all that difficult. At worst, you have to create a new world with different rules for operating. At best, you just need to respect a narrative logic. Get invited to a party. Convince Valentina to come along. Introduce her to Laia. Leave the two of them talking on their own for a while. Get them a bit drunk. Create an atmosphere of complicity. Persuade them to go to our apartment after the party. Go. Keep drinking. Offer them the pills. Take them. And, all of a sudden, the impossible has materialized: discover that the three of us are naked in bed and hear Laia say to me: You like to watch, Mexicano? before sinking her mouth between Valentina's legs, while Valentina, stretched out on her back, moaning, leans up slightly on her elbows, just enough to catch my eye, and when she does, when her gaze fixes on mine without dodging it for the first time since we arrived in Barcelona, she says: Juan Pablo would have loved this, too.

TWO

THE LA VIRTUD DIARY

Wednesday, December 22nd, 2004

I cross the Plaza del Sol again and again in the hope of warming up, skirting round the squatters and their dogs, who never leave this place, surrounded by beer cans and garbage. I watch their movements and their habits; this is my main entertainment.

I've discovered this call shop on Torrent de l'Olla where they charge thirty cents per fifteen minutes for using the internet. One euro an hour or fifty cents for half an hour, just like everywhere else, except here you can pay for only fifteen minutes. There is no mail from Juan Pablo. One message from my brother. A whole heap of spam. A friend of my sister's writing to tell me she's planning to come live in Barcelona and asking if we (that's how she says it, using the plural pronoun) might put her up for a few days, till she finds her own place. If I didn't have to ration my fifteen minutes, I'd have answered: Oh, of course, idiot, I can put you up in my two-by-two room, I'll just get my bed and suitcases out so you can fit. You're going to love my bedroom, it has lovely views of an inner courtyard and the aroma of all the fry-ups in the building. Oh, and you need to keep the lights on all day if you want to see your hands and it's so cold it gnaws away at your toes, though I guess the two of us will stay relatively nice and warm together. Instead, I wrote an email to Juan Pablo. Subject: Juan Pablo is a dickhead. Message: Dickhead Dickhead Dickhead Dickhead Dickhead Dickhead Dickhead. I went on writing 'Dickhead' till the fifteen minutes expired. At least it warmed up my fingers. I went back to my room to freeze to death.

5:30 p.m. All my blood has gone to my stomach after eating a can of sardines and a whole baguette. Half a bottle of two-euro red wine. My legs are freezing. My toes especially. I'm not allowed to turn on the heating.

'You going to pay the gas bill yourself, princess?' said Gabriele. 'Buy yourself a blanket from the Chinese store.'

The advertisement had said the apartment had heating, and when I went to look at the place I saw the heaters, and even though they were turned off I didn't ask. I guess I assumed you just had to turn them on.

I went down to the Chinese store, the blanket that looked warmest cost twelve euro. Twelve euro I can live on for two days. I can't risk running out of money before I've decided what I'm going to do.

Thursday 23rd

Almost two hours putting up with the cold outside Julio Verne. I hid in the doorway of the building on the corner, from where I could watch without being seen. It was getting on for seven o'clock when Juan Pablo finally came out. Alone. Smarter-looking than usual. It looked like he'd cut his hair, too, but I'm not sure. It also looked like more rashes had appeared. He had a new coat on, black, in thick wool, a long one that went all the way down to his knees, European-style. Must have cost him a fortune, seventy, a hundred euro, at least.

A bag from the La Central bookstore with a Christmas bow hanging from his left wrist (both hands in the lovely warm pockets of that coat).

He went down Calle Zaragoza to Guillermo Tell, then turned right toward Plaza Molina. He walked mistrustfully, as if he was about to be attacked at any moment, with that scared-dog look he's had constantly since we started packing our suitcases in Xalapa. When he reached the square, he went into the train station and boarded a train uptown toward the mountain. He got off at Sarrià. I couldn't believe what was going to happen. But it would. I knew it was going to happen. I knew what was going to happen.

In the tunnel out of the station, I felt an urge to run and catch up with him at the stairs, yank on the tail of his overcoat, scream like one of those hysterical women from the telenovelas I try so hard not to be, and stop him getting to his meeting. But I restrained myself. I settled for not losing sight of him. He went into a café on Avenida Bonanova where a coffee must cost three euro. I positioned myself on the sidewalk out front, waiting, like him, except that I was outside, in the cold, and he was inside, lovely and warm, ordering a café con leche or a tea. Maybe a hot chocolate. I gave a start when I saw a Mexican flag flying on the next block. It was the consulate.

Five minutes later, Laia arrived. With a big smile on her face. I could even see her crooked teeth. I knew it. Son of a motherfucking bitch.

Friday 24th

Christmas Eve. I went to the call shop to call my folks. I warned them as soon as they answered that I wouldn't be able to talk long, that the call was expensive, that there were a lot of people waiting to use the phone (it was true). I didn't want to lie if they insisted on asking me how things were going. A half-truth is always better than a lie. I told them Juan Pablo couldn't talk because he wasn't there with me. That was not technically a lie. I didn't tell them he said hi or sent a hug either. His greetings or hugs were taken as read.

Then I asked for a computer and checked my email. There were no messages from Juan Pablo, not even a crappy Christmas greeting. I did send him a present, a delightful little fragment from Fray Servando he knows very well (we used to laugh at it together) and which he now wouldn't find funny at all (I find it even more so than before): 'Returning from this digression to the subject of the Catalans, their appearance seems to me the ugliest of all the Spaniards. Their noses are of a single piece with their foreheads. The women are mannish, too, and I've never seen a truly beautiful woman in Cataluña, with only some few exceptions among the poor of Barcelona, owing to all the foreigners or to the army who are always to be found in that city from other parts of the kingdom.'

I came back to the apartment. On the way I spent five euro on half a roast chicken. Another two on a bottle of red wine. One euro on a bag of potato chips. I shut myself up in my room to eat and listen to the noise of Gabriele's Italian friends. They invited me to have dinner with them. They were making a risotto. I said no, Gabriele was quite capable of billing me twenty euro for the meal.

I spent the night thinking about the past weeks, trying to find some logic to everything that happened. Of course, I've done nothing else since leaving Julio Verne, but now I set about doing it in a systematic way. I felt such an asshole, like one of those women's-magazine readers, that in order to escape being the cliché I've so despised I started to analyze things as if they were a narrative plot. All that studying literature had to come in useful somehow. Todorov could explain everything. Or Genette. I was a bit drunk (I am now too).

The problem is, trying to reconstruct the narrative, it turns out I'm not an omniscient narrator. I don't know what happened to Juan Pablo on his trip to Guadalajara, from where he returned to Xalapa acting so weird. I also don't really know how the change of country affected him, or the change of city, the doctorate, what anxieties these awoke in him, how they changed his ideas about the future. But it's not all that hard to imagine, either.

After going round and round several times, even up to the point of jotting down notes and diagrams, I came to the conclusion that this story is like the classic tale of a hero transformed, which is ultimately the essence of all novels. The hero who in order to transform his future has to betray his past and his own people. For hero, read asshole.

Conclusion: I shouldn't have come to Barcelona. Juan Pablo had in fact warned me. He told me not to come. Or that I shouldn't *go*, at that point. Said he wanted to go on his own. And he was coming on his own, he would have come on his own if I hadn't been so innocent as to imagine this could be fixed, that it was all just stress from the trip, from the changes, that Juan Pablo was under a lot of pressure. And also because of the business with his cousin, which had really gotten to him. That's what I thought when at the last minute he kneeled down to ask my forgiveness for all the things he'd said. And he said he was confused, but that it would pass. And he started crying at the exact moment when the taxi came that I'd called, because despite everything I wasn't going to stay, I didn't think I had the strength to go back to Xalapa and explain to my family and friends that I wasn't going to be going with Juan Pablo to Barcelona after all. At that moment, I don't think Juan Pablo was lying, I think he truly had repented and wanted me to come. But the hero's crisis was already there, lying in wait, and it was going to get worse: the nightmares, the silences, the evasions, the ludicrous steps taken not to be near me, his incapacity to reconcile with me (or lack of interest in doing so), that permanent attitude of someone who senses he's going to come to harm and is waiting for his punishment. It all adds up now. The gastritis. The rashes. The hero's somatizing.

All that was missing was the appearance of the promised future. The motive for the transformation: Laia. I've met a really cool chick, he said one day when he came back from class, she's inviting us to a party. And on that confused night, the past, present and future all three went to bed together, but when morning came the past was the past and the future was already razing it all to the ground.

I'm really drunk.

I went out into the living room, where the Italians were singing Italian ballads at the tops of their lungs and smoking hashish and in the middle of all that racket I asked the first one I found, who was neither very handsome nor very ugly, not very tall or very short, very fair or very dark, nothing special, not even particularly Italian:

'Do you want to come with me to my room?'

Sex between people who are drunk, stubborn, persistent, the sex between those who really just want to go to sleep knowing they've screwed someone, that they're not alone, even though they're alone. Sex on the verge of failure (he wasn't all that hard and I wasn't all that wet). Two positions and less than ten minutes and good night and thank you. All the same, the Italian was kind as he picked his pants up from the floor before leaving the room:

'You're a great fuck, girl,' he lied.

I got dressed and went down to the streets as if possessed by the energy of the orgasm I hadn't reached and which I was carrying wedged between my legs and which was gradually transforming into an emptiness in my chest that threatened to explode through my breastbone. I found a public phone and called Juan Pablo's cell, totally freezing (I'd forgotten to put on my jacket).

'I want my Christmas present,' I said, when he answered.

In the back, I could hear music playing, some Charly García song.

'Don't do this to me, Vale,' said Juan Pablo, and the music moved into the distance, as if he'd shut himself in the bathroom.

'I'm cold,' I said.

'It's not that cold,' he answered.

'I've had my jacket stolen,' I lied.

'Where?' he asked.

'I don't have enough money to buy another one,' I said. 'I don't have enough money for anything. I want you to give me your coat, that real nice black one you bought yourself.'

'What?' he asked, with that scared voice that is such a good match with his scared eyes, his scared gestures, with that Juan Pablo I didn't know before and who appeared out of nowhere, from inside the empty suitcase that we were filling in Xalapa, and who has swallowed up the affectionate, jokey Juan Pablo I'd fallen in love with when he stood in for my narratology professor and I heard him spending an hour and a half – an hour and a half! – analyzing Monterroso's famous one-line story using Chomsky's generative trees.

'I'm coming over,' I warned him, 'I'm coming to collect it.'

I hung up before he had the chance to say anything and ran the ten minutes it took me to get up to Julio Verne, maybe it was seven or eight. I buzzed 6D.

'I'm coming down,' said a voice I couldn't recognize amid the noise of the party.

I waited, shivering. The door was opened by Facundo.

'Here, shithead,' he said, 'shithead upstairs sent you this.'

He shut the door in my face. I put on the coat and went back home.

I'D BEEN IMAGINING A LESS CONVENTIONAL STORY

The lawyer called me up and said: I'll see you at eleven in La Barceloneta. It was nine in the morning on December 25th and I'd just dug my phone out from the pocket of my pants that had been discarded in the furthest corner of my room. My head was throbbing with a concerto for bass drum and cymbals by a schizophrenic composer. I'd only gone to sleep three and a half hours earlier.

What? I said, You're in Barcelona? No, asshole, said the lawyer, I'm boarding the plane this minute. What? I said again, staring hard at a shoe and trying to lower the volume of the racket in my head. You were still sleeping? he said. Like, I said, so, yeah, it's just I went to bed late. It's Christmas, I said. Is it really? he said. You know, I hadn't noticed that I had to leave my family to come over and fix your fuck-ups, he said. So who the fuck is going to wring the turkey's neck now, eh? Who's going to prepare the móle now? he said. What? I said again, still focused on the shoe (I hadn't even untied the laces). The Chinaman will be waiting for you at eleven outside the metro station, he said. Where? I asked. Barceloneta metro station, fuck's sake! he said, Why've I always got to repeat everything for you? and he rang off.

I took a long, hot shower and drank a café con leche which between them had no effect on me except to shift the concerto in my head into its second movement, which at least was slower and more measured. My temples boomed every seven seconds. I boarded the metro like a sleepwalker, the two hundred meters of the Paseo de Gràcia tunnel felt like the road to hell, literally. I looked at the graffiti on the ceiling of the tunnel, trying to find one saying DANTE WAS HERE written in a Latin Kings font.

The Chinaman was leaning on the stair rail, smoking. I greeted him with a pout that really concealed a retch. Man, just look at you, he said, and walked off toward the beach. I followed him without a word. We stepped onto the sand and he escorted me over to the sculpture of some metal cubes that reminded me, ironically, of Los Cubos in Guadalajara, the crossroads where my cousin is supposed to have been run over. Wait here, said the Chinaman, and he left. While I waited, I kept myself entertained kicking cigarette butts, which were as plentiful as grains of sand, and doing my best to bear the icy Mediterranean wind.

At nearly eleven-thirty, as I'm starting to wonder whether the call and the walk with the Chinaman might not have been merely the product of mixing red wine and tequila, I see the lawyer approaching, gray overcoat down to his knees, lapels up, dark glasses like a policeman or a criminal (there's no difference), hair slicked back with gel, hands stuffed into his coat pockets. I start to walk toward him. The other way, he says, when we meet and I hold out a trembling hand, don't stop. And I don't need a fucking greeting, asshole. We start walking toward some factory chimneys in the far distance. What's happened to your face? he says. Dermatitis, I say. Nervosa, I add, after a pause, separating the noun deliberately from the adjective so the adjective might acquire more dramatic weight, but the lawyer ignores my superhuman rhetorical effort. He walks with purpose, as if he's not just going for a stroll, because we aren't just going for a stroll, but as if he's headed someplace, even though we aren't, or at least not so far as I know. Further on, four seagulls are fighting over the remains of what must have been a nighttime picnic. My mother would never believe European seagulls feed on garbage, too.

And might we know what the fuck you think you're doing? he says, with no preamble and no indication of any concern over the state of my nervous system. I'm normally a fan of stories that start *in medias res*, I've always thought they suggest a greater respect for the reader's intelligence, but to tell the truth, when you're talking about real life I'd honestly rather have things explained to me properly, starting at the beginning. Carrying out your orders, I say, because I truly believe that's what I'm doing, that this is what my whole life comes down to. You're sure about that? he says, as we step onto the wet sand to avoid the seagulls, which are so obstinate in their hunger that they don't take flight when they see us approach. I didn't tell you to dump Valentina. How could you want to dump Valentina, honestly, poor Valentina. She was the one who wanted to leave, I say. After what happened with Laia, I explain. It's still your fault, he says, you shouldn't have let her go. What were you trying to do, protect her? You still haven't understood the only way to protect her is to carry out my orders? So, like, I begin, I can't exactly force her, but the lawyer interrupts me: You're fucking kidding me, he says, don't tell me you've started believing all the bullshit you've been reading to catch Laia.

A Pakistani man with a green plastic bag hurries over to meet us. He's going to say *cerveza beer* when he reaches us, offering us beer, and hashish, if we look interested, and I get ready for the lawyer to shoo him away the way you do a street dog before it gets too close, but he doesn't, and nor does the Pakistani guy say *cerveza beer* when he reaches us, instead he says good morning to the lawyer as if they know each other. You're early, says the lawyer, I said twelve. Want me to wait? says the Pakistani. I want you to look like you've come to offer us beer and we've said no, get out of here, says the lawyer. I'll see you at twelve. The Pakistani ignores him and keeps following us. He has a thin little moustache and a prominent double chin in distinct contrast to his slim body. Talking about contrasts, the sun that's just appeared between the clouds unleashes the third movement of the concerto in my head. Turns out now that the first two were harmonious after all. Oh man, says the Pakistani to me, that thing you've got, is it contagious? What the fuck are you waiting for? says the lawyer to the Pakistani. Get out of here. But I'm already here, the Pakistani starts but the lawyer interrupts him. You see that jerk over there? The lawyer doesn't take his hands out of his pockets, he doesn't point anywhere, but the two of us are still able to identify the old man walking along the edge of the beach. White beard. Detective's raincoat. He's pretending to take a French bulldog for a walk but the dog isn't a very convincing fake either (I could have sworn the dog never stopped staring at us). He's not the only person around, but he's the only one who looks like he's watching us. The dog, white with a black head, barks as if in confirmation of this fact. He's following us, says the lawyer. Get out of here, now. The Pakistani beats a retreat at once and the lawyer pulls out a cell phone. You're seen him? he says into the phone. No, it's all good. But don't lose him, he says, and hangs up.

Who's following us? I say. The lawyer watches the Pakistani's departure before answering: That motherfucker's been sent by your girlfriend's family, he says. Your new girlfriend. What? I say. Laia's family, asshole, he says. My head's going to explode any moment and I even give myself a pinch to see if I wake up, though apparently, I think, I sense, I'm already awake (I hope not). I don't know if she's my girlfriend, I say. How come? he

says. Well, so, like, I don't know if boyfriends and girlfriends
are still a thing in post-modernity. I've already told you I don't
want to hear any of that bullshit, he says. Are you going out
with her or not? I say yes. You've made yourself seem suspicious, asshole, he says, exactly what we didn't want to happen.
I pinch myself harder. I don't wake up. Or I stay awake. And
extremely cold. And all just because you ignored me, he says.
Wasn't that hard, either. When the fuck did I tell you to break
up with Valentina? he insists. I didn't break up with her, I say
again, she was the one who went. And you let her go, asshole,
he says. I thought it was for the best, I say. The best for what?
he asks. For getting access to Laia's inner circle, I say, repeating
the lawyer's own phrase from memory. What the fuck do you
know about what's best? he says. Know the only thing worse
than an asshole with initiative? I say nothing, respecting the
pause in his rhetorical question. An asshole with a *lot* of initiative, he says. Now we're going to have to do damage control.
Though most likely you've already fucked up the whole project.
My cousin sent me a letter, I say, without even realizing I'm
doing it, as if it's merely a reflexive act on hearing mention of
the word 'project'. The lawyer pauses for a fraction of a second,
like a car just about to run over a reckless pedestrian, and
sets off again. And enough about your asshole cousin, he says.
Dead people don't write letters. He sent it before he — I start,
but the lawyer interrupts me: Your asshole cousin didn't have
the first fucking idea what he was getting himself involved
in. Are you threatening me? On the contrary, I say, I want to
make a proposition, for a project. Now he does stop (I do the
same), pushes his hands deeper into his pockets, as if digging
a tunnel in there, shivers at a gust of wind that still, seriously,
doesn't manage to muss his hair. Now suddenly I'm talking
like my cousin. Mainly because I don't know what the fuck
I'm talking about. What the fuck are you talking about? the

lawyer does indeed say. About a long-term project, I say, as if the spirit of my cousin had taken advantage of my shivering, my horrible hangover, my lowered defenses, to get right inside of me. You're not going to tell me you plan to marry Laia and have babies and a happily-ever-after, he says. He starts walking again, and I follow. Fuck's sake, he says. The lesbian heir to a politician who's a supernumerary in Opus Dei isn't going to marry a Mexican immigrant. You have any idea how bad that sounds? I don't know what face I make but I ought to learn to pretend. The lawyer grabs my forearm and forces me to stop. Don't tell me you didn't know Laia's family was Opus, he says. Sure, I say. *Sure*, the lawyer repeats mockingly. You really are a bad liar. You know how many siblings Laia has? says the lawyer. I say nothing (I don't know, incredibly I've never asked and, curiously, she hasn't told me). Or how many sisters, to be precise? Eleven daughters-of-a-bitch. The entire fucking Barça women's team. And she's the pubilla. The what? I say, thinking I must have misheard. The heiress, asshole! says the lawyer. Haven't you been studying Catalan? The conductor of the orchestra orders all the bass drums and cymbals to crash to an apocalyptic climax. I'm actually going to faint, I think, from the cold, or the gastritis. But I don't faint. Pity.

I cannot believe you truly are this much of an asshole, says the lawyer. Can we go inside someplace? I say, I'm freezing to death. You haven't got a coat? he says. With that tiny fucking jacket you're going to get yourself pneumonia. Seriously, I cannot believe you're such an asshole, he says again, ignoring my request for shelter. So, what, you're actually horny for her now? he says. I say nothing. Do you like Laia? he says. I keep quiet. Dead quiet. Just what we need now, to have you to fall in love with her, he says. So totally quiet as if I'd swallowed a million seagulls filled with garbage that were flapping around in my belly. Didn't we think Laia was a lesbian? he says. The fact she'd never had a boyfriend doesn't mean she was a lesbian, I say. The fact she'd never had a boyfriend and had only ever had girlfriends does mean she's a lesbian, he says.

We walk on for another two, three minutes, in silence. Tell Laia your godfather has come to visit and wants to meet her, says the lawyer. It's not too soon to introduce you to her family? I say. She's going to get spooked. You should have thought about that earlier, he says. He's silent for a moment, pondering. Tell her I know her father, he says. That it's this amazing coincidence we've only just realized, that your godfather did his master's in Barcelona and her father was his professor. We're going to have to go all in, on a single hand. You'd better hope it works.

This is unacceptable, says Laia's father as we're sitting alone in his office. Alone: the lawyer, Laia's father, and me. I'm not going to put up with it, he says, absolutely not. Absolutely not, he says again, this time in Catalan. Son of a bitch. I'm glad to see you again too, Uri, says the lawyer. My name's Oriol! says Laia's father, though he pronounces it *Uriol*. What is it you're trying to prove? he says. That you're capable of infiltrating my family? I look from one to another, astonished, getting confirmation now of what the lawyer told me on the beach: that my asshole cousin, my total mega-asshole cousin may he rest in peace, did not have the faintest idea what fucking project he was getting himself (myself) into. And discovering now that the lawyer, contrary to all expectations, hadn't been lying when he told Laia he knew her father, that he'd taken the foreign investment seminar her father taught for the master's at an Opus Dei business school, he said, as we'd sat having a coffee at the lawyer's hotel, a five-star one, or six or seven, on Paseo de Gràcia, this very morning. And then he'd started buttering her up, talking about Rosa Luxemburg and about the museums in Berlin, dropping in little phrases of Catalan, telling her that his companies in Mexico always respected gender equality and that actually there were more women than men in leadership roles, and that it wasn't a matter of ideology, or not only ideology, but for the simple reason that women were smarter, more efficient, more productive, and that in fact these businesses wouldn't have grown as they did had it not been for the advice of her father, a genius at analyzing capital flows, he told her, until Laia, enthusiastic about the coincidence (*sic*) and about my most charming godfather (double *sic*), ended up inviting us to come by her parents' house for coffee that afternoon, after lunch, four-thirty or five, she couldn't invite us for the actual meal, Laia apologized, because it was a family lunch, being St Stephen's Day.

So like, I say, so you mean you really did know each other? But the lawyer and Laia's father don't even turn to look at me because they're deep in a staring contest like I used to play with my sister when we were little. Whoever blinks first loses. I make the most of the fact they're oblivious to my existence to start scratching. Honestly, says the lawyer, I'd been imagining something different, a less conventional story, a toxic relationship with some girl, Juan Pablo's ex-girlfriend, actually. And he finally blinks. But you can't trust these people, he adds, they're all literature people, they believe in feelings, they're romantics, they're bohemian, they fall in love. Assholes, says Laia's father. Exactly, says the lawyer, *pendejos* we call them in Mexico. You know the funniest part, Uri? You're the one who got Laia mixed up in this. Laia's father gives the desk a slap as if to dispute the slander. Didn't you ask me to look after her when she took her Caribbean trip? asks the lawyer. What were you afraid of? That she'd get kidnapped? That we'd send her back home to you in little pieces? I ensured she returned home intact, I kept my promise, I looked after her for you,

I gave her the best room in our hotel in Cancún and I arranged to have a young man totally at her service. And what a coincidence, it was Juan Pablo's cousin. Regrettably, he's recently passed away in an accident. Terrible story, so sad, he was a good lad with a great future ahead of him. Can we have that whiskey? he adds, because that was what we were supposed to have shut ourselves in the study to do, to take refuge from the din of Laia's eleven sisters and their boyfriends (the older ones') and their snooty cousins and their maiden aunts of the perpetual veil and their godfathers (actual and political) like something out of *The Godfather*. Stop scratching, fuck's sake! says the lawyer to me. You're like a mangy dog! Laia's father turns his glance toward me for just a second (I hide my hands in my pants pocket), then goes back to wedging himself protectively behind his desk, tense as a stone in a slingshot, unable to blink. Don't get defensive, Uri, says the lawyer, I tried to do it nicely, but there was no way to get you to listen to me. Consider the possibility that this could turn into the opportunity you've been waiting for. And if you don't want to consider that, he says, at least now you know how far I'm prepared to go. Is that a threat? says Laia's father. The fact we're sitting here, in your study, on the afternoon of St Stephen's Day, that's the real threat, says the lawyer. But all I want, at this moment, is to have a whiskey.

Laia's father gets up to serve the whiskey. I'll give you five minutes to explain what it is you want, he says, and you'd better hope it's of interest. Otherwise I'm calling the Mossos. And you know that in this country, unlike yours, justice still works. The lawyer laughs. Roars with laughter. Real laughter. Until he slaps his knee, almost overdoing it. That's the Uri I know, he says, always joking around.

There's a knock on the door and Laia's father says: Come in, in Catalan. The woman who puts her head round the door is a uniformed maid, a Latina, who says in a Bolivian or Ecuadorian accent (I can't tell them apart) that the lady of the house would like to know if we want coffee or if she can get us anything. Nothing, says Laia's father, without consulting us, but before the maid closes the door the lawyer says: Wait. Take the kid over to Miss Laia. And then to me: You should have a chat with your mother-in-law. Let's see if you can get her to stop looking at you like you're a cockroach. Explain that what you've got isn't contagious. I get up and walk over to the door. Before I leave, I hear the lawyer say: You're giving me the twelve-year-old stuff, Uri? Really? And then I close the door which opens up an ellipsis that shouldn't exist if I want to tell this story whole, or rather, an ellipsis that would not exist if I were able to tell this story whole.

There's a Mexican, a Chinaman and a Muslim and they're in a meeting with a Mexican mafioso in the office of an abandoned wine store in Barcelona, except the Muslim isn't exactly a Muslim, he's a Pakistani atheist. The Mexican, the Chinaman and the Pakistani don't know each other, it's the Mexican mafioso who's brought them together to explain how a bit of business is going to work. Or not exactly how the business is going to work, but rather what each of them has to do to make the business work, though in reality none of the three of them understands precisely how the business works and the Mexican, in particular, doesn't understand anything at all.

The Mexican mafioso tells them that for the business to work depends on all of them doing exactly and exclusively as he tells them from now on. And by exactly and exclusively he means exactly and exclusively. No room for interpretation. And if any one of the three of them thinks they've come up with a better idea, they can shove that idea up their ass and quick. He will tolerate no deviations from the plan. The least disobedience will be punished and the three of them have had plenty of opportunities to know for sure that he's not joking. Am I laughing? he asks. The three of them all say no. What's more, just so you can be sure I'm not laughing, so you can see the difference, I'll tell you a joke.

There was once this dickhead who was studying for a doctorate in literary theory and compulsive literature, says the Mexican mafioso. You'd think the dickhead was real smart, which was why he was doing the doctorate, but the reality is the dickhead was a real dickhead. Real asshole, he adds, so you get my drift. Real retard. The dickhead was such a dickhead he even thought the ideas he had were better than the orders he received. What the dickhead didn't think about was the consequences of his brilliant ideas and the real joke in this joke is that the dickhead thought his ideas really were better. Because that is what you think, dickhead, isn't it? says the Mexican mafioso, gesturing with his chin toward where the Mexican's standing. You think it all worked out well, don't you? The Mexican says nothing, he stays totally quiet, because even a tiny blink would mean accepting he's the subject of this joke. Well, I'm here to tell you we have a tiny little problem, says the Mexican mafioso. And you're going to fix it.

The Mexican mafioso takes a cell phone from the inside pocket of his jacket (he's wearing a dark suit) and makes a call. He waits three, four seconds. Bring him in, he says, when they answer the call. Two, three minutes pass, during which time the Chinaman tries to light a cigarette, but his lighter doesn't work. He asks for a light. Nobody gives him one. The Pakistani moves closer to the Mexican, but not much closer. Hi, he says, I'm Ahmed, you saw me the other day, remember? You didn't say whether what you've got is contagious. Before the Mexican says anything, the Mexican mafioso shouts at them: What the actual fuck?! But if we're gonna work together

I need to know what illness he's got, says the Pakistani, if he's got leprosy and isn't getting treated for it we might catch it. You may think we're in your shitty country now but we're not, are we? shouts the Mexican mafioso. Just shut it! Jesus, you're going to ruin the damn joke! Then a Mexican thug enters the scene pulling an old man by the arm, an old man with a white beard, wearing a detective's raincoat. This old man is cuffed and there's a piece of gray duct tape covering his mouth. You remember Chucky? says the Mexican mafioso to the Mexican. Say hello to Chucky, don't be impolite. Hi, says the Mexican, confused because the joke's getting too complicated (there's a Mexican, a Chinaman, a Muslim who isn't really a Muslim but a Pakistani atheist, a Spanish detective, a Mexican mafioso and his hired thug . . . too many characters, this joke can't end well). How's Valentina? says the Mexican thug. Who's this guy? says the Pakistani, gesturing toward the old man. This damn jerk is the asshole that the family of this asshole's little girlfriend sent to investigate him, says the Mexican mafioso. He has a name, he adds, but we're going to call him Damage Control. Or maybe Bawling-Out. Or alternatively Let's-See-Dickhead-If-You-Understand-How-Things-Are-Done. The poor jerk didn't investigate very much, he says, but this doctor of compulsive literature here has got to learn. Chucky, he says, nodding toward the Mexican. The Mexican thug pulls out a gun and holds it out to the Mexican, offering it to him. The Mexican doesn't move a centimeter. Take it, says the Mexican thug. Not a millimeter. You're meant to take it, fuck's sake, says the Mexican mafioso. The Mexican holds out his right hand and accepts the gun, trembling.

If you want me to believe the project can work, says the Mexican mafioso, I need proof. I don't trust people who study so much, who have so much respect for theory. Ultimately they don't actually do anything, he says. They get indecisive.

Contemplative. Skeptical. And there's nothing worse for a project becoming reality than having a skeptic involved. So you're going to stop thinking, he says. And you're going to obey, he says. Understood? he says. The Mexican gives a slight nod, stunned by the unusual presence of the weapon in his right hand. Kill him, says the Mexican mafioso. What? says the Mexican. You shoot, for fuck's sake, says the Mexican thug. Who? says the Mexican. What do you mean, who, dickhead?! What do you mean, fucking who?! Who'd you think?! says the Mexican mafioso. You got him involved in this, with your brilliant idea, you're taking responsibility. So, like, the Mexican begins, but he can't think of anything else to say. Chucky, says the Mexican mafioso, nodding once again toward the Mexican. The Mexican thug takes a second gun out of the inside pocket of his black woolen coat he's wearing, an extremely elegant coat, which whoever's telling the joke hasn't noticed until now, nor any detail of his clothing, oh he's quite the thug dandy, and he holds it out toward the Mexican, only this time pointing it. Do you need a hypothesis to shift into action? says the Mexican mafioso. The dead person ending up being you, that's a valid hypothesis. I don't know how to use it, says the Mexican, looking at the gun. You're kidding, says the Mexican mafioso, everybody knows how to use a gun. The Mexican raises the weapon. The old man moans under the tape that's covering his mouth and tries to shake himself loose, without much conviction, possibly because he knows any effort is pointless if the joke has a Mexican, a Chinaman and a Muslim, even if the Muslim doesn't really practice that religion. There's no way he's getting out of this joke alive. The thug dandy moves away as best he can from the position in which he has the old man immobilized, extremely worried about getting his clothes stained. Hurry up, he says to the Mexican. And aim well, he says. The Mexican adjusts the position of the gun. Take off the safety, asshole, says the Mexican mafioso. The Mexican looks at the gun. On the top, says the dandy. The Mexican takes off the safety and points again. Wait, says the Mexican mafioso. Last words, everybody has the right to say their last words, he says, and he looks up at the dandy. The dandy moves back toward the old man and in one go pulls off the gray strip of duct tape covering his mouth. The tape pulls out some of the old man's moustache. Filthy cunt immigrants, says the old man. Most edifying, says the Mexican mafioso. Anything else? he adds. Don't kill the dog, says the old man, none of it's her fault. You brought the dog? the Mexican mafioso asks the dandy. She's tied up outside, says the dandy. You people are all trash, says the old man. Oh, just shoot already, fuck's sake, says the Mexican mafioso to the Mexican. Shoot before this damn jerk ruins the joke. The Mexican fires. Again, says the Mexican mafioso. The Mexican fires again. One more, says the mafioso. The Mexican obeys.

Fuck, says the dandy, letting go of the old man's body and wiping the blood-specked lapels of his coat with the back of his hand. The Chinaman and the Pakistani look at the floor to ascertain the state of the body: two shots to the chest and one in the neck (the first). The Mexican mafioso approaches the Mexican and takes the gun from his hand. Huh, not just a pretty face, he says. Then he looks (first) at the Chinaman, who's trying really hard to make the lighter work (failing), and (next) at the Pakistani, who reaches down to the floor to pick up a green plastic bag in which he's got six cans of beer. Can I keep the dog? says the Pakistani. End of joke, says the Mexican mafioso. You can all laugh now. Nobody laughs. He said you can all laugh, *man*, says the dandy. That's a fucking order.

TELL YOUR MOTHER MORE ABOUT HER

My dear son, what a surprise to receive your message with so much news, even if your mother would have preferred it if you'd called to tell her on the telephone. You know of course that your mother isn't one of those melodramatic mothers, but would it have killed you to call her on Christmas Eve? Believe your mother when she tells you your call would have made that night a little less dreadful, mostly because your mother had to put up with the unpleasantness of going for dinner at your aunt Concha's house. Yes, I know what you must be thinking, why did your mother go only to complain about it afterward, but you know what your father's like, your uncle called him to invite us over and he didn't have the nerve to say no, which is a shame, and then he came to your mother with a whole story about how the family has got to stick together now more than ever. As if your cousin's death erased all the rudeness and the mean remarks your aunt has made to your mother in the past! Remember that time she got up in the middle of dinner to prepare a sauce because she said your mother had dried out the turkey? Your mother remembers. It was a recipe from Provence and your aunt chucked a guajillo chili salsa on top of it. These are the sort of details, my son, that reveal differences of birth very clearly.

And to top it all your father was giving your mother a really tough time with emotional blackmail. Imagine if it'd been Juan, he said to your mother, with a face like a little puppy who's just been run over (do forgive your mother for the simile, but you as a literature student know better than anyone how important it is to be precise when using language). Imagine Juan had died, your father said to your mother. Your father is truly incorrigible. If you were dead the last thing your mother would want would be to have your aunt sitting in her dining room waiting for your mother to serve her dinner. But your mother told your father such a thing would never happen to you, for starters because right from when you were little you and your sister learned that you cross over the bridges and not under them, that's the one useful thing you learn from having been born in that ghastly town in Los Altos.

Would it have been so hard for you to call, son, your father wanted to wait till eight o'clock that evening to see if you did, your mother said you weren't going to, that in Europe it was already three in the morning, but your father doesn't understand that whole business with the time zones. Finally he resigned himself to the idea and took the two bottles of cider out the fridge that he'd bought to take to the dinner and which your father knows perfectly well gives your mother heartburn. Your father was so hurt, Juan, write your father when you can, or better still, call him, make up some complicated excuse to explain why you didn't call, make some use of all those books you've read, make something up for him, your father will swallow anything. The other day your father must have spent a good half an hour staring intently at the living-room window, without saying or doing anything, and when your mother asked what he was looking at, do you know what he answered? That the winter light was captivating him. The light was captivating him! Honestly, your father does drive your poor mother up the wall. If he'd spent that half-hour in his office instead of stuck at home, he'd have seen three or four patients.

But your mother isn't writing to tell you about the problems with your father, you know of course she's not that kind of mother, your mother's writing to tell you your news was the best Christmas present she could possibly have received! Oh, how happy you've made her, my son! If only you'd told your mother before the dinner she could have told the whole family that you've gotten yourself a European girlfriend now. Your mother would have loved to have seen the looks on your cousins' faces, and on your aunt Concha's face!, your mother had to settle for imagining it when she phoned to tell her the news after receiving your message. You should have seen the silence, son, after your mother made the announcement, and please note it was quite without boasting: Concha, I'm calling to tell you two things. First, Juan Pablo and Valentina have broken up. And second, my son now has a Catalan girlfriend from a pedigreed European family. Your mother could practically hear the maid mopping the floor under your aunt's feet.

Son, your mother knows it's not good to flog a dead horse, but in this case your mother thinks it's important you realize your mother always knew Valentina wasn't a suitable choice. If your mother is only telling you this now, son, it's not meant to be a reproach, not at all, your mother could never do such a thing, your mother isn't that kind of mother, but rather your mother's saying it in order to congratulate you. How good that you've reconsidered, Juan, this Valentina who was so short, and named after that salsa brand, those sad little eyes and that hair flattened down like an Indian girl, poor thing, truth is it's not her fault, what with that family who've only just come down from La Huasteca. But your mother can't worry about her, after all our family isn't a charitable institution for going around gathering up poor little girls and giving them opportunities in life. Your mother will leave that to the

Veracruz government. Your mother only has enough heart and energy left to worry about your future, son, and that is why your mother is so pleased.

Your mother won't hide the fact that besides being pleased she's also relieved, your mother has always worried about your character, that tendency you have just to bow your head and obey orders, you've taken after your father's family in that. All exactly the same. All so rebellious in Los Altos, only to turn out utterly weak-willed. Please don't be annoyed, son, your mother's telling you the truth, don't let your mother's honesty cloud your good sense. You were the one who gave your mother plenty of reasons to be distraught, with all those wrong decisions you kept making, studying a subject with no future, going to live in an underdeveloped city, falling in love out of pity, your mother knows you know perfectly well what she's talking about. All these things somebody who doesn't know you the way your mother does might think were signs of rebelliousness, a person with a strong character who knows what he wants out of life, but in reality they were just the opposite, tantrums to disguise your lack of self-confidence. When you were just a boy, the thing that most tormented your mother was exactly that, you not having the confidence to defend yourself, whether it was from your sister, who even though she was younger than you was constantly humiliating you, your schoolmates who made your life impossible (remember when they used to make you cry and you didn't want to come out from under my skirt?), or your cousins, who've been savages ever since they were small.

And to see you now! With a European girlfriend! And very beautiful from what I can see in the photo (though your mother asks you to send another photo where I can see her from closer up, because in the one you sent Laia's smile is a bit funny).

You mother has to admit that until very recently, until you told her you were going to study in Europe, the uncertainty about your future prevented her from living. The truth is, your mother was wrong. But how was your mother to know that behind all those mistakes there was a plan, a proper life project? You must acknowledge that your mother had plenty of reasons to be heartbroken. Your mother was already imagining you giving Spanish classes at a public high school in Pachuca or a private one in Guadalajara (where all the students would have laughed at you), married to poor little Valentina for whom living in a two-room apartment with drinking water and electricity was moving up in the world. But your mother was wrong and your mother has no problem admitting this, what matters isn't how proud your mother is, what matters is your future. Your mother is so very proud that that scared little runt who wet his bed until he was eleven has become a successful adult living in Europe.

If only you'd told your mother before dinner, it would have been the happiest Christmas of her life! Instead, your mother had to put up with your aunt Concha, who's so selfish she won't let anybody talk about anything but the string of misfortunes that's befallen them since your cousin died. As if it hadn't been two months already. I told her it was time to start getting over it. But there's no way to make your aunt listen, the only thing she's interested in is unburdening herself about the aforementioned foundation they're allegedly setting up, the foundation in your cousin's memory, an institute to teach people to cross roads, I did tell you about that, didn't I? We spent the night looking at logos for the foundation, your aunt wanted us to vote on which was the best, and they were all horrible, they were designed by your cousin Humberto who hasn't even completed his degree (or has he?), all just to save a thousand pesos, how much do you think people charge to design a logo? You can imagine what the foundation's going to be like if they want to do the whole thing by calling in favors. Your mother found your cousins in a corner roaring with laughter at a logo that they hadn't shown your aunt and uncle. It was a photo of somebody run over which they'd stuck your cousin's face on and underneath it said: The Ed Krusher Foundation. Honestly, your cousins are simply savages.

By the way, before your mother forgets, let your mother tell you that your aunt said that her maid told her that your cousin had sent you a letter to Barcelona before he died, that he'd asked the maid to take it to the post office. Is that true? Your mother told your aunt that surely the maid was making it up, you know how it is with these people having these fantasies and hallucinations from the hunger. Besides, nobody sends letters, they're from a different time. And that he supposedly also sent a letter to Valentina. Your mother found all this extremely peculiar. Did your cousin know Valentina? Your aunt kept rattling on to your mother about how these letters showed how close you and Lorenzo were and she even decided to embrace your mother and start crying on her shoulder. You can't imagine what that moment was like, son, your mother had no idea how to wriggle out of it.

Well anyway, son, your mother is telling you this because, in case it does happen to be true, you should be careful now you and Valentina have broken up, who knows what it was your cousin wrote, if he really did write her, you know what a liar your cousin was and also how jealous. You didn't notice because you were always very naive and very trusting.

But your mother isn't writing to talk about your poor cousin, may he rest in peace, or about your aunt's snootiness or the tales the maid is telling. What your mother wanted to tell you was how happy your message made her, and that she'll be anxiously waiting for you to send her another picture of

114

Laia so she can get to know her better. Tell your mother more about her, her family, her character, what her father does. It's quite clear from the photo, even though it's from kind of far away, that she's from a good family, your mother doesn't need a close-up to be able to tell that, you can make these things out from a distance. Sorry to ask, but was Laia chewing something in the photo or what's she got in her mouth that looks slightly twisted? A piece of chewing-gum? Send your mother a portrait shot of her face, don't take too long about it, don't make your mother wait too many days, you know the curiosity sends her sugar levels sky-high.

Moving on to other subjects, less pleasant ones, your mother doesn't know if you've spoken to your sister or if you've been writing to each other. Your mother is telling you this in case you don't already know. Well it turns out she's gotten it into her head that they're underestimating her at the firm and that, if they don't give her a raise and better benefits, she's going to quit. Write your sister when you can and tell her to stop this nonsense, if she ends up without a job then what will she do, your sister needs to be aware of her limitations, it's not nice for your mother to be saying this, but your sister wasn't born for great things. Your mother doesn't want your sister stuck in the house all blessed day, your mother has enough of her own troubles to worry about already.

Ah, no, my son, your mother's ended up writing another long message but you have to understand how excited she is, it's not every day a mother learns that at last her son has set his life on the correct path. So your mother will leave you now, son, since you must be really busy. Your mother sends you a big hug and reminds you not to forget to send her the picture of Laia.

A picture of her face, please, for your mother who misses you.

IF YOU DON'T WANT TO TELL ME
THEN DON'T TELL ME

Sunday, December 26th, 2004

Spent all day yesterday in bed, asleep. I got up at 9 p.m. I ate a tin of sardines and a packet of cookies and went back to bed. I was going to go out to stretch my legs but the prospect of having to climb back up the stairs on my return prevented me. Five flights demand a degree of willpower I haven't got right now.

If I sleep with the overcoat on, I don't get cold.

As was to be expected, I woke at 4 a.m. and couldn't get back to sleep. I turned on the light and from the little pile of books I have on my little table (my circumstances and the dimensions of the room condemn me to littles), I chose the one that would hurt me the most. Quick as a sigh, I reread the 'Diary from Escudillers'. I ended it with the consolation that I live in a better neighborhood than Pitol, though the last line left a bitter taste in my mouth: 'The truth is, I wouldn't trade Barcelona for any other city on earth.' I'd swap it for any.

I remembered Pitol's enigmatic smile on the day we came over and told him we were going to live in Barcelona. It was at the end of a lecture and he made a very good pretense of remembering us, from when we'd taken his course on cinema and literature at the arts faculty. At that time I thought it was a smile of complicity, a strange smile but a complicit one. And I also detected something else in his reserved attitude, a certain fear that we would ask him for something (a letter of recommendation, to introduce us to one of his Catalan friends). Early this morning, after rereading the diary, this smile was transformed into a sly irony. As if Pitol had warned us Barcelona wasn't a good idea. He had gauged our naivete. He knew what would happen to us.

At 11 a.m. I felt a need to go out to feel the cold on my face, even if it was only to buy a baguette. In Plaza del Sol there were fewer squatters than usual. Had they gone to spend the holidays with their families? I stood watching one who was sitting on the floor playing the recorder, with a coffee cup to ask for money, without any dogs. I looked at the other squatters and noticed he was the only one not surrounded by dogs. I watched him a while without bothering to hide it, understanding for the first time how one might get to this condition. I could get there myself. I'm headed the right way.

'Nice coat, girl,' the squatter says, interrupting his music and my thoughts. 'Where are you from?' he asks.

When I didn't immediately reply, he added:

'I'm from Italy, from Milan.'

'And what are you doing in Barcelona?' I said, barely even realizing it, with genuine anthropological curiosity.

'We have got Berlusconi in Italy,' he said. 'A fucking fascist. You're out on the street not doing anything and he sends the police over to beat you up.'

'That doesn't happen here?' I asked.

'People in Barcelona are good,' he said. 'Kind of dumb.'

'The police too?' I asked.

'No,' he said, 'the police are always sons of bitches, here you've got the Mossos d'Esquadra and the municipal police and the secret police. All sons of bitches,' he said. 'But here people give you money, it's great in Gràcia, we don't have lots of problems with the neighbors. You live near here?' he asked.

I said yes, that I was on Calle de la Virtud, raising my arm to point toward where the street was.

'*Virtue Street*,' he said, 'that's quite a name. You aren't going to tell me where you're from?' he asked again.

'Mexico,' I replied.

'Oh, I love Mexico,' he said. 'Chiapas, Subcomandante Marcos . . . Hey, *una birra*?' he offers, slipping momentarily into Italian as he points to a tall bottle with a red sticker, thinner than our large bottles back home. 'Why don't you sit down? It's easier to get warm here if you stay put where there's sun, look at the dogs, the dogs know. Dogs are very wise, huh, you should always pay attention to the dogs.'

'You don't have dogs?' I asked.

He picked up a carton of wine and took a long swig.

'I'd rather not talk about that,' he said.

'What's your name?' I asked.

'Jimmy,' he answered. 'You?'

'Not exactly a very Italian name,' I said.

'I'm really called Giuseppe.'

Thursday 30th

Three days without writing in my diary. I don't keep a diary to make a fool of myself, to feel sorry for myself, so it wouldn't have done me any good at all to write about the last few days. I don't want to read myself a little while later and feel ashamed. Better not to write. The only things I've written have been emails to Juan Pablo. One a day. Juan Pablo is an asshole.

Juan Pablo is a motherfucker. Juan Pablo is a fag. I tap and tap away until my fifteen minutes are up. On Tuesday I even paid for a half-hour.

When I crossed Plaza del Sol I found Jimmy in his usual place. He offered me a tumbler of red wine, which I didn't dare turn down. Box wine that went down my throat as if it was shaving razors making little cuts in my esophagus.

'Where are your friends?' I asked, because the square was half-empty.

'Back home,' he said, 'visiting their families.'

'In Italy?' I said.

'Or in France, in Germany, there are people here from all over Europe.'

'And how do they get back there?' I asked.

'Like anybody else, by plane, by train, by bus, what did you expect? That they'd walk? Hitchhike? We're normal people, huh, squatting is a choice, a way of life. What do you do for a living?' he asked.

'Nothing,' I answered. 'Nothing right now.'

'But you've got to live on something,' he said, 'or where'd you have gotten that fancy overcoat. That's an expensive coat, huh.'

'I'd rather not talk about that,' I said.

'So you don't work?' he insisted. 'Barcelona's expensive, you'll run out of money quickly.'

'I haven't got papers,' I said.

'You don't need papers to work,' he said, 'I'm sure you could get yourself a job, in a restaurant, for example. There are lots of Mexican restaurants here, in this actual neighborhood.'

'Maybe,' I said.

'But what were you doing in Barcelona, why'd you come?' he asked.

'I'd rather not talk about that,' I said again.

'Ah,' he said, '*amore*, huh.'

I didn't say anything.

'I've watched you every day,' he went on, 'going round and round the square dragging your overcoat with you, like a lost soul. It makes me sad, but if you don't want to tell me, don't tell me. Not a problem.'

'OK,' I said.

'How'd you get the coat? Did you steal it?' he said, presumably noticing that I wore it with the sleeves rolled up.

'No!' I answered. 'A friend gave it to me.'

'A friend, huh,' he said. 'The thing I most like about your coat is it has a lot of pockets, it has pockets all over. Have you checked all the pockets?'

'What for?' I asked.

'One time I found an overcoat in Milan and when I checked one of the pockets there was some dough inside,' he said. 'The owner had thrown it away without noticing. Maybe your friend forgot something. Have a look, you've got nothing to lose.'

'I've already checked,' I said.

'All of them?' he asked. 'Are you sure? There are a lot of pockets, huh.'

I pretended to be checking them again and then, with my heart suddenly in my throat, I discovered an inside pocket I hadn't seen before. I undid the little button. I took out a fifty-euro bill.

'I knew it,' he said, 'your friend really is pretty forgetful, huh.'

'Now it's my turn to invite you for a drink,' I said. 'I'll go buy a bottle of wine.'

'If you like,' he said.

I walked over to the supermarket, but on my way stopped off at a public telephone. I called Juan Pablo on his cell.

'What do these fifty euro mean?' I asked him as he said 'Hello?' (he didn't say 'Yeah?' anymore).

'Vale?' he asked.

I repeated the question.

'You told me you didn't have any money,' he said.

'And what, so you're going to give me money whenever I need it? That way you'll have a nice clear conscience?'

'No,' he answered. 'But if you want I can pay for the cost of changing the date of the flight, so you can go back to Mexico. It costs a hundred euro,' he said.

'I know,' I said. 'But I'm not going back to Mexico.'

Friday 31st

Last day of this strange year. Gabriele went to Rome to see in the New Year with his family. The Brazilian couple in the other bedroom, whom I haven't met yet, are still on vacation in Morocco and aren't back till after Epiphany. I've got the whole apartment to myself!

In a burst of optimism I went to Calle Torrijos, where I'd seen two Mexican restaurants. I managed to get work in one of them, as a waitress, I start Sunday. The pay isn't great, but I've worked out that it'll be enough to survive till I find something else. I might have to get a different room, living in Gràcia's expensive, I can't allow myself to pay two hundred euro a month for a prison cell. Maybe I'll find somewhere on Calle Escudillers – why not? I like that roguish atmosphere of El Raval, the closest I've found to Fray Servando's Barcelona. I only came to Gràcia because it was close to Julio Verne and what I need now is to get far away.

I bought two shawarmas on the Plaza del Sol and sat down on the ground to have dinner with Jimmy. For dessert he offered me chocolate. I ended up learning that's what they call hashish. Even though I'd smoked, I'd never tried it before. I never liked pot much, it made me anxious and paranoid. The ecstasy I don't even want to remember. Hashish loosened my tongue, as if somebody had opened a floodgate that was about to burst. Maybe it wasn't the hash, maybe it was my having decided to stay, the sense of expectation of being in the apartment on my own, having gotten some work, having decided to stop walking around dragging my overcoat with me.

I told Jimmy everything (well, nearly everything), with no bitterness and no melancholy, not expecting his advice or his solidarity, just for the pleasure of telling him, because I felt he deserved it. I talked for hours, nonstop, and he interrupted me only occasionally to ask me who Pitol was, or Monsiváis, Monterroso or Ibargüengoitia. I explained that Juan Pablo had told a joke about Monterroso the day I met him. That Monterroso had written a one-line story called 'The Dinosaur'. That the story was eight words long. And that in the joke a reader tells Monterroso that he was a big fan of his work and Monterroso asks what he's read. 'The Dinosaur', says the reader. 'And what did you think?' asks Monterroso. 'I haven't finished it yet,' says the reader, 'I'm halfway through.' And that then Monterroso came to the university to give a lecture and he'd told the story of a reader who'd come up to him to confess that she was a great fan of his work. And his anecdote was identical to Juan Pablo's joke.

'That gives you some idea of what Juan Pablo's like,' I told Jimmy. 'Or used to be like.'

'Well he sounds like a jerk to me,' said Jimmy. 'You, girl, are awesome, and after seven years together he traded you in for a Catalan girl with crooked teeth. You came here to be with him, you left your family and your job. He's a jerk, girl, you're beautiful. Yeah, you're nice-looking, and fuck, you're smart, too.'

And I laughed and asked him if he was hitting on me.

'Don't you go falling in love with me, Jimmy,' I said, almost pissing myself laughing, from the effect of the chocolate and the euphoria of a new life.

'If you want I'll give him a scare, girl,' said Jimmy. 'You just say the word and I'll give him a real fright, you'll see, he's so gonna shit his pants.'

'Don't talk crap, Jimmy,' I said, 'that's all in the past now. Time to turn the page, it's New Year's.'

2:30 a.m. I came back to the apartment and dragged the mattress from my bed into the living room. I turned the heating up to the max. I turned on the TV and left it on a channel showing porn.

Saturday, January 1st, 2005

I woke up at 3 p.m. with an emptiness in the pit of my stomach. I cried until four-thirty, without even the strength to get up. Then I went down to the square, had a café con leche and waited for Jimmy to show up.

'You remember what you offered to do yesterday, Jimmy?' I said before even saying hello – 'Were you serious?'

THE LAWYER ISN'T GOING
TO LIKE THIS ONE BIT

Ahmed called me up and said: It's the dog, she doesn't want to eat. It was one-thirty in the morning on New Year's and I was at a party of some friends of Laia's in an apartment close to Plaza Joanic. I told him to wait, excused myself from the friend of Laia's who was taking her turn to bug me, covering the tiny cell phone completely with my hand, and went out onto a terrace where people were clustering together smoking. I saw Laia at the back sharing a joint. I told Ahmed to wait again and made my way across the living room and the kitchen where people were packed around the fridge and went out to the laundry area, which opened onto the building's inner courtyard. I closed the door.

Well? I say. What? says Ahmed. What's going on? I say, with fear radiating its poison to my extremities, the arm holding the phone suddenly limp and weak. I tighten my hand so the phone doesn't fall. The dog does not want to eat, says Ahmed. Is that code? I say. What? says Ahmed again. I don't understand the code, I say, I think I've missed something. The dog hasn't eaten anything in four days, says Ahmed. I don't understand the code! I say, in a whispered shout. What code? shouts Ahmed. What dog? I say. Oh man, the dog, he says. She's started yelping and there's nothing on earth that'll shut her up. You kept the fucking dog? I shout, whispering again. Didn't they say they had to get rid of her? Chucky said I could keep her, he said. I live on my own, the dog keeps me company. The blood returns to my body and with it the itching in my scalp, in my left arm, and all the way up my back to my neck. Man, she's so cute, Ahmed insists, you saw her. I swap the phone from one hand to the other and start to scratch.

What did the Chinaman say? I say. That if I want to keep her it's my problem, he says. The lawyer isn't going to like this one bit. What do we do? he says. Wait, I say, because I hear noises behind me. I take the other cell phone out of my pants pocket, just in case. The door opens and Laia sticks her head out: Everything OK? she says. A friend from Mexico, I say, showing her the cell phone she knows about. What time is it in Mexico? she says. Her eyes are sad-looking from the joint. I look at the watch on my wrist. So, like, I say, six-thirty in the evening. Oh, that's right, she says. I'll leave you to talk. I wait for her to go, but she doesn't go. She stands there looking straight at me for two, three seconds, four, saying nothing, and I think she's smoked too much, but then she says: Your rashes have come out again. I grimace as though apologizing for not having controlled my bodily responses (that's my intention). At least I'm not itching so much, I say, repressing the urge to scratch my back furiously. I'll be on the terrace, she says, and finally shuts the door.

The Chinaman's right, I tell Ahmed on the telephone, it's your problem, man. You should have thought about it earlier. Hey, I saw what you did, man, Ahmed interrupts me. I saw what you did, you got to help me. What are you talking about? I say, though I know what he's talking about. I saw what you did to the dog's owner, he says. Shut up, I say, my scalp in flames. The lawyer said these phones are secure, he says. Shut up, man! I shout, covering my mouth with my hand. You got to help me. Take the damn dog out, I say, before your neighbors call the police. Where do you live? I ask. In Sant Antoni, he says. Then go to the Ramblas, I say. Or to the Rambla del Raval. With the chaos there must be there tonight, no one's going to say anything. But man, the dog's not eating, he says. I'll see you tomorrow morning, I say. Soon, I mean. At eleven, at the Zurich. Tell the Chinaman. Where? he says. At the Zurich, man, on Plaza Cataluña, don't you ever go out?

I put the hot cell phone in my pocket and bring the other to my ear. I close my eyes and in my head I recite the names of Mexican Revolutionary writers. Martín Luis Guzmán. José Rubén Romero. I say uh-huh to the cell phone from time to time. I take a deep breath. José Mancisidor. Mariano Azuela. Francisco L. Urquizo. I haven't stopped shivering. I focus on making the itching subside, as though I really believed in the power of the mind over the body, as though I didn't know that this power does exist but only the other way around. Rafael F. Muñoz. I should sign up for yoga. What could that F. stand for in Rafael Muñoz? Fernando? Francisco? And Francisco Urquizo's L.? Luis?

I open the door to return to the party and in the kitchen I'm intercepted by Laia's friend again, I think I remember her saying she was called Núria, the same friend I'd been talking to when the secret cell phone in my pants pocket had started vibrating. Núria's a friend from middle school, a very dear friend, said Laia when she introduced her, so dear I suspect she's an ex-girlfriend. Are you hiding? she says. I show her the cell phone that I've still got in my right hand. A friend from Mexico, I say. What I was going to tell you, she says, starting to talk in Catalan and then backtracking to translate herself into Spanish (noticing the rashes on my face and repressing the automatic instinct to ask what the everloving fuck is happening to me?), what I was going to tell you is that I know Laia very well. I nod. Really, really well, she says, in Catalan now. I nod and try to remember where I left my beer. There's something really weird about all this, she says. Laia's not like this. She stops talking and looks me in the eye and then looks me in the mouth, forcing me to say something. Like this how? I say, hoping this will mean she stops looking at my face. This, she says, in Catalan. Heterosexual? I say. Among other things, she says. People change, I say. Not their sexual preference, she says. They don't? I say. Not Laia, she says. I know her. Extremely well, she says, in Catalan again, as if the adverb was more emphatic in Catalan. You know what's going on? she says. I respect the rhetorical pause, but she has stopped talking and compels me to ask, What, what's going on?, feigning interest, though I'm still thinking about Ahmed and the dog, realizing it's likely the dog has been tagged. It's because of her father, says Núria, Laia's gotten tired of fighting. She's been fighting for years to assert her identity. And I'm not just talking about her sexual identity, I'm talking about everything. When you meet her father, if you get to meet him, you'll see what I mean. A damn chip, I think, which would allow any vet to connect him to his dead owner. Laia's gotten tired of fighting, Núria goes on, forgetting to speak Spanish. Sorry, I say, trying to interrupt her. So sad, she says. Really. But you guys won't be happy, man, Laia's going to be real unhappy. Seriously. And you too. If you get my meaning? she says, in Catalan. Yes, I say, thanks for your good wishes. Hey, I say, to interrupt her. I'm real sorry, man, she says, in Catalan, we Catalans are like that, we like to call things like we see them. And this is just a no-shit serious drama. Real, real sad. They say drama plus time equals comedy, I say. Maybe in your country, says Núria, stubbornly, you guys laugh at everything, even death. Things are different here. Here drama plus time still equals drama. Or sometimes melodrama. Anyway, that's what Woody Allen said. Woody Allen's a piece of shit, he's a misogynist dick. The cell phone rings again, but this time it's the phone that's still in my hand. Sorry, I say to Núria, and I start to walk back over toward the laundry area.

Yes? I say. Happy New Year, asshole! says Rolando. Hello?! I shout, Hello?! I pretend I can't hear and cut off the call. I turn the cell phone off, pull out the other one and dial. Hi, babe, who's this? says Babe. It's the Mexican, I say, you remember me? You liked the pills, huh? he says. You want to see in the New Year on a high? I told you they were the shit, babe, but if you want more you're going to have to pay me. Have you got a dog? I say. What? he says. I'm asking if you've got a dog, I say, I need a vet I can trust, no one too sketchy. At this time of night, babe? he says. No, I say, tomorrow morning. Soon, I mean. I've got this pal, he says, but you'd have to come to Badalona, why don't you go to a vet's in the city? I need somebody I can really trust, I say, do you know your friend well? We're neighbors, babe, he says, we've been pals our whole lives, we smoked our first joint together, babe. Where do I find you? I say. Outside the train station, he says. At twelve, I say. Sure, if you want, babe, he says. But bring cash, it's a holiday, it's gonna cost you. I hang up and call Ahmed again. Change of plan, I say when he answers, and as I explain I scratch myself with masturbatory pleasure.

I go into the kitchen and before walking through it I survey the landscape. I don't want to run into Núria again. As far as I can tell, either Núria has already given up, after two interruptions, or, more likely, she thinks she's conveyed her message now. With some relief I start toward the terrace to look for Laia, but before I'm out of the kitchen another of Laia's friends intercepts me. Núria has just passed her the baton.

She's the fourth in a row; the first was the other Laia from the doctoral program, who constructed a theoretical framework to defend the hypothesis that I was part of a repressive phase in Laia's sexuality; the second, the one before Núria, was some girl called Lluísa, a very very close friend from high school, she said, who focused on showing me via negative dialectics that I represented a classic case of the abnormality annulment impulse (including that cacophony). And now a squat, dark girl intercepts me en route and grabs hold of my arm and calls me by my name to show that she hasn't got the wrong person. Listen, man, she says, so you, you don't know me, but I'm one of Laia's best friends. I'm Mireia, we're very very good friends, if you get me? I say yes, nodding my head up, down. I've got to tell you something, man, she goes on, it's pretty heavy but you got to hear it. I sigh and glance away, as far away as I can, looking for something or someone who might save me. I consider throwing my beer over myself, but I lost my beer hours ago. When I look back at her I see that she's staring hard at my face. OK, man, that's dermatitis nervosa, she says. I thank her for her diagnosis but tell her she's wrong, it's an allergy. I know what I'm talking about, man, that's a case of dermatitis nervosa, she insists. My father's a dermatologist, I cut her off. Would you excuse me, I say, and try to move her out of my way. Wait, she says, I need to talk to you, it's very very important. Laia's using you, man, you're part of a plan and you have no idea. Aha! I say, affably. That was all I needed: her conspiranoid friend. You don't know anything about what's going on, man, she continues, and I'm really sorry you've been taken in, you've even got yourself a dermatitis nervosa, man, that's heavy. That was all I needed: her conspiranoid friend who feels sorry for me. Laia's using you, she insists, squeezing my arm and shouting into my ear to be sure I can hear her clearly over the music and the clamor of the party. You're her doctoral thesis, she says. What? I say. I said you're her doctoral thesis, she says again. You know what Laia's thesis is on? she says. So like, I say, it's about

Mercè Rodoreda. That's what she told you? she says. And you believed her? There are more theses on Mercè Rodoreda in Catalan literature faculties than camels in the Raval, man, she says, you have no idea. They've even stopped accepting proposals on Rodoreda, it's all been said already. Laia's thesis is on heteronormativity and multiculturalism, she says, oh man, you have no idea. You're her guinea pig, she says.

A gypsy and a Moor walk into a bar, says Sketch, in the empty reception room of his office. It smells of wet dog. Cat piss. Dog kibble. A revolting mixture of all these things. They sit at the counter, says Sketch, and the gypsy orders two coffees from the woman serving there, a Spanish woman who's lived in the neighborhood her whole life. Hey man, watch this, says the Moor to the gypsy, and when the Spanish woman turns her back to make the coffees the Moor takes a cupcake from the counter and puts it in his jacket pocket. That's nothing, says the gypsy, who's irritated now, just look at me. Hey, lady, says the gypsy to the Spanish woman, I'm going to do a magic trick that's gonna make you totally shit yourself. The woman looks at the gypsy kind of pissed off, but she doesn't say anything so as not to annoy him. The gypsy takes a cupcake and gobbles it down in one bite. So where's the magic trick? says the Spanish woman. Look in the Moor's jacket pocket, says the gypsy.

Nobody laughs. You shouldn't say Moor, man, says Ahmed, you say Maghrebi. In my neighborhood they're still mother-fucking Moors, bro, says Sketch. If you're not having a laugh about it, it's because you're foreign. You didn't get the joke. Even your pal here isn't laughing, says Ahmed. I'm not laughing, babe, says Babe, because I've been told that joke a thousand times. It's not funny at all, says Ahmed, besides perpetuating the stereotype of Maghrebis and Romany people as thieves. Romany people? says Sketch. Where the fuck'd you find these cretins, Babe? The joke doesn't mention thieves, says the Chinaman. Thieves aren't the same as wise-guys, he says. Either way, it's a derogatory depiction, says Ahmed. Depends what world you live in, says the Chinaman. Where I live, cunning is highly valued as a virtue. Where you live in China, babe? says Babe. Man, I was born in Hospitalet, says the Chinaman. And is your name Jordi, babe? says Babe. Are you one of those Chinese with a Catalan name? My name's the Chinaman, says the Chinaman, and he takes a pack of cigarettes out the pocket of his jacket. Before his hand reaches for a lighter, Sketch stops him: You can't smoke in here, Chinaman, he says. The Chinaman's about to complain, but instead of arguing with Sketch (a lost cause) he gives Ahmed a warning: Get to the point, I get nervous if I can't smoke, he says. Wait for them outside, babe, says Babe, outside you can smoke the whole motherfucking pack. I can't, says the Chinaman, I'm these assholes' babysitter. Jesus, says Sketch, if you guys don't want to laugh at my joke then don't laugh, but don't bust my balls, OK? It was a motherfucking joke I just remembered when I saw you, he says. Because you look like the start of a fucking joke: There's a Mexican, a Muslim and a Chinaman. I'm not Muslim, says Ahmed, I'm an atheist. And the worst part of the joke is you say the owner of the bar is a Spanish woman, he says. It's like you're saying we immigrants have come to steal from Spaniards. You're the one saying that, man, says Sketch, now you're going to start on about me being racist just for telling you a fucking joke. Just because I laugh at a joke about Blacks doesn't mean I'm going to go straight out and give some Black a beating, man, seriously. But it's immoral, says Ahmed. Immoral, babe? says Babe. Didn't you say you were an atheist?

So, like, can we check about the dog? I interrupt them, though I could get enough to write a whole chapter of my doctoral thesis if I let them go on. My thesis – the one I actually wanted to write, I mean. She's a bitch, babe, says Babe, didn't they teach you at school how to tell the difference between males and females? How are you ever going to stop being an underdeveloped country if you get such a piece of shit education? I know she's a bitch, I say, it's just a manner of speaking. And what the fuck's happening to your face? says Sketch, who seems not to have noticed my presence before now. It's an allergy, babe, says Babe, don't worry, it's not contagious. It's from living in Mexico City and breathing all that pollution, babe, poor guy's poisoned on the inside. Didn't you tell me it was dermatitis? says Ahmed. You wouldn't be telling me lies because you've got leprosy, would you, man? Everybody looks at me waiting for an answer. I've got both, I say, I've had the allergy since I was a kid, and now this dermatitis has come on, must be the change of climate, and water, and food. Poor babe, babe, says Babe, that's what the crowd's like in the third world, babe, they start getting new illnesses on top of the ones they've got already. My grandmother can cure you with acupuncture, says the Chinaman. Jesus, babe, says Babe, you sure you're actually for real? You're not a cardboard Chinaman? A plastic Chinaman you buy for a euro in one of those Chinese stores? Sketch and Babe roar with laughter.

So like, I say, so, can we see about the bitch? I ask again, before the lack of nicotine and the other men's rough backstreet rudeness drive the Chinaman up the wall. What's wrong with the bitch? asks Sketch, looking at the end of the leash Ahmed's holding in his right hand. The animal is lying on the floor, dozing. She doesn't want to eat, says Ahmed. What's her name? says Sketch. We all look at Ahmed. I don't know, says Ahmed. You haven't given her a name? I say. Not yet, says Ahmed. Shit, man, says Sketch, she's a pretty grown-up dog not to have a name yet. This jerk got the dog from a guy who wasn't able to look after it anymore, says the Chinaman. And your guy didn't tell you what she's called? says Sketch. The guy croaked without revealing this information, says the Chinaman. And the bitch is starving herself out of sadness, babe? says Babe. That's lovely, babe, dogs are fucking awesome. We've really brought her, I say, to see if she's got a chip in her. A microchip, Sketch corrects me. So basically you're worried somebody might be able to identify the previous owner, he says, you're worried they might connect this bitch to the dead man. Didn't you say we could trust this guy, Babe? I say to Babe, in a tone I think is recriminatory. Sure, babe, says Babe, this babe here's been a pal my whole life. The fact you can trust him doesn't mean he's not going to ask questions, it means he's not going to spill the answers to nobody, he says. And why don't you just kill it? says Sketch. Looks like you've left this little job partly unfinished. What are you talking about, babe? says Babe. Don't be a dick. You want me to put her to sleep or take the microchip out? says Sketch. To put her to sleep, says the Chinaman. No, says Ahmed. Putting her to sleep costs two hundred euro, says Sketch. And sending her off to get cremated is another two hundred. Plus another hundred for taking out the microchip, as we'd have to take the microchip out anyway so she can't be identified at the crematorium. Fuck that, says the Chinaman, for a hundred euro I'd do it myself, just knock her out in one go and toss her on the Garraf dump. With a karate chop, babe? says Babe, laughing. You laugh, says the Chinaman, but you wouldn't laugh if you knew I know ninety-three of the hundred and eight dim mak points. But that's no use on dogs, babe, says Babe, they're points on the human body. I've tried them on cats, says the Chinaman. Man, what in the name of unholy fuck are you talking about? says Sketch. Kung fu, babe, says Babe, according to kung fu there are a hundred and eight points in the body where you can deal somebody a mortal blow. Wushu, says the Chinaman, kung fu's for westerners. And Hospitalet isn't in the west, babe? says Babe. That's all nonsense, says Sketch, conspiracy theories taken from Bruce Lee movies. I don't expect anyone to believe me, says the Chinaman, want me to do a demonstration? We want to take the chip out, says Ahmed. Taking out her microchip costs five hundred euro, says Sketch. Didn't you say it cost one hundred euro? says Ahmed. It costs a hundred if I've got to put the bitch to sleep and cremate her. If it's just taking out her microchip, it costs five hundred. Cash, he adds. First we need to check that she has a chip, I say. I'm sure she does, says Sketch, this is a pedigree dog, he says, and she's very well taken care of, just look at her nails. We all look down toward the ground. This bitch received a pedicure not long ago, says Sketch. Ahmed hands me the leash and puts his hand in the back pocket of his pants. We all watch as he pulls out his wallet and then extracts a purple banknote from inside it, one we've never seen before, a five-hundred-euro bill. He hands it over to Sketch, who holds it up to inspect it against the ceiling light. Man, you're such a jerk, the Chinaman says to Ahmed. The European Union's greatest invention, babe, says Babe. Come through, says Sketch, putting the banknote away in his pants pocket. I'm going to have a smoke, says the Chinaman, he opens the door to the street and goes out, leaving it ajar.

We go in to the office and Sketch pops out to the back of the store, the back of the office, that is, and immediately returns with something that looks like a remote control. White. With a little screen. And a fork at the top. Actually, the only way it resembles a remote control is that it has small buttons on it. Put the bitch up here, Sketch says to Ahmed, pointing at a metal table. Ahmed obeys. But the bitch does not: she resists and Ahmed has to hold her down to stop her hurling herself off the precipice of the table. Sketch passes the device over the dog's back. He hears a beep. Here it is, says Sketch. He shows us the screen of the gadget which shows a series of numbers and letters. This is the code, he says. Wait, I say. So like, this code allows people to investigate the details of the owner? I ask. Sketch says yes. Name, address, phone number. Oh, and the dog's name, too. I want to see them, I say. And leave a trace of the search? says Ahmed. Man, you're so dumb. Give me the code. The system's part of the Veterinary College, says Sketch, not just anybody can get in. You need a password. Write down the code, Ahmed says to me.

Three days later Ahmed phones me and says: I've got the info, come down and I'll give it to you. It was nine-thirty at night and I was scratching and having a slice of pizza in bed as my dinner. What? I say. I said come down, he says, I'm at the entrance to your building. How the fuck do you know where I live? I say. On the council record, he says, I went to the website of the local council. You haven't brought the bitch, though, right? I say. Where do you expect me to leave her, man? he says. She whines if I leave her on her own. Christ, I say. Holy Jesus fuck, I say, to make sure he has understood. Walk down Calle Zaragoza, I say, then you go down Vía Augusta. I'll see you at Gala Placidia. I hang up.

Ahmed was sitting on one of the benches at the side of the square, chatting to a teenage girl who was walking a beagle. The two dogs were sniffing one another's tails. I had to keep my distance, loop around the playground, waste some time pretending to look in the window of a closed shoe store on Travessera de Gràcia. I returned to the square, where Ahmed and the bitch intercepted me halfway. Hi, says Ahmed. Is that what you wanted the dog for? I say. To pick people up? Oh man, I wish, he says, but the only people who come talk to me are girls. The guys keep to themselves, your dogs can be killing each other or start screwing and they still don't say a word. I'm about to ask him if he's gay, purely as a reflex, but it's obvious he's gay: because of what he's just said and because I don't know how I'd never noticed it before. That's why I left Pakistan, man, says Ahmed, guessing my thoughts. No way you can live there if you're a fag. I ask him to give me the info he's gotten hold of before he goes on. The dog's on a new food now, he says, the vet was right, it was just a question of buying the more expensive one. I was asking for the info, I say. Such a hurry, he says. He takes a folded sheet of paper out of his back pocket and hands it to me. I put it straight into my coat pocket and turn around. Hey, he says. What? I say, spinning back to face him. My mother says the best thing for itching is to eat raw food, he says, fruit, vegetables, don't eat junk. You should listen to me, my mother's a doctor in Lahore, she works at a children's hospital. I nod silently. Oh, he says, the bitch's name is Viridiana.

I turn around again, and without saying goodbye I change my return route, I take a small paranoid detour, as if I was hoping to throw somebody off my track and, paradoxically, this is how I discover that I've got somebody on my tail. It's impossible that anybody should just happen to be taking the same route, for the simple reason that this course, halting and ludicrous even for somebody taking a stroll, makes no sense. When I reach Guillermo Tell I turn around for a good look at the person who's after me: it's a squatter. Without a dog. He's wearing an olive-green military jacket. He's carrying a cardboard container of wine which he tilts up to cover his face when he realizes I'm looking at him.

I go up Calle Vallirana, which is deserted. I hear the squatter's footsteps behind me. Hey, man! he shouts. I don't even pause. Yeah, you, Mexicano jerk! he shouts again. I freeze but I don't stop walking (it's a freezing of my spirit, which becomes paralyzed with fear). Man, are you deaf?! he shouts again. I'm talking to you, jerk! Juan Pablo! He has an Italian accent. I break into a trot. I know what you're up to, asshole! he shouts. I'm watching you! I know what you're up to with your Catalan girlfriend with the crooked teeth! You think nobody's noticed, you're going to live happily ever after, but I'm going to kick the living crap out of you, I know what you're up to! I start to run without looking back till I've arrived at the door to my building.

Once inside, I make sure the door's properly closed and I don't stop running till I've gotten myself into the elevator. I press the button for the sixth floor. The secret cell phone in my pants pocket starts to vibrate. I look at the little screen: number withheld. I hesitate before answering, thinking the siege might be continuing by phone, like in a bad horror movie. I don't answer. I'd rather start scratching. The vibrating of the cell phone stops. It starts shaking again.

Yeah? I say, my trembling voice still halting from being out of breath and the army of ants marching all over my back (I should go to yoga, I should exercise, I should go to the doctor, I should eat fruit and vegetables). The Chinaman's been here! shouts Laia's father, enraged. The idiot says he's only obeying orders, and that I should talk to you. So like, about what? I say. About what he's just brought me! he shouts, what else could it fucking be? Is there some problem? I say. He's brought me a hundred and thirty! he shouts, and we'd agreed on fifteen! Where in fuck's name am I going to stick a hundred and thirty?! This isn't how things are supposed to work! he says. Tell your idiot boss that there's no way for us to put away a hundred and thirty without getting Interpol onto us. A hundred and thirty what? I say, when the elevator opens on the sixth floor. Million euro, cretin! he says. That's twenty billion pesetas! he shouts and hangs up.

I walk across the hallway and into the apartment, which does seem empty, and do a check of the place to make sure there's really no one there. I find the phone number that the lawyer gave us for emergencies, the Barcelona cell number, only if it's absolutely urgent, he said, we shouldn't contact him under any circumstances, except for emergencies, and we'd do well to understand what constitutes a real emergency. I pour myself a glass of water, breathe, sit down in the living-room armchair, breathe, and finally dial the number.

Are you calling to tell me that the fag ended up keeping the dog? says the lawyer, answering. So like, I say, Laia's father's just phoned and he was really upset, the Chinaman's brought him— I say, but the lawyer interrupts me: Tell the fag to go see him, the fag knows what needs to be done. What? I say. I said tell Ahmed to go see Oriol, asshole, he says, Jesus, why do I always have to repeat everything? Am I your mother or something? That's what you called me for, for Christ's sake? Didn't I tell you all that you should only call in case of an emergency? he says. One other thing, I say. What? he says. So, like, I say, and I'm thinking about how best to describe what's just happened so it doesn't look like it's my fault. What, fuck's sake? he says. I think they've found us out, I say, counting on the possibility that the impersonal verb and the plural direct object might at least seem to give me the benefit of the doubt. What the fuck are you talking about? he says. I give him a summary of what's just happened, about the Italian chasing after me and what the Italian shouted at me. Are you sure he was Italian? asks the lawyer. I don't know, I say, I think so. So was he or wasn't he? he says. I think so, I say. Fucking hell, he says, to hell with every Italian fucker. To hell with the whole of Italy. So like, I say, what has his being Italian got to do with it? Only that the Italians want to swipe our project, dickhead! he says. The apartment door opens, and Facundo comes in, carrying Alejandra, who's asleep. He gestures with his chin for me to help him close the door and unhook the backpack from his back. We've got to identify this Italian, says the lawyer. I'm calling Riquer. Who? I say. The head of the Mossos, dickhead, he says. Listen out for the phone, he's going to call you. Him or one of his people. Do what they tell you, he says, and he hangs up.

I put the little cell phone in my pants pocket without Facundo seeing it and walk over toward the door to help him. Though there's an imperative for silence, Facundo's verbal diarrhea spills over, in whispers: She's going to stay with us a few days, he says. Her shithead mother's going to Buenos Aires, an emergency. Brother's been injured. On his motorbike. Shithead slipped and ended up under a lorry. I'm sure the shithead was up to his eyes in pills. I know that shithead. Alejandra opens her eyes, gives her little arms a stretch and says: The landscape is so real it's like it's pretend! I look to Facundo for an explanation. More shit from her mother, he says. Alejandra is just staring at my face. Yo, shithead, she says, what's happened to your face. Come on, be a pal, Al, says Facundo, you don't call the shithead a shithead.

Riquer called me up and said: Come to my office first thing tomorrow morning. We agreed to meet at eight at his office on the Paseo de San Juan. When I arrived, I found him on his own: it wasn't the station of the Mossos d'Esquadra, it was the off-ice where they finish off (*sic*) private matters, he explained. I shook his rough hand and breathed in the alcoholic fumes that emanated from the pores of his skin. One of two possibilities: either he'd breakfasted on gin or he hadn't slept and had just had his last drink of the day. Of the previous day. He had very little hair, really very little indeed, a buzz cut, and nicotine-yellowed teeth. Fiftysomething, closer to sixty than fifty. Navy blue suit, no tie. Shirt not very well ironed. Let's get to it, he says, got to hurry, and he asks me to follow him.

The place is made up of two office rooms and a reception. Old, heavy furniture, made of real wood, from a different time when there used to be carpenters and trees. A fine layer of dust, a calendar from the '92 Olympics, bundles of documents in various shades of yellow, the curtains fraying at the bottom, everything suggesting that its use is only occasional, or clandestine.

The secretary arrives at nine, he says, and gestures that I'm to sit myself at the desk, facing the monitor of a computer. The leather chair, from a real animal, creaks when I sit down. The files of the antiestablishment agitators, he says, calling the first pictures up onto the screen. How do you know he was antiestablishment? I ask. Because you said so, he said, didn't you say he was a squatter? I don't know, I say, that's what he looked like. That's what he looked like, he repeats, and that's why we're here, to find out for sure, he says. Click the button on the mouse to move to the next photo. I obey. I look at the first. Several seconds. I move to the next. I take a good look at that one. Hurry up, says Riquer. There are more than eight hundred files on Italians alone. If you don't find him we'll have to check the others. I accelerate the pace of my clicks on the mouse, one every five seconds or ten at the most.

Riquer drags a stool around from the other side of the desk to sit next to me. Those Italians are trash, he says, they think Barcelona's a sewer where they can show up to dump all their crap, specially since Berlusconi started sorting them out. Nothing but riffraff, he says. He opens a desk drawer and pulls out a cigar. I hear him remove the wrapping, cut it, light it, and suck on it with satisfaction while I keep pressing the left-hand button on the mouse.

Have you been working for the lawyer long? he asks. For a moment I'm not sure if I should reply. Jesus, he says, we're on the same side here, do me the fucking favor of returning the courtesy I'm showing you. I hesitate again. Holy Jesus fucking Christ, man, he says, you think you'd be here if I wasn't somebody the lawyer trusted completely? So like, I say, not taking my eyes off the screen, I really came to Barcelona to do a doctorate. A doctorate? he says. Oh fuck, that's a good idea. The lawyer is the shit, man, seriously. Doctoral students. This is going to end up making it even harder to catch you guys! he shouts, and bursts into a metallic laugh followed by a bout of coughing.

What's the doctorate on? he asks, once he has recovered. I don't say anything. Have you actually registered or did you just get the acceptance letter so as to process your visa? he asks. I press the mouse's little button faster and faster and keep quiet. The stink from the cigar is starting to make me nauseous. I give a deep sigh to regularize my breathing. Riquer doesn't bother waiting for my answers, he's just following the thread of his speculations out loud. Just what we need now, for the national police to be issuing student residency cards to delinquents, he says. Wouldn't surprise me, from assholes like them.

Then I see the face: a little chubbier, a little more tanned, a little healthier than that of the man who threatened me, but no question at all, it's the same face. The same face, but aged and haggard from a dissolute life. This one, I say. Are you sure? says Riquer, waving away the cigar smoke and bringing his face right up close to the screen. Sure, I say. Well, that's that, then, he says, and he gets up and pushes away the chair in which I'm seated. So what now? I say, following him to the exit. He opens the door and gestures for me to step through. Now you go, he says.

*

In the most frequently recurring dream, the old man appears to me with his raincoat and his dog, I mean, his bitch, and he says, anguished: Did anyone laugh at the joke? I tell him no and I tell him I'm sorry, that's not what I'm like, what I was like, not until now, somebody incapable of killing even a character in a story. I tell him one time I was writing a story for a competition in college and that at a given moment I realized that the protagonist, a private detective who'd been sticking his nose into other people's business, had to die. And that I hadn't had the nerve to kill him, because I'd become attached to him. That I'd preferred to stop writing the story despite the prize being two thousand pesos. The old man scratches at his raincoat to remove a stain from his lapel and in his face I see the saddest look in the world: the empty gaze of the dead. But you did kill me, says the old man. And it wasn't a story. It was reality. You people are just cynics, he says. All of you. Book people.

And each time I wake up feeling like I'm under the dead man, as my grandpa used to say, with the weight of the old man's corpse hugging around my whole body, and I turn on the little bedside lamp and I start to scratch and I grab any old book from the pile I've got on the table, *Cartucho* by Nellie Campobello, but it's full of corpses, the stories of Julio Torri, but the best one is a humorous tale about firing squads ('Even to die they make you wake up early,' writes Torri), and then I get up and turn on the computer and without much conviction start typing the essay I've got to hand in in February for Dr Ripoll's seminar, a historical account of the invention and evolution of blow-up dolls, which I'm thinking of relating to Felisberto Hernández's 'The Daisy Dolls'. I only tap away for a few minutes and then I give up and open a new document and start writing down everything that's happened to me in the last few months, as if I was writing a novel, as if my implausible life could ever be the material for a novel. I write with no guilt, no shame, like a liberation, with itching. I'm not writing to ask forgiveness, I'm not writing to justify myself, to give explanations, it's not a confession. I'm writing because deep down I'm a cynic who's really only ever wanted to write a novel. I want to get to the end. Whatever it takes. And though I exaggerate slightly (there's no comedy without hyperbole), everything I describe in my story is true. There's no place for fiction in my novel. I can prove it all, I've got evidence. It's all true. I don't expect anyone to believe me.

IT'S ALL FOR MY COUSIN'S BENEFIT

Whassup, cousin?, how're you doing, girl?, how are those Catalans treating you?, have you hit the sales yet?, you best keep your eyes open cause they put the price of clothes up before offering the discounts and you end up paying more.

Hey, cousin, you won't be put off if I call you cousin, right, cousin?, my cousins' girlfriends are my cousins too, just like they were really part of the family, I guess you've already noticed we're a real close family. No matter that we haven't been able to spend time together, that we've never met in person, I know you like I've known you my whole life, know everything about you, everything, because my little cuz's told me, we're real close, my cousin and me, and I guess he'll have told you everything about me too, I've always been his favorite cousin.

I hope you read this, because that means the letter will have gotten to you, they said at the consulate they could pass it on to you if you go in to do your consular registration, write that down, that's what they call the procedure, it's important you do it so they can track you down in case there's any problem and also that way you make the most of it to pick up this letter. Or if the letter arrives later then they have some way of notifying you. So don't put your registration off till tomorrow, hurry over to the consulate, do it today, and tell my cousin he should register too, those kinds of practical things are the ones he never bothers with, you already know my cousin's always got his head in the clouds thinking about the immortality of shellfish.

But don't go telling my dumbass little cuz I've written to you, cousin, don't go telling him about this letter, it's important that you and me, cousin, we open up a channel for direct communication, without my cousin finding out, but don't go thinking it's so's we can do stuff behind his back, how could you even think that, cousin, my cousin and me we're like brothers, everything's for my cousin's own benefit, cousin. You maybe think you know him well, that cousin of mine, but I know him better than you do and that's why I'm writing, to tell you a few things and so's you can help my cousin in this new phase you guys are starting. I know you'll understand, I know you're smart and you understand what a shithole life is like, sorry to use that kind of language, but you're from a modest background and you know very well life isn't like in those books my cousin likes so much, where even the dumb cockroaches have existential crises. And I hope you're not going to get defensive, cousin, I'm on your side, and now you and my cousin and me are all going to be a team, we got to stick together, I know you must be thinking I'm against you, but I'm not like my aunt and uncle, or my cousin, your sister-in-law, if you know what I mean?, you got to learn to see things clearly and see that I'm on your side, we're a team from now on, you really can trust me. I'm going to defend you against the family and to me you're already one of the family, another one of us, like you were born out of the belly of one of my aunts, no word of a lie, as if you were from Los Altos and light like the rest of us, as if the whole world was like that ice cream parlor in Veracruz where they call every one of their customers Blondie, you know it?, what'll you have, Blondie? they say, a vanilla for you, Blondie, even if their customers are darker than Moctezuma.

Talking about Veracruz, and so you know I'm not just saying it, I can tell you that two weeks ago I took a trip to Veracruz to see where you lived and meet your family. Two weeks ago from when I'm writing this letter, to be clear, not two weeks from now when you're reading it, because I don't know when you're going to read it, I hope you are reading it, it did reach you, right? Don't go getting a bad vibe about this bit, it's all for my cousin's benefit, when it comes to my cousin's benefit there's nothing I wouldn't do, but it's also for everybody's benefit, now that we're a team, now you're part of the family, if I say you can depend on me it's because I know you and because I also know I can trust you and that was what I needed to be sure of. That's what I'm like, you'll get to know me in time, though I'm sure my cousin must have told you just what I'm like, that I'm someone who when he suggests something he sees it through, but for that the first thing you need is trust, loyalty, and how was I to know we could really depend on you?

I really kind of liked your brothers, and your folks, and that fatso cat that scared the living shit out of me when he appeared from his hiding place, apparently he spends all his time hidden away in the bathroom. Obviously I didn't tell your folks I was my cousin's cousin, what do you expect, they wouldn't have understood me showing up there asking questions, they'd have thought I was spying on you, there'd have been some misunderstanding because they weren't to know we're a team and that you're part of the family now, Blondie. I knocked at the door and told them I was doing a survey, that's what I said to your folks, that if they answered the survey they'd be put into a raffle for a car, and they were incredibly nice to me, they invited me in, we sat in the living room and they offered me a hibiscus water and a coffee. I really kind of liked them, your folks, seriously, I thought they were perfect, I've always thought that the simpler people's lives are the happier they are, and the more dignified, more decent, even if some people think the opposite. I swear it, cousin, sometimes I just want to go live on a desert island and eat coconuts, make sushi from the fish or at the absolute most a tuna tartare.

What I want is to tell you about my cousin and about us, now that we're a team and we got to stick together, we're going to be a team and I need you to do your bit, giving my cousin some serious support, you know my cousin's personality doesn't help, that's why we're going to back him up, you and me, because otherwise he's not going to be able to do it all on his own, real big opportunities are always too big for him, my cousin has no idea about how to become a success, you know how inclined he is toward failure and unhappiness, because that's what the characters in his favorite books are like, all just total fucking neurotic slacker dicks (pardon my French).

One time, I'm never going to forget this, we were at my cousin's wedding, this is a different cousin, and when my cousin was kind of drunk he started quoting me some lines by his favorite writers from memory. You should have seen it, these mega-loser lines, about how man is excellent manure for sowing papayas, or how basically everyfucker and his sister likes posterity because of how you'll be dead and resting by the time they get there. I said to him: Look, cousin, if those are the books you like, you're never going to make anything of yourself in life, life's enough of an utter bitch for you not to also be dumping more depressing things on top of it. And sorry about the language again, cousin, it's just I feel like I know you well even though we've never met, and I really kind of liked your family, they're honest people, real simple folks, your folks, if only there were more people like your folks in this country, that's what we need.

That's just what my cousin's like, cousin, I'm not making it up, I'm telling you I'm the only person who defends him in this family, even my aunt's treated him real bad his whole life, criticizing everything he does, but I do understand my aunt, because it's a pain in the ass defending him (sorry about the language) when he's always taking wrong decisions, like studying a subject that's useless, like going to live in Veracruz, don't get offended but that's basically like going to Honduras or Guatemala. Or going out with you, cousin, I'll always defend you and we're a team, but my cousin did exactly the opposite with you to what he should have done. Now don't go taking this the wrong way, but you can't deny getting married is also a way of ensuring a good future, accumulating some assets, making new business contacts, I'm sure you understand, because there had to be some reason you chose my cousin, and it wasn't because he's handsome or smart. Sorry if you're offended, cousin, but I think it's important we're honest with one another, now we're a team we can't go being hypocrites.

The good news, cousin, is that your cousin here does see things differently, your cousin sees the glass full when every fucker else sees it empty, even better, your cousin sees it full of champagne, and your cousin will never forget about his cousin, about my cousin, even if he's made me lose some business deals and has no aspirations in life. If my cousin wants to settle with being a literature professor, you know what, cousin?, your cousin isn't going to just abandon him, your cousin would know how to transform a useless doctorate into a business opportunity, your cousin has some serious projects going on and your cousin isn't going to forget his cousin, your cousin has always included him in his plans, even when he didn't deserve it, because we're cousins and that's what families do, they support each other and when one person has an opportunity he shares it, which is what I'm doing now, taking advantage of the fact you and my cousin are going to live in the country of the jerks, your cousin is making the most of his cousin's shit to use as manure for making the business grow, I'm inviting my cousin into some real high-level business, real serious business, this is the kind of business anyfucker at all would kill for, the kind of business if it works out well we're all going to be loaded with banknotes, you, cousin, and my cousin and me, and you'll even be able to help out your folks, send them some euro via Western Union, that's why I'm writing to you, because I need you to support my cousin, to give him some solid backup so as to bring home this project we're working on.

I can't tell you the details of the business because that's the way these projects are, you got to keep things confidential or other investors will hear about it and steal our idea. But what I can tell you is that our partners are seriously heavy guys, ultra high level, both the Mexican partners, who are people I trust who I've done other serious business with before, as well as the Catalan partners, who're the ones my cousin's going to be working with. The only thing I can tell you is that you got to support my cousin come what may and even if my cousin does things that are STRANGE, don't be thinking this is a normal office job, when you're involved in ultra-high-level business you got to be prepared for anything, you really think Carlos Slim made his fortune sitting in an office from nine to two, and four to seven? You got to be ready for anything, cousin, and you got to trust me, I trust you, I've already made the investment of going to Veracruz to meet your family and investigate whether you might be a trustworthy person, and when I saw that I could put together a totally positive file on you, cousin, to give to our Mexican partners, where I told them you were someone who's coming up from below but who's really aiming to get on, that you got ambitions in life. As you can see, it's not just talk with me, I'm also a doer, it should show you that you can trust me too, that I'm also my cousin's favorite cousin. And the thing you've most got to support my cousin with is giving him SECURITY, because he's very insecure, and making him be PERSISTENT, because I worry about him starting the project then giving up halfway. You and me both need for my cousin to be strong for the project to work out, and I also want to ask you that if you notice anything strange, if you see that my cousin might be acting against our interests, yours and mine, cousin, that you tell me right away, at the end of this letter I'm going to put my office phone number. If you see my cousin deviating from the plan you call me and if you don't find me you leave me a message, you say my cousin called, just that, don't give your name, just that my cousin called, that way when they tell me a woman called who said she was my cousin I'll know it was you and you just leave me a phone number or something so I can find you. Don't go thinking I don't trust my cousin, it's not that, we two are brothers, but when you're doing high-level business there are a lot of temptations, and I hope my cousin's only a bit of a pussy and doesn't turn out to be a TRAITOR too.

Well then, cousin, I'm not going to take up any more of your time, go straight to the consulate to register and take advantage of the visit to pick up this letter. Don't delay, we don't want some busybody opening it, you know what diplomats are like, nothing to do all day, those guys totally live the high life, I've even thought maybe I ought to try being an ambassador, I've got a friend who's the Secretary of Foreign Relations' cousin's brother-in-law's neighbor, I'm going to give him a call and see if he can hook me up.

I'm sending you a big hug, cousin, and a lot of luck, do it for your folks, they deserve a better life and if everything works out well you're going to be able to help them. I hope we get to meet in person soon, I know you're going to like me, you'll see.

FOUR SUNNY DAYS

Monday, January 3rd, 2005

One in the morning. It's raining. My tiny room catches all the noises from the neighborhood. Really fierce depression this evening, and tremors. I'm not going to drink again. I've got to learn to say no to Jimmy's box wine.

First day of work yesterday. And last: I quit after two hours, I didn't even make it through the day. I didn't come to Barcelona to serve nachos and guacamole. I didn't leave my family just to put up with people treating me like an under-developed cockroach because the food's too spicy. Who am I trying to kid? I didn't come because I wanted to. The doctoral plans were just an excuse to be with Juan Pablo.

Maybe it's time to accept that being here makes no sense. To take the money Juan Pablo's offering me and change my flight. There's no way I can make it to the end of the month. Not financially, not mentally. Tomorrow, or rather today, later, I'm going to call him.

Wednesday 5th

Two awful days. Terrible insomnia. Two days of not being able to summon up the nerve to call Juan Pablo because I can't swallow my pride. Because I'm devastatingly scared of hearing his voice, in the same phone booth. The big thing that's changed is that I've stopped being the dummy from the telenovela, the idiot, and now I'm a poor jilted maiden from one of those country songs. And drunk. All I do is sit in the Plaza del Sol drinking with Jimmy. Checking my email a couple times a day. Eating (when I remember to). I don't read anything. I feel like a burden's been lifted off my back.

Yesterday Gabriele came back from Rome.

'You ought to give yourself a shower, gorgeous,' he said when he saw me.

Or, rather, when he smelled me.

Thursday 6th

9 p.m. and the fear's still in my body, I can't calm down. I feel like my nib is short of air, like my writing's suffocating. But now's not the moment to start making literature. Even my eyelashes are trembling.

It must have been five in the afternoon and I was at the square, sitting on the ground with Jimmy, when I saw a police car stop on one of the side streets. I saw a few squatters slip away, a black man offering passersby bootleg movies, a German couple who sometimes get very violent shooting up heroin. I could have gotten up, I could have walked calmly home and maybe nothing would have happened. I stayed sitting where I was, not reacting, because I'd come to a mistaken conclusion: this had nothing to do with me. In truth it wasn't even a conclusion, it didn't even occur to me. The bad habit of not being in the habit of getting into trouble with the police. I presumed that raid, if you can call an action carried out by just two cops a raid, must have been to seize drugs. But the two cops crossed the square, making straight for Jimmy. Straight for us, I mean.

Juan Pablo Villalobos

They were a man and a woman. The policeman called Jimmy by his full name, which he had written down in a notebook, like in the movies, and asked him for his papers. Jimmy, snorting, handed him a piece of cardboard that wasn't even laminated. With a photo of him from a million years ago where he had short hair and looked like a student of business admin. He said it was his Italian ID. While the policeman checked the information on the little card, the woman clocked my presence. The fact that I was with Jimmy.

'Papers,' she said to me.

I took my passport out of one of the inside pockets of my overcoat. I don't normally carry it around with me, for fear of losing it, but this morning I was absolutely resolved to call Juan Pablo and thought that at the offices of the airline they might ask me for it to change my flight. (I didn't call him, needless to say, my determination evaporated no sooner than I'd crossed the square.) When the officer had taken my passport, she interrupted her colleague, who had started questioning Jimmy about his registration, telling him that he was required to register.

'She's Mexican,' she told him, in Catalan.

It sounded like an accusation. She handed my passport over to her colleague as if it was evidence of a crime. The sequence of actions suggested the man was her boss, as if there was some hierarchical connection between them. And if there wasn't they were just behaving in accordance with the roles of machista supremacy.

'Do you live in Barcelona, Valentina?' asked the policeman, flicking through all the pages in my passport.

He was looking for the immigration entry stamp. I said yes, for a bit. Just three months. That I'd arrived at the end of October. Finally the officer found the stamp and checked the date.

'Are you registered with the municipality?' he asked me.

154

I said yes, but not at my current address, that I'd previously been living in a different apartment and hadn't yet made the change.

'What's the address where you're registered?' asked the policewoman, with pen and notebook, ready to note it down.

I said it was Julio Verne, number 2. The policeman closed my passport and put Jimmy's ID inside. The two officers exchanged a look. Both of these actions alarmed me.

I started to tremble.

'In apartment 6D?' said the policewoman, pronouncing it *parmen*.

I sobered up in an instant.

'We seem to have a motive,' said the policeman to the woman, both of them staring hard at us.

'What?' said Jimmy.

'It's just that your new Mexican girlfriend's ex-boyfriend has reported you for threatening him,' he replied. 'The plaintiff, Juan Pablo Villalobos Alva, identified his assailant as Giuseppe Colombo.'

A burning hole opened up in my belly.

'Threatening behavior in a public place,' the agent went on. 'The plaintiff was walking down Calle Vallirana on Tuesday the 4th at 10:30 p.m. when he was accosted by the accused.'

'She's not my girlfriend,' said Jimmy.

'Why did you leave the apartment on Calle Julio Verne?' the policewoman asked me.

The hole started spilling lava down toward my legs.

'Did you and Juan Pablo have a fight?'

Somebody put a rock inside my head, in the place my brain was supposed to be.

'Don't answer,' Jimmy said quickly. 'I know the law, man, don't say a thing. At that time on Tuesday I was here in the square,' he went on, now also speaking to the police officers,

'I've got masses of witnesses. We could report you for slander, we're going to report you for harming our image with our friends here and the people in the neighborhood.'

I stared at him, amazed.

'I studied law in Bologna, man,' he said to me, 'I'm a lawyer.'

'Is this a joke?' said the policeman.

'Am I laughing?' replied Jimmy.

The policeman tutted loudly and looked over to the other sides of the square where those squatters who hadn't slipped away were bunched together to comment on what was happening.

'The things we've got to put up with,' he said to his colleague, 'Jesus, these Italians are really something.'

'And you lot are fascists,' said Jimmy. 'And racists. You're hassling my friend because she's Latina. You stole all the gold from the Americas and now you complain about immigration. Nazi fucks.'

'Whoa there, pal,' said the officer, 'you'd better shut your mouth if you don't want us to arrest you right now.'

'These ones are Mossos, man,' Jimmy said to me, 'the ones from the Catalan police, they're the worst.'

'I'm being serious, man, shut your fucking mouth,' said the officer.

Then he asked me if I had a return ticket to Mexico. I said yes.

'For what date?' he asked.

I said it was for January 27th. He asked me to show it to him and I said I had it back at the apartment where I was living.

'Have you registered at the consulate?' he said.

I said no, I didn't know what that meant.

'Well,' he said, 'since you haven't updated your local registration, and you also haven't done your consular registration, we're going to have to accompany you back to your apartment. We need to confirm your place of residence.'

Jimmy was about to say something but the officer cut him off:

'This is for you.'

He held out a sheet of paper.

'It's got the date, time and place where you've got to show up,' he said. 'If you don't come, we'll come and fetch you. A notification's been sent to the Italian police, too.'

'Here it is,' I said to the police officers when we were outside the building on Calle de la Virtud. 'Apartment 4A,' I said.

'We need to go inside,' said the policewoman, 'we need to check you really live here.'

'You go in,' the policeman said to her, 'I'll wait for you out here. I'll go get a coffee.'

The woman accepted his suggestion as if it was a matter of obeying orders. The two of us went into the building and started climbing the stairs.

'That's the problem with Gràcia,' said the officer on the landing of the second floor, which is really the third if you count the mezzanine. 'It's a really cute neighborhood but the houses are old and they don't have elevators. At least you get your exercise,' she added.

I said nothing. I didn't know if they were now going to go all bad cop (the one who'd gone for a coffee) / good cop, or if the policewoman really was making an effort to be nice, to show her empathy, as if now her colleague was no longer around it was just a matter between us girls. I was so scared I decided to follow Jimmy's advice and keep my mouth shut, not so much because I trusted his legal counsel, but out of a basic survival instinct telling me that if I did nothing, things couldn't get worse.

Finally we reached the fourth floor, with me somewhat breathless as always, and the police officer cool and glowing, she was in great shape. I noticed what she looked like for the first time while I recovered and rummaged for my keys in my overcoat pockets. A redhead (she'd taken off her cap when she came into the building). Olive-colored eyes. Unremarkable features. Cheekbones dotted with tiny, almost imperceptible freckles.

I turned the key in the lock, pushed the door and immediately heard Gabriele's voice.

'Oh, you're back,' he said, 'hey, let me introduce you to the Brazilians, they're back from Morocco.'

The two backpacks were still dumped in the middle of the living room and the Brazilian couple were drinking beer on the sofa.

'Hi,' I said.

The three of them saw the officer who was following me in and for a moment the effect of the police uniform produced total silence.

'Afternoon,' said the policewoman. 'Just a routine matter,' she added.

Then she asked me, in a kindergarten teacher's voice, to show her my plane ticket. I went into my room to fetch it. While I rummaged among the papers in the bureau I heard the officer saying it looked like it was going to rain. The Brazilians agreed. Gabriele said it might look that way, but it never rained in Barcelona.

'There's just this damn humidity,' he said, then apologized for having said damn.

'No problem,' said the policewoman, 'complaining about the weather isn't against the law yet.'

I came out of the room with the piece of paper folded in four. The officer looked it over. The Brazilians took advantage of the silence to drink little sips of their beer. The officer folded the sheet of paper up again, and handed it back to me along with my passport (I hadn't even noticed they hadn't returned it yet).

'Everything seems to be in order,' she said.

She said goodbye. At the door, she asked me to step outside a moment. I walked out and pulled the door closed behind me.

'Listen,' the policewoman said, her voice a high-school teacher's now, 'for the moment there's no problem, but if the Italian squeals or if your ex-boyfriend finds out you're going to be in for it. Giuseppe's summons is for March. By that time you'll be in Mexico. If you're really planning to use that ticket. My advice, if you'll allow me, is that you go tomorrow first thing to your country's consulate and register with them. So they know how to track down your family if anything were to happen. Keep out of trouble, as these things never end well. Trust me, I know what I'm talking about. It looks like just some petty little jealousy right up until some piece of shit loses his mind. I've seen it many times before. And on the 27th you get on the plane. There are people who stay as illegals for years and nobody notices. That's not an option for you. If you don't go, on that same day, the 27th, there'll be an expulsion order for you.'

She put her hand on my shoulder. I said nothing, though I felt uncomfortable, as if she wanted to make me feel totally helpless. And she needn't have bothered, I was totally helpless already, I was basically getting a doctorate in that.

'Listen,' she said, 'is there anyone you trust you can call if things turn sketchy?'

Still I kept quiet.

'Man,' she said, 'I don't know what things are like in your country, but I'm guessing you've seen the news here, we've got cases of violence against women happening every day. You'd be amazed if you knew how the stories start that end up like that.'

She was so insistent I ended up wondering whether it was possible, in some parallel universe, that good policemen might actually exist. Or good policewomen, to be more accurate. This one, at least, did seem genuinely concerned.

'No,' I said, finally, 'I don't know a lot of people.'

She took out a notebook and jotted down her name and a couple of phone numbers. On top of everything, she was called Laia.

'Here,' she said, tearing out the page and handing it to me. 'Call the bottom number in case of emergency. The other's my cell, you can call me anytime you like if you think there's something I can do to help.'

I went back inside the apartment, crossed the living room without looking over to where Gabriele was waiting for an explanation, and shut myself in my room.

Friday 7th

I stayed shut up in my room until nine-thirty because I wanted to avoid running into Gabriele, who normally leaves the house before nine. I didn't hear the Brazilians leave, but I had to go out because I was practically peeing myself. I opened the door and was hit by the smell of coffee and of butter in the frying pan. The Brazilians invited me to join them for breakfast. They were so insistent I couldn't say no.

'We did not get a chance to present us yesterday,' he said, supplementing his bad Spanish with his better English. 'She is Andreia. My name is Paulo.'

He emphasized the Spanish pronunciation of his consonants as if afraid I might think he was Argentinian. We exchanged a pair of kisses and I apologized for looking a bit odd (and smelling a bit odd).

'I'm going through a confused phase, where hygiene is concerned,' I said.

They laughed heartily, and I saw their beautiful teeth. In

order to make me feel good, or rather, to make me not feel bad, they showed me their arms and legs, covered in insect bites (and tattoos). The bedbugs had feasted on them in Morocco. He's dark and she's very fair, with that milky coloring that other people feel sorry for on the beach. They must be over twenty-five and under thirty. While they spread a baguette with butter they told me they'd come to Barcelona to do a master's. They'd arrived at the end of September last year.

He's an architect, and even though he'd only come over to study, within two weeks he'd already gotten himself a job in construction.

'The firm builds traffic circles where there's nothing else around,' he said, laughing. 'We did a traffic circle in a town near Alicante and there are no roads to get to it. So what you're left with is a gigantic sculpture that cost a pretty penny. All paid for with European money.'

She's a physiotherapist. She's studying for a master's in kinesiology. When we sat down at the table she lit a joss stick. I was slightly offended, though I acknowledge that instead of taking offense what I should really do is take a bath. Neither of them mentioned what had happened the previous night, nor did they insist I tell them about my life or the reasons I'd come to Barcelona. I liked that. They contented themselves with telling me about their vacation in Morocco, they showed me photos on a laptop, and we laughed at the close-ups they'd taken of the bedbugs in the mattress of a guest house in Tangiers.

'Pesky little bed-buggers,' I said, just a silly bit of wordplay, but which they loved and repeated over and over.

They laughed a lot, each time revealing their beautiful teeth. When we finished I offered to clear the table and do the washing up. They accepted without making me think I owed them anything. I really liked them. Before heading out to do their things they warned me not to move the backpacks. Not to touch them. The backpacks were still dumped in the middle of the living room.

'We're going to take all the clothes out to wash in hot water,' said Paulo.

'And we've got to chuck the backpacks,' said Andreia.

'Bed-buggers,' they said, in chorus, laughing again.

They were so happy I was starting to hate them a bit.

Having breakfast with the Brazilians did me good, sticking my confused little head back into normality, remembering that outside this deep hole I'd gotten myself into there's a world where people are happy with their perfect teeth. I waited for the bathroom to be free and went in, intending to take a shower. I hadn't counted on the Brazilians having used up all the hot water. Five days without a bath and when I finally decide to do it there's only freezing cold water. I scrubbed my armpits, between my legs, my face. I put on clean clothes. I brushed my teeth furiously. Then I spent a little while taking the fluff off my overcoat with the brush I found in the living room. I needed to talk to Jimmy.

I went down to the square at midday and he wasn't there yet. I took advantage of his absence to stop in at the call shop to go online to look into this consular registration thing, which is really called 'consular matriculation'. I made a note of the address of the consulate and their office hours so I could go on Monday. Truth was, that business yesterday had left me very scared.

When I came back to the square I found Jimmy where he always was, as he always was, as though nothing had happened. He patted the ground with his right hand, inviting me to sit. I stood still, in front of him.

'Are you off to tea with the queen, girl?' he said. 'Where are you headed looking like that?'

'Did you hit him?' I asked, with no preamble and no beating around the bush.

'Who?' he answered. 'Your jerk ex-boyfriend? I didn't do anything to him, man, only what you asked me to. I gave him one hell of a fright, the jerk isn't only a jerk, he's also a chicken, what kind of dickhead would go to the police because some guy's given them a fright?'

'I didn't ask you to . . . ' I said.

'To what?!' shouted Jimmy before I was able to complete my phrase. 'What's this now? You're going to start on how the whole thing was my idea now? I'm the only person defending you, man, all I need now is for you to turn against me. Don't feel bad about it, you're screwed while this jerk is on top of the world, it's not right, did you know the asshole's bought himself a new coat? Another coat just as sweet, just as expensive, where does he get the cash, huh? You're right to want the fucker to be given a fright, don't feel bad about it.'

His face had turned the color of box wine and a vein in his neck was about to explode.

'I'm also right to be asking you for explanations, Jimmy,' I said, 'I've got trouble with the police now.'

'So that's what this is? The Mossos scared you? You're going to fuck me over just to get free of the Mossos? You're a fucking traitor, man. Screw you, man.'

He drank a long swig of beer, avoiding my eyes, his gaze lost on the ground of the square.

'How did you find him?' I said.

'Jesus, man, it was the easiest thing in the world, you don't stop talking about him every second of the fucking day, you told me the address where he lived loads of times, you showed me photos that day you brought your laptop computer, don't you remember?'

'You should have told me,' I said, 'you can't just go doing something like that and not tell me.'

'I forgot, man!' he replied. 'You think the only thing I'm worrying about is how to carry out your sentimental revenge? I've got shitloads of things to think about. You think I spend the whole day in the square doing nothing, but you don't know me, you don't know who I am. Besides, how was I to know that stupid son of a bitch was going to go to the police? I wasn't expecting that, man, honestly I don't know how you could go out with that jerk. Besides his whole fucking face is covered in marks, man, he's seriously butt-ugly.'

'I didn't ask you to threaten him, Jimmy,' I said. 'I mean, yeah, of course we talked about it, but I was a total mess, you should have realized I didn't mean it.'

'You didn't mean it?' he said. 'Those Mossos really scared you that much? You Mexicans are really something, you know that, man? You don't deserve Zapata. Pancho Villa invaded the US and now you lose your shit when you meet the Catalan police. And now you think you can show up disguised all fancy to bawl me out? You've even taken a shower to come over here and complain, you've showered so you could feel like you're better than me, I know what that fascist mentality's like. But who's the only person who put up with your ass when you were totally reeking, man? Me, man! Me! Girl, you're a coward. Forget that jerk, man, forget him, he's a dick. He left you for a Catalan girl with crooked teeth, get over him already.'

'Look who's talking!' I said. 'You think I haven't noticed why you're always on your own in the square? Why you don't have dogs and you're always looking over at that group? Because, *man*, that girl left you, and she kept the dogs,' I said, reaching my arm out to gesture toward the group of French squatters.

'Don't point, asshole!' he shouted.

'Am I wrong?' I asked. 'And you haven't got the balls to go talk to her or to move off to some other square. And I bet you were even using me just to make her jealous.'

'Shut up!' he shouted. 'You know what you should be doing instead of sticking your nose in where you're not wanted? You should be asking yourself how that jerk managed to identify me and how the Mossos managed to figure out my name and know that I come to the Plaza del Sol. Now that really is weird. I've been thinking about it all night. Where'd they get my information? Something doesn't add up, girl. But we're not going to leave it at that. I'm going to investigate.'

LOOKS LIKE A PANIC ATTACK

The dog talks, man, says Ahmed as he shows me the coat stand where he's hung the leash, in the entrance hall of his apartment. What? I say. I'm telling you, man, the dog talks, he says again, I know you'll think I'm crazy, but it's the truth, man, the dog talks. I look at him with the sympathy of knowing that he's not crazy (or not yet) and that his survival strategy (disconnecting from reality) might actually be healthier than mine (suffering a nervous breakdown). I guess Ahmed's conversations with Viridiana must have been a sublimation of his fears, the schizophrenic expression of the threats from the lawyer. And what does she say? I say. I don't know, man, he says, the dog speaks Catalan. I don't understand Catalan, he says. Do you know any? he says. Some, I say, I can understand it well enough. That's great, man, he says, so you can tell me what the dog says to you. Sure, I say. Are you going out now? he says. No, I say, later. Don't take too long, he says, if you don't take her out soon she'll wet herself. Take her to the Rambla del Raval, she loves peeing on the paws of the fat cat sculpture. Botero's cat? I ask. Whose? he says. Forget it, I say. Don't take too long, he says again, if she pisses herself you're cleaning it up, and careful with the rugs. Don't worry, I say, I'm sure she'll tell me when she's got to go. Christ, man, he says, it's true. I got to take some Catalan classes.

He opens the door to go out. I close it before he's gone out. So look, I say. Why've you got to talk to this guy? I say. I'm referring to Laia's father, who's waiting for him in an office on Avenida Diagonal. It's my job, says Ahmed. Are you a hacker? I say. You watch a lot of movies, man, he says. Is it you who cleans the cash? I say. What? he says. I'm asking if it's you who launders the dough, I say. Don't use that kind of language, man, he says. So it is you, I say. You don't know who I am, man, he says, I went to Yale, man, I used to work in a bank, he says, you don't know who I am. In a bank in Pakistan? I say. In London, he says. Is that where you met the lawyer? I say. The guy I know is the lawyer's boss, he says, but I'm not going to talk to you about that, he says. It's for your own safety. I look at his neatly trimmed little moustache, his wool sweater, his scarf, the rat-gray overcoat he still hasn't put on, folded over his forearm. Only now do I think about how well dressed he always is (perceptiveness to fashion is always diminished in emergency situations). He bends down to pick up the green plastic bag with six cans of beer from the floor. Hey, *man*, I say, you're dressed kind of fancy for someone who's supposed to be selling beer on the street. Doesn't matter, he says, people don't look at your clothes, man, they look at your face. You don't notice because you're white, you've got blue eyes, it's not till you open your mouth that people even realize you're Mexican. I'm going, man, he says, it's getting late. And will your work take long? I say. What? he says. I'm asking how long you're going to be? I say, I've got things to do (I'm supposed to be reading an essay by Jung). I don't know, he says, it's not up to me, it depends on this guy. I really got to go, he says.

I go fetch the dog while Ahmed's on his way out and I find her sprawled in the middle of the living room, dozing. I take the opportunity to have a look around. It is, very evidently, one of those apartments on short-term rental, furnished, deco-rated in the standardized taste of the petit bourgeoisie. The pictures are a reminder that this city is still the capital of the Informalists. I find three, four laptop computers in drawers (two), closets (one) and backpacks (one). I turn them on but they immediately ask for a password. I put them back where I found them.

There's nothing unusual to be discovered in the apartment, it's just as you'd expect: a place for a businessman who's passing through, working in the city for a few days. In my pants pocket, my cell vibrates. I make an automatic associa-tion: right pocket, social cell phone. I pull it out. It's Laia. Hi Mexicano, she says, have you got plans for this afternoon? I tell her I don't have anything special on, but that I should get to work on some stuff for the doctorate. I need to ask you a favor, she says. I ask her what, by means of a protracted silence that she doesn't understand. Are you there, Mexicano? she says. Yes, I say, tell me, tell me. I've got to go to my uncle's place and I don't want to go alone, she says. It's a weird situation. Now it's her who falls silent. Because? I say. We haven't heard from him in days, she says, he's, she says, and she pauses, he's kind of a bit disappeared. I wait for her to say something more, but she says nothing, it's my turn. Maybe he's gone on vacation, I say, just to say something. No, she says, he'd have told us, and also he didn't bring gifts. What gifts? I say. Happy Epiphany, Mexicano, she says. And does he not have a family? I ask. We're his family, she says. His own, I mean, I say. He's not married, she says, will you go with me? Where? I say. I don't understand? To his flat, she says, my mom's managed to get the key from the building manager but she didn't dare go in. Another pause, a longer one this time, enough for the image of a decomposing body to establish itself between us. Why's she calling me? I think. Why doesn't her dad go or one of the domestic staff? Instead I ask her if her uncle's very old. Not really, she says, he's seventy-two. Will you go with me? she asks again. Isn't there anyone else who can go? I say. I want to go myself, says Laia, emphatic. My uncle and me, we're super-close. In the living room, Viridiana is whining. I cover the microphone on the cell phone. Forget it, says Laia, I shouldn't have asked you the favor. What time? I say. At five, she says. I'll see you at the corner of Còrsega and Enric Granados.

I walk over to the coat stand to fetch the leash, a leash with the Barça colors and crest. Let's go, I say, poking my head into the living room, with the front door already open. The dog gets up, lazily. She allows the leash to be put on her, uncomplaining. Do you know what it is Ahmed does? I say. I repeat the question in Catalan, in what I think is Catalan, in broken Catalan. But the dog doesn't answer.

It's this one, says Laia, stopping outside a yellow building. On the top floor there's a relief of modernist flowers. At the mezzanine level, a balcony with Doric columns. I know this building, I know it very well, so well that suddenly my heart is in my throat and I feel the rashes rising one by one to announce their itching torture. Are you sure? I nearly say, but I don't say it, because I'm sure of what's going to happen, all of a sudden I understand everything, that when I ask her which apartment her uncle lives in, she'll answer Penthouse A.

So like, I say, which apartment does your uncle live in? Laia puts the key into the lock of the wrought iron and glass door, which also has modernist details on it. Oh man, she says, you've become covered in rashes in like a second! she says, and she holds the door half-open without going in, to look at me in the fading light of the winter evening. Are you not well? she says. It's my bastard allergy, I say, my motherfuck-ing bastard allergy, to be precise. Why's it happening now?

she says. What are you feeling? Like I'm suffocating, I say, like I can't breathe, it's a feeling that makes me real anxious. It looks like a panic attack, she says, don't you maybe have dermatitis nervosa? It's an allergy, I say, pressing toward her to make her go inside (let's just get this over with), it's a bit like asthma, I say, the allergist explained it all to me, I lie. You've already been to the allergist? she says, pushing the door and finally stepping into the building, and while we walk to the elevator, call it and wait for it to come down from the third floor I explain that I got an emergency appointment to ask for something for the itching and by pure chance there happened to be an allergist on duty. An allergist at the community health center?! says Laia, outraged. So like, no, I say, like, no, I try to correct my lie, I try to breathe normally, I went to a private clinic, I've got insurance with my scholarship (as in literature, a small insignificant truth in the middle of a whole heap of lies creates an illusion of reality). Still, it's weird, isn't it? says Laia. Neus is allergic and when my mother tries to get her to an allergist they give her an appointment for like two or three weeks later, at least. Well, I don't know, I say, seems like it might be low season now, I say, as if allergies were hotels or cruises. What? says Laia. Yeah, I say, it's just that allergies are at their worst when the seasons are changing, so like, specially in spring (I read this on the internet). Well, you'd best take care, Mexicano, she says, running her hand over the back of my neck, if you're already like this in winter, just think what you'll be like in spring. I might not even make it to spring, I say, as if joking, but serious. Don't be such a moron, Mexicano, says Laia.

The elevator arrives, we get in, and Laia does indeed press the button for the penthouse. I don't even bother asking her again which apartment we're headed for. The elevator climbs slowly, with a stateliness well suited to the bourgeois solidity of the building. I use these moments to try to calm myself. I close my eyes and breathe normally, the way I imagine people breathe normally, if I can even still remember what normal's like. Laia puts her hand on the back of my neck again, she says nothing, instead of saying anything she gives me a gentle squeeze with her fingers, respecting the silence.

I need to calm myself down. What could possibly happen now? Nothing. Nothing. I breathe normally, apparently normally. Nothing. Nothing's going to happen now, no cause for alarm. Laia's uncle's corpse isn't going to be rotting in his bed, and we aren't going to find him bleeding to death in the bathtub, as Laia and her mother must be fearing, though they don't dare admit it. This I'm sure of, I couldn't be surer: Laia's uncle's corpse was taken away by Chucky right after I fired three shots into it. Two in the chest. One in the neck. How else to explain that we're now at the same address, Enric Granados 98, that's registered on the dog's microchip?

But nothing's going to happen now, no, I breathe with all the normality of someone still totally panicking, just like nothing happened yesterday either when I spent a while watching the building, seeing the neighbors come in and out and imagining how that one there might be the detective's wife, that one his teenage son, her the maid. And if there wasn't a police car yesterday or any strange movement to worry about, and there was nothing of the kind on our arrival now either, nor would there be later when we leave, because what we're going to find is an empty apartment, suspended in its curtailed everyday-ness, like the house of somebody who's just run down to buy cigarettes and never come back (if Laia's uncle did in fact smoke), the way people do in the suburbs in North American novels.

The elevator reaches the penthouse. Are you feeling better? asks Laia, stopping her massage and taking her hand from my neck. She pushes the elevator door and walks falteringly toward the right, toward the door to apartment A, hesitating out of nervousness, not indecisiveness. Yes, I say, it's passing now, I say, as if making a wish. You really don't smell anything, right, Juan? says Laia, scared. It's the first time she calls me Juan, like my mother, it's the first time I've seen her acting like a little girl. If I didn't know that she really was scared I'd think she was a terrible actress. Your uncle's gone on vacation, I say, you'll see, we're going to go in and not find anything. Whenever he goes away he always tells my mother, she says. Besides, he's got a dog, when he goes on vacation he leaves her with us. He must have hooked up with some girl and set himself up in her place for a few days, I say. My uncle's gay, she says. Oh, I say, well then a *guy*. She passes the keys from hand to hand, hesitating.

Could you go in first? says Laia. If you don't find anything, you can tell me. OK? Please. I answer yes. Laia opens the door and takes two steps back, three steps, as if a long-dreaded truth was about to pounce on her and flatten her. I push the door and immediately feel a suspicion gnawing at the pit of my stomach. I turn to Laia. So like, I say, so wait for me here, I'll tell you, and I shut the door.

I walk across the entrance hall, where several overcoats are hanging from the coat stand. As I cross the living room I kick something that wets the ankle of my right sock: a plastic bowl of water. Next to it there's another container with kibble. Two of the walls have floor-to-ceiling bookcases filled with books, my instinct wants me to stop to take a look at them (a bad habit of mine), but I don't. I go all the way around the apartment, frantic, jumpy, hysterical, on the verge of a respiratory and dermatological breakdown, and paranoid, but I find nothing, however paranoid I may be my paranoia doesn't manage to produce a piece of proof or evidence to incriminate me. I go around the whole apartment one more time, and another, checking there's nothing that might compromise me, I go through the drawers of the desk in the study, in the chest of drawers in the master bedroom and in the guest room, I even inspect the larder, the drawers with the cleaning products, then finally I return to the front door, recover my breath and open it.

Laia's sitting on the floor of the landing, in tears. I told you, I say, nothing's happened. I told you, I say, there's nothing wrong. You're such an idiot, she says, sobbing, you're such an idiot. You took ages. So like, I'm sorry, I say, I wanted to check the place properly. Last time I saw him we had an argument, she says. I don't want my uncle to die, she says. He's the only person in the world who's always supported me, she says. He isn't going to die, I say. You promise? she says, and sniffs, breathes in hard and then out again, to try to regain her composure.

The sound of her cell phone rescues me from making a false promise. Laia looks at the little screen and tells me it's her mother. She answers. Don't worry, Mamá, she says, in Catalan. He's not in the flat. Yes, she says. I'm going to do that now. I'll call you later. She holds out her right hand for me to help her up, I pull her and when she's on her feet she hugs me. Thank you, Mexicano, she whispers in my ear. I've got to admit, it is nice feeling protected, she says (could this be one of the findings of her research? The confirmation of a hypothesis?). She moves away. She takes a piece of toilet paper from her bag and blows her nose. All that militant feminism, she says, laughing sadly, only to end up as a helpless little girl in the arms of a manly Mexican (I like the idea of this phrase as the subtitle of her thesis). Let's go inside, she says. Maybe we'll find something to explain where my uncle is.

I push the door, let Laia go in and then follow her respectfully, or feigning respect, or caution, at least: the care of the guilty. What does your uncle do? I say, when I again see the hundreds of books in the living room. Nothing, says Laia. He lives off his rental income. Oh, I say. My mother's family is loaded, she says. Or rather, it was. Look, she says, picking up a photo frame from on top of a display cabinet, that's him. I take the photo and nod, recognizing the protagonist of my nightmares, some ten years younger. And that's his dog, she says, showing me another photo. What's his name? I say, realizing I ought to ask. Pedro, she says, didn't I tell you? He changed his name to Pere after Franco, on his ID card, on his papers, but everyone went on calling him Pedro. I meant the dog, I say, I saw your uncle's name written on the gas bill that's on the desk in the office, I say (I don't say, of course, that that was where I saw it for the second time, or that the first time it had been written on a document from the Veterinary College). Sorry, I say, as if that intrusion were the worst of my sins. No problem, she says. She's called Viridiana.

Laia wanders around the living room and stops to look in an address book. Then she goes into the master bedroom, then the guest bedroom, the study, and glances into each of the bathrooms. Meanwhile I fake an interest in the library (that's something I do know how to do). He's got good taste, your uncle, I tell Laia when she comes back to the living room (it looks like the western canon, with Mexican literature represented only by the most obvious things: the two Rulfo books, Paz's poetry and a handful of Fuentes novels, the worst of them all, curiously). I'm not sure he's read all that, she says. I pull out four books at random: three of them are new, one has definite signs of having been read. I don't see anything strange, says Laia, half-opening a drawer. You? she says. I don't know, I say, like, I don't think so. Look, she says, and she points at the little puddle of water that spilled from the dog's bowl. That was me, I say, I tripped. No, she says, the food. What about it? I say, looking at the bowl half full of kibble. Laia's cell phone rings again.

Hi Mamá, says Laia. No, she says in Catalan, nothing. It's like he just went down to walk the dog or buy the paper and didn't come back, she says (he clearly doesn't smoke or she would have said that inevitable thing about his having just run out to buy cigarettes). We've got to notify the police, says Laia. Yes, she says. Yes, she says. Tell Papá, she says.

The master bedroom has a balcony, fifteen square meters, that seems to float over the Mediterranean. But it only seems so – in reality the Mediterranean is just eight meters away (or at least that's what's promised by the large advertisements at the front of the building). The lawyer stares straight out at the beach, his back to the empty apartment. I thought we'd be alone, I say, when I discover the Chinaman sitting in a corner, smoking, and two other people, both ethnically undifferentiated, roaming around the apartment pretending to be deep in their pretend thoughts. To judge by their outfits, they're liberal professionals. One of them is holding a folder crammed with documents and another is tapping into a tiny little phone. The lawyer turns around to address the guy with the folder. Write that down, too, he says. The one with the folder opens up the folder and rummages among the papers. Man, says the Chinaman to me, you're worse every time I see you. I'm going to talk to my grandmother to get her to give you an appointment. I tell him there's no need. What do you mean, no need? he answers. You look like you've got mange. Wait here for me while I talk to this asshole, says the lawyer. He crosses the apartment toward the exit and I follow him.

We climb the building's marble staircase in silence to the upper floor, we go into another apartment identical to the previous one, and identically empty. The door is wide open, though, and once we've stepped through the lawyer shuts it behind us.

The detective was Laia's uncle, I say, immediately, following the lawyer as he walks across the entrance hall, the living room, the master bedroom and out onto the balcony. He wasn't a detective, I mean, I say, he was Laia's uncle, her mother's brother. Why'd you call me, asshole? says the lawyer, resting his elbows on the guardrail, adopting the same contemplative position he'd taken in the apartment downstairs. Was that the totally urgent thing you couldn't tell me on the phone? he says. You could have saved yourself the trip, there's nothing to see in this shithole town. How did you get here? he says. So like, by train, I say, recalling the forty-minute journey from Plaza Cataluña station on the line that runs up Maresme. To the building, asshole, says the lawyer. Don't tell me you took a cab at the station. No, I lie, I walked. Sure about that? he says. It's a long way. Sure, I say, lying again. Every motherfucker's the same, says the lawyer, looking away at the row of buildings running along the coast. I think he's about to say that everybody lies, like a jilted bride, but he's actually already changed the subject: I don't know why the fuck people like the beach so much, he says. It's the most uncomfortable thing in the world, getting sand everywhere, smeared in suntan lotion. People are serious assholes. When I lived in Cancún I had it up to here with them, there's no worse race on the planet than tourists on a beach. Worse still if they're foreign.

He was Laia's uncle, I say again, interrupting this sociological digression, returning to the subject that made me, yet again, suspend for this latest emergency the plan I had for the evening (rereading Albert Cohen's *Les Valeureux* and underlining all the passages that allowed me to relate it to the idea of laughter as a sign of superiority from Baudelaire's essay on the comic). The lawyer turns his head to look at me. He was her uncle, I insist. You think I didn't know that, asshole? he says. You think I'm such an asshole to ask an asshole to kill another asshole without knowing who he is? You think I didn't know the asshole was Laia's fag uncle? You told me Laia's family had hired him, I say. I told you Laia's family had *sent* him, he says, not that they'd hired him. But I was wrong. Poor old bastard had started following you of his own accord, fucking unemployed people are just the worst. Or at least that's what he told Chucky, this fucking European middle class, they can't bear anything, a couple little knocks on the nuts and out pours the whole story. About how Laia had talked to him about you and it'd all seemed real suspicious. How his lesbian niece suddenly came out with this crap about some asshole she was dating. A fucking Mexican immigrant, on top of it. They were real close, you know, they were the family weirdos. You know why he started following you? he says. I say nothing. Or rather, I say that he should tell me by raising my eyebrows. Because he thought you were a hustler, that you wanted to take advantage of the family's money, her father's political influence, that you were going to use her to get yourself some papers. He was real prejudiced against immigrants, the son of a bitch. I'm going to tell you a secret, he says, but you aren't going to tell your little girlfriend: we've still got hold of his ears and fingers. What? I say. Chucky cut them off before getting rid of the corpse, asshole, he says. We're keeping them in the freezer of a Chinese restaurant. If Laia's father starts being an asshole, we send him one of his brother-in-law's ears. If he rebels, we send him a thumb. If he disobeys us, we send him the ring finger, for him to stick it up his ass. The serene tone with which he's describing these atrocities is giving me a troubling sense of calm, which is what I suspect the terminally ill feel when they're told they're in the hands of the greatest specialist in the world. We were about to send him an ear to stop him making such a fucking noise about the initial capital of the project, says the lawyer. Just as well Ahmed managed to persuade him, I wouldn't have wanted to have to spend one of our ears so early on. He's a genius that fucking fag, he says, you really think I'd have let him keep the bitch if he wasn't a fucking genius? And he's as patient as an elementary school teacher, he had to explain to him how you do divisions and how you calculate percentages. Persuading him that 3 percent of a hundred and thirty is better than 3 percent of fifteen. That asshole Oriol gets scared because he's Catalan and Catalans are naturally pessimistic. We're giving him the opportunity of a lifetime, if he makes the most of it he could end up as a minister, or president of the autonomous government, if that's what he wants, or rather if that's what we want, and instead of seeing things like that the asshole starts imagining they're going to put him in prison. You know what Catalans think when Barça's five–nil up? That the other guys are about to bring them to a draw.

And what if they notify the police? I say. So like, they must have told the police about the disappearance already, I say, but the lawyer interrupts me: They're not going to tell the police yet, he says. He gives a rhetorical pause, then smiles, amused. His teeth are perfectly aligned and natural, without the fixes that are so obvious in the smiles of the nouveaux riches. That fucker Chucky has been sending the asshole Oriol messages from his cell phone, he says. From Pere's cell phone, or Pedro's, or whatever he's fucking called. Total garbage. He laughs, somewhat unenthusiastically, as if he's just been told a joke that's a very good one but super-well known, one of those puns that an average Mexican will repeat twenty thousand times in his lifetime. About how he's shut up in an orgy in Sitges, he says. An orgy with Brazilian transvestites. That Chucky's such a dick, he laughs. Laia's father hasn't said anything, I say, Laia doesn't know anything about this. Oh, really? he says. Why do you think that would be? Seems to me fucking Oriol's canoe has also sprung a leak. Those Opus types always turn out to be the real crazies. Forget about Laia's uncle, it's all under control.

He straightens up and stretches his back, turning his head that way and this, then up and down, he puts his right hand over his shoulder and links it with his left behind his back. I should go to yoga, he says. It's just with all this fucking traveling I can't, damn it, he says. He takes off his dark glasses and starts to wipe them clean.

I've talked to Riquer, he says. He turns around and leans on the guardrail with his back to the seascape. It's the first time I've seen his eyes: his eyes are the color of coffee, quite ordinary. To who? I say. To the head of the Mossos, asshole, he says, do I have to keep telling you the same things over and over? They've found the Italian, he says. They found him with Valentina. What? I say. He's a lawyer from Milan with a record of minor offenses that look like an alibi to hide something else, he says. I told you, he says, you shouldn't have let Valentina go. He finishes cleaning his glasses and puts them back on. I told you, he says again.

The mention of Valentina's name distracts me from the explanation, and though the lawyer keeps talking I only take in isolated fragments of what he says: squatter, Plaza del Sol, plane ticket, another Italian called Gabriele. How come Valentina's with the Italian? I say, when I manage to return from my astonishment. Fuck's sake, says the lawyer, don't you understand what I'm telling you? I don't say anything, because I don't understand anything. Those Italians are trying to take our project away from us, fuck's sake! he says. It doesn't surprise me, he says, but what we've got to find out is how Valentina fits into all this. What Italians? I say. The Italians from

Italy, asshole, he says, which ones do you think? Valentina's real smart, not like you. I told you, he says, you shouldn't have let Valentina go. I told you, he says.

I'm dumbfounded, looking without looking at the Mediterranean, contemplating the ludicrous suggestion that Valentina has been recruited by the Italian Mafia. Or that my cousin could have involved her in this in some other way. Answer me, asshole! shouts the lawyer. I don't know what he's talking about. What? I say. Can you not hear me? he says. I say nothing. I'm asking what you've heard from Valentina, asshole, he says, and don't make me ask again. So like, nothing, I say, I haven't seen her since she left the apartment. His mouth twists into a grimace, annoyed, really annoyed. I never wanted it to come to this, he says. I like people who come up from below. But there's no other way around it. You shouldn't have let Valentina go, he says. I told you.

I JUST CAN'T BELIEVE I'M DEAD

Aargh, my dumbass little cuz, I don't want you telling me you've received this letter, or that you're reading it, because if it's reached you that means I'm fucked already. I hope this letter never gets to you, seriously, but if it has to get to you I hope it does, because things can't go on the way they are, seriously, how do you expect me to stay so calm if these assholes fuck me over?, no way, if those assholes fuck me over I'm going to fuck them back.

I don't think this letter's ever going to get to you, I'm sure of it, but still I've got to write it, because if it does get to you then you got to help me, asshole. But don't tell me this fucking letter did get to you, little cuz. Even just imagining it's gotten to you gives me a real fucking downer, for real, but you'll see it's never going to get to you and I'm wasting my time writing it like a dick.

It really hasn't got to you, right?

Really not, right, little cuz?

It hasn't got to you, I'm sure it hasn't, and it's not going to, you just see it won't, do me a favor and be an optimist for one damn time in your life, don't come to me now with your fucking negative attitude, let's be together on this one, let's agree that it'll never get to you, cause if the letter gets to you it means your cousin's dead. That's right, man, DEAD, for real, so it'd be for the best if you don't get to read this letter EVER.

We got to make a deal, the two of us, my dumbass little cuz, you got to promise me. I promise to write the letter even though I know really there's no need to write it, and you promise that if you receive it you'll help me, promise me, my dumbass little cuz, I've done a fuckton of favors for you and now's the moment for you to pay me back, asshole.

And if this letter is never going to get to you, then oh man, why am I writing it?, don't go thinking your cousin's a dickhead who hasn't got anything more important to do than write you some fucking letter you're never gonna read. If I write it it's only because your cousin's real farsighted, your cousin has learned in business to consider all the variables, to analyze all the possible scenarios, there can even be some projects that turn out bad, but not because your cousin's a fucking pessimist like you, your cousin's got his feet firmly on the ground and he knows that the tough blows we receive in real life are serious shit, little cuz, and if things go to shit your cousin can't allow things just to go on the way they are, no, your cousin wants REVENGE. We're in this together, cousin, I told you already in the other letter, that other letter I sent you at the university did get to you, right?, if it did get to you and you haven't told me then call me right-a-fucking-way, right this minute, come on, asshole, what are you waiting for? We're in it together, the whole thing, little cuz, good times and bad, but if this letter's got to you don't go being such an ungrateful little shit that you make yourself be a dick just because I'm dead and you think I'm not going to realize you ignored me, you owe me, asshole.

That's why you got to help me now.

You can't let me down.

But here's hoping this letter never gets to you, little cuz, I swear just imagining you reading the letter on some terrace next to the Sagrada Familia brings tears to my eyes. And don't say I'm exaggerating, asshole, how could I not cry if I'm dead and you're living it up eating patatas bravas and drinking a beer as you read my letter?

See that thing up there? That little damp stain? Know what that is?

It's a fucking teardrop, asshole! A motherfucking tear from your cousin who's dead and you living it up in Barcelona knocking back a vermouth with olives! So the least you can do now is help me, or are you going to back out now?, have some respect for the dead, asshole, you owe me that, don't think just because I'm dead I'm not gonna find out, I can assure you I'll find out, little cuz, even if I'm a fucking ghost.

You got to help me, little cuz, you can't imagine what it's like being dead, for real, I just can't believe I'm dead, no word of a lie. And if I'm dead then the least I want is REVENGE, things can't just stay the way they are, how do you expect me to stay so calm if on top of fucking me over they're taking advantage of my projects, it's one thing for them to fuck you over and something completely else for them to take you for an idiot.

I didn't want to write this letter, my dumbass little cuz, I didn't want to do it, but if I'm writing it it's not because I want to, I'm not such an asshole as to write a letter that's my death certificate, if I'm writing it it's because there's a fucker who wants to fuck me over, and if the letter did reach you it's because the utter fucker did fuck me over, for real, I can't believe I'm dead, I can't believe the total fucker did what he'd threatened and totally fucked me. At this point, if you're reading this letter, you must already know who I'm talking about, yeah, the motherfucker lawyer, the son of a bitch we thought was our partner and who it now turns out fucked me. The asshole has got it in for me, little cuz, all because of a project that went badly, well, it didn't go badly, what happened was the partners gave up hope and didn't want to put any dough into it before we'd even got out of the start-up phase. How the fuck were we supposed to not lose any dough if they didn't want to wait for the project to take off?

I just can't believe I'm dead, little cuz. I can't believe it, no word of a lie.

How'd it happen?

Did they run me over? Those sons of bitches are always making it look like they've run people over.

So they did run me over?

Aw, no shit, I just can't believe I'm dead.

I wanted to be an optimist and that's why I sent you that other letter where I talked about our partners and about the project in Barcelona. And if I didn't explain to you in that letter how that fucker the lawyer wanted to fuck me over, it was because at that moment it was important for us to stay positive. My only chance not to get fucked was if the project worked out well and I wasn't going to tell you about how things were going all to shit, since on top of every fucking thing you're mega fucking prone to failure, my dumbass little cuz, you're a super fucking serious pessimist. But even though things worked out badly I'm not going to have a chip on my shoulder, and I don't hold a grudge against you, now I think about it they probably fucked me over because of you, probably you screwed it up and I was the one who ended up paying for it, little cuz. All the more reason you got to help me, dickhead, we can't let things go on the way they are, I've trusted you and invested a lot in this project, I gave it the most important thing I had, little cuz, I gave it my life and now you got to help me.

The most important thing you got to understand, first things first, is that you're not to be thinking about going to the police, listen closely, you're not going to the police for any possible reason, the damn police are controlled by them, for real, what fucking world do you think you're living in? If you go to the police you're the one who's going to end up in prison, dickhead, that's if they don't fuck you too, for real, cousin, oh don't tell me you've gone to the police, don't tell me they've fucked you too, last thing we need is for this letter to never get to you because they've fucked you too.

For real.

If they've fucked you too then there really is no point me continuing to write this letter, little cuz, so don't go going to the police, OK?, pay attention to what I'm telling you if you want to live, the only way to survive is to put yourself on the same level as those sons of bitches, and that's what I'm going to explain to you, how can you fuck them over by yourself, assuming that is they don't fuck you, they haven't fucked you yet, cousin, right?, tell me you really are reading this letter?

I don't want them to fuck you, seriously, cousin, you got to believe me, I've done everything for your benefit, you don't know how worried your folks were because you kept doing such total and utter crap, how were you going to get on in life if you were devoting yourself to investigating the influence of some dead asshole writer on the books of some other dead asshole writer. Nobody's ever going to give you money for that, my dumbass little cuz, you got to react, the tough blows we receive in real life are the shit and it's like you don't want to know about how reality even exists, only some fucking dumb literature simulation. But me, I'm positive, little cuz, and I want to think they haven't fucked you yet and you're going to read this letter, you're gonna read it and quick, you will, you'll see, I'm sure of it, little cuz, you got to be positive too because this is about your own life, bro, or don't you want to live? and you're going to get REVENGE for your cousin and along the way you'll get your cousin's money back to give it to my folks and you'll give five thousand pesos to the maid at our place who did me the solid of sending you the other letter and twenty thousand to the other guy who sent you this letter and promised he'd check out your address if anything happened to me, and that he wouldn't say anything about this letter to anyone (I'm going to give you his details at the end, don't go forgetting to pay him, I told him you were going to pay him twenty thousand pesos for sending the letter and if you don't pay him he might tell Mom and Dad).

You got to see this is a chance to pay me back for everything you owe me, little cuz, I've always invited you onto my business projects even though you were an ungrateful little shit who wanted to boycott me, but I don't hold a grudge, what I want is for you to return those favors now, but you got to do things the way I tell you, I've already said you can't go to the police because they'll fuck you over, listen to what I'm telling you for once in your life. Also, if you go to the police, my family will find out what happened and my folks won't understand, they're from a different generation, they don't know that to get into projects on this level you got to take risks, that's the only way to do business in this fucking country, you're not to go going to the police, I'd rather have them think I'm an asshole who doesn't know how to cross a road. Was it a truck? Those sons of bitches totally love flattening people with trucks, that way nobody can find out what they did to them before that.

What you got to do is get yourself onto the same level as them, those sons of bitches, and that's what you're going to do, I'll tell you how you're going to do it, pay attention, little cuz, the key to the whole thing is this fucker who goes by the name Chucky, if you're reading this letter you must know who he is already. Chucky's the key to everything, if you convince Chucky to help us that fucker the lawyer is going to get fucked so good, and I know how we're going to do it, because I became friends with Chucky, and even though he's a very bloodthirsty motherfucker the motherfucker is a good thing, don't think just because these people are killers they haven't got a heart. And fucking Chucky's already had it with the lawyer because the lawyer's *totally* a dick, he can't take him anymore, and he's even been thinking about going it alone or about fucking him over to take his place, about being the guy in charge of the projects, he's a serious motherfucker, that Chucky, real well prepared, and yeah so maybe you see him carrying, doing whatever the fuck he does, but you wouldn't have guessed he did an MBA in the US, I swear, little cuz, he got honorable mention for his study of the flows of international capital, he designed this whole fucking system for not paying taxes that now all the damn investors are using, you see, asshole, just so you see how tough blows can be in real life. Fucking Chucky should be the one in charge of the projects and not the lawyer, fucking Chucky is a real leader, he was in the Boy Scouts his whole fucking life, he's a black belt in limalama karate and he was even president of the Student Society at the Ibero, when he was studying administration and finance, and all the asshole lawyer's got is one good contact, a real shit-awesome contact, I'm not saying he doesn't, but the asshole's lived off this contact his whole life like a parasite, this contact's the only reason he's climbed up and everything he's done is because this contact's put him there and is protecting him.

When I met him, the lawyer was the fucking manager of a fleapit in Cancún, apparently five stars, but, no word of a lie, Cancún's got much more awesome hotels than that one. And the fucking lawyer would have stayed there sending towels off to the laundry and supervising the mayo consumption in the hotel kitchen if it wasn't for that fucking contact, he was the son of a bitch who paid for him to go do a master's in Barcelona and then when he came back he set him to run a few of his projects. And if I'm not telling you who this dumbass contact is, little cuz, it's for your own safety, to protect you, so you can see I really am positive and I believe you're alive reading this letter, if I wrote you the name of the lawyer's contact, of the big cheese, not just you and me would be fucked, even the fucking mailmen would be for it just for having touched this letter. All you need to know is that the big cheese isn't an asshole, how could he be an asshole if he's the big cheese?, for real, and the big cheese is already realizing the lawyer's a 360-degree motherfucker and that Chucky's better prepared to be running his projects.

So what you need to do, when the lawyer and Chucky move into Barcelona for the start-up phase of the project, is start getting close to Chucky, gain his trust and make him see he can trust you in his plan to fuck the lawyer. You won't find it too hard, the asshole's already had this in his head for a long time and we always talked about it, about how he should be the one to notify the big cheese that the lawyer's a motherfucker, but if you're reading this letter that means something went wrong, that the lawyer's gotten ahead of us or some other thing happened (probably you were the one who screwed it up, fucking dumbass), but you can rest assured Chucky didn't betray me, Chucky and I became real good pals, soul brothers. So you got to help Chucky, so you got to help me, we can't let things go on the way they are, you owe me, my dumbass little cuz, you owe me because that's why we're family and I've always done you a ton of favors and stood up for you.

You can't let me down, little cuz.

You can't let me down, pal.

You got to commit to me even if it's just this one time in your life, now that I'm dead.

THREE

YOU SURE THIS GUY ISN'T RETARDED?

Sunday, January 9th, 2005

Noon. I went out just to wander aimlessly because the walls in my room were closing in on me. I never cease to be surprised by the sepulchral calm of Sundays compared to the hyperactivity and noise of the everyday. This city, or at least this neighborhood where I live, only knows two states of mind: the hysteria of an amusement park and the desolation of a cemetery.

There was practically nobody out on the streets, apart from a handful of squatters on the Plaza del Sol (Jimmy hadn't arrived yet), a few old people sitting in the sun, some parents with their children in the playgrounds, and a few people doing an emergency shop in the little Pakistani stores.

The cold in my lungs did me good, it woke me up, seemed to clarify my ideas, my lungs were grateful for the icy air after a day and a half shut away. As I walked, I did the math again in my head: there was no way I could make it to the 27th of January with the forty euro I had left. I needed to do something. Call Juan Pablo to ask him for money. Beg with Jimmy (those recorder lessons I took in elementary school might prove to be some use after all). Or work. But doing what?

I was crossing the Plaza de la Revolución when I heard Alejandra's squeal:

'Look, Daddy, the brown girl!' she shouted, sitting on top of a slide.

Facundo was tapping away on his cell phone, leaning up against the fence that separated the playground from the square. I stopped but didn't move closer, keeping a safe distance, two or three meters from Facundo.

'You good, shithead?' he said.

'How are you, Ále?' I called to the girl, ignoring her father's question.

'I'm bad,' she shouted, with the overdramatic voice of a rude little girl. 'Very bad.'

'What do you mean, bad?' I asked. 'Why?'

'My mommy's gone to Argentina and my daddy isn't looking after me properly.'

'Ah, be a pal, Al,' Facundo interrupted her. 'The girl's pissed because I can't stay with her or go fetch her at school,' he explained. 'So? What am I supposed to do? I'm on the job at five.'

'The brown girl can look after me, Daddy, the brown girl can look after me!' shouted Alejandra.

'Stop it, Ále, you've already got a sitter, have you already forgotten? What would we tell poor Pilar?'

'I don't like Pilar!' shouted Alejandra. 'Pilar's dumb. I want the brown girl to look after me.'

Facundo came toward me, so he could also move away from Alejandra, and told me that her mother's brother had died in Buenos Aires in an accident, that she'd had to go urgently last week and that Alejandra was unbearable.

'Truth is, the sitter can't handle her either,' he said, 'they get along horrendously, don't suppose you could take care of her? I'd pay you, of course, seven euro an hour.'

I knew at once I couldn't turn down the offer, seven euro would allow me to survive one more day, but all the same

I resisted. I told him that, in truth, I did need the work, but it would be really weird going back to the apartment, that I didn't want to run into Juan Pablo.

'Come on, don't be a shithead, OK?' he said. 'Look, you go fetch Ále from school at five and take her to the park for a bit. Then you go to the apartment, I'll stick a key in her backpack. You give her a shower and spend a bit of time drawing with her or doing whatever shit she wants. I get back at eight at the latest. That shithead Juan Pablo is never around at those times. How would you like to have twenty euro a day? How about we agree on twenty? But with a bit of flexibility if I'm running late, and if I arrive earlier you'll still charge twenty, so the days will even each other out. What do you say?'

I hesitated again, silently.

'Listen, shithead,' Facundo insisted. 'If you need the work, then to hell with the shithead Juan Pablo. It's not my business to tell you what to do, but you got to think of yourself. This is a very beautiful city, but she's like a real high-class hooker. If you don't have money this can be the worst city in the world, listen to what I'm telling you, shithead, take the job.'

I hesitated again. I said nothing.

'You need an apology, shithead? Fine, but you're seriously a shithead, you know? I screwed up, fine, I was a shithead, I'm sorry, but you could have taken it as a compliment, too, the fact I wanted to . . . '

'Best if you don't try to make things better,' I interrupted him. 'Truth is, I really do need the money. I accept.'

Monday 10th

The day when nothing made any logical sense. Or the day when at last everything started to make logical sense. Though I don't understand any of it. Or not yet. But at least I do know there's some logic to explain everything that's happened up to now.

I went to the consulate to deal with my consular registration and when I signed in at the reception desk I was told there was a letter for me. That they'd had it there for months, since the start of November. I thought it all had to be some mix-up, but the only way of knowing was to open the envelope, which didn't have a sender on it, though the postage stamp was from Guadalajara. It was a letter from Lorenzo, Juan Pablo's cousin! I put it back in its envelope, fear gripping my chest as if I'd received the letter from a dead man, which was indeed what had just happened. The receptionist asked if I wasn't feeling well, I must have looked very upset. I turned around and left the consulate without completing the process. I hurried away in no particular direction, went into the first café I found and read the letter.

The one thing that was clear was that Juan Pablo was involved in something weird, in some apparent business project his cousin had gotten him into, that is. I don't know why I immediately sensed it was some kind of extortion or blackmail. Something illegal, even criminal. Maybe it was the tone in which the letter was written, like the ravings of an idiot with delusions of grandeur (business grandeur, to cap it all), like a kind of delirium. I didn't know Lorenzo and I couldn't remember much of what Juan Pablo had told me about him. He was the cousin who lived on the Caribbean coast, and not much more than that.

It took me some time to get out of the daze enough to register that Lorenzo wrote he'd gone to meet my parents. I panicked momentarily, how long had it been since I'd spoken to them? Since New Year's. I paid for the coffee I'd ordered (two euro!), and only then did I notice I'd come into the same café where Juan Pablo had met Laia before Christmas.

I ran back to Gràcia, finding my way down by instinct, and I stopped at the first call shop I found. I phoned home. My mom answered. She asked me, alarmed, what had happened. I said nothing, I was just calling to say hi.

'Child,' she said, 'it's five in the morning.'

I was sure she could see me shaking at the other end of the line, on the other side of the Atlantic.

'Is there something you want to tell me?' she insisted.

I was about to take this opportunity to tell her Juan Pablo and I had broken up, but suddenly realized that Lorenzo's letter changed everything. There was some mystery that explained everything that had happened to Juan Pablo, that had happened to us, and I had to find it out. Maybe I'd read too many novels, or maybe the conclusion I'd drawn was a strategy for upping my self-esteem, maybe believing in the existence of some outlandish explanation would prove to be just another way of deceiving myself.

I told my mom I missed her a lot, that was all, and I said goodbye, attempting to give the impression of a melancholy normality, though I'm sure she didn't believe me, the poor woman must have been kept awake fretting that something bad was happening to me.

I ran to the Plaza del Sol, straight to Jimmy.

'At last the princess deigns to speak to me,' he said, by way of greeting.

I started telling him what had happened, hurriedly, I sat down next to him and read the letter out loud, hardly pausing to breathe, and whenever I did take a breath Jimmy took advantage of the moment to say, in exactly the same words:

'You sure this guy isn't retarded?'

I finished reading the letter and got up as if I had a spring in my butt.

'Where are you going, girl?' Jimmy held me back.

I told him I had to talk to Juan Pablo to tell him I knew everything, even though I didn't know anything, or though I didn't understand anything, but that he would have to explain it all to me.

'Don't talk to anyone about anything, girl,' he said, 'you don't know what you're getting mixed up in. You know what a pal told me? You know what I've been able to dig up?'

He took a long swig straight from the bottle of beer, before continuing:

'That your jerk ex-boyfriend identified me by going through the files of the Mossos d'Esquadra.'

'How do you know?' I asked. 'Who told you?'

'The asshole was received by the head of the Mossos in his private office, so how do you get seen by the big boss to report some crappy little threats? The jerk is well connected. There's something totally heavy behind all this.'

'And when were you planning to tell me this?'

'I only found out yesterday. And you weren't talking to me, man, you're such a selfish bitch, you chucked me aside because you were crapping yourself. But I'm going to forgive you because none of it's your fault, it's the fault of your jerk ex-boyfriend.'

I told him I needed to know how he'd found out, that it was very important, that I needed to be sure in order to decide what I had to do. He looked from side to side, paranoid, ahead of him and behind him. He lowered his voice, forcing me to move in closer, the stink almost dissuading me.

'I asked a pal, a guy I know.'

'A Mosso?' I asked.

He nodded. He hesitated between the bottle of beer and the carton of red wine. He chose the latter: he took a slug, but the container was empty. He threw it out toward the middle of the square.

'You can't tell anyone about this, girl,' he said, 'I'm warning you. It's hard for people to understand. Sometimes we talk so I can help him, other times he helps me. There's a real nasty war against the antiestablishment movement.'

'You're his informer?'

'Shut up, man, fuck, what's the matter with you?'

He got up and walked toward the nearest street. I followed him. Halfway along the block he stopped, pressed himself against the wall, lowered his zipper and started to pee.

'Don't talk to him,' he said, as if he was talking to himself, or having a conversation with his dick. 'Not now,' he said. 'First you got to know what he's mixed up in.'

4:30 p.m. Purely out of curiosity I went to the call shop and rang the number Juan Pablo's cousin had put in the letter in case I needed to contact him.

'Chick-Out?' somebody answered.

I asked who I was talking to, pretending I'd made a mistake. They told me I'd reached the offices of Chick-Out, the leading roast chicken home-delivery franchise in Mexico and Central America.

First afternoon looking after Alejandra. There was no one in the apartment and I couldn't resist the temptation to peek into Juan Pablo's room. What if I could find some clue to help me understand what was going on? After giving Alejandra her bath, I tried to slip away from the bathroom while the girl was drying herself, but she wouldn't let me: the scrawny little thing clung to my leg like a tick. Then we started drawing and at the bottom of a pretty abstract doodle (which in theory was a tree), Alejandra wrote: 'The truth is structured like a fiction.' This time it didn't alarm me, it barely even surprised me, except for the beauty of the words, perfectly luminous.

Facundo arrived at eight-thirty. Alejandra was already starving and the only thing I'd found in the cupboard was a pack of chocolate cookies. Half an hour late on the first day . . . I showed him the drawing.

'Is this one also from Pizarnik?' I asked.

'It's from Lacan, shithead,' he said.

'Another tattoo?'

'It's a sign my shithead ex-wife's got hung up in the living room of her apartment.'

'Your ex is a psychoanalyst?'

'Nah,' he said, 'she's just a shithead.'

Tuesday 11th

11:20 a.m. Juan Pablo came out of Julio Verne. I was ready to follow him along Calle Zaragoza, but he walked in the opposite direction, toward the Ring, and turned right toward Plaza Lesseps. I was completely exposed, the open expanse of the Ring gave me nowhere to hide, if Juan Pablo turned around he'd easily spot me. I decided to risk it. I could pretend it was a coincidence. Or confront him once and for all.

We reached Plaza Lesseps, where there was construction going on, Juan Pablo stopped at a junction, waiting for the lights to change, and I positioned myself ten meters away, half-hidden behind a small digger. The lights changed, but Juan Pablo didn't move. Nor did I. From a distance, it looked like his dermatitis, his so-called allergy, had gotten a whole lot worse. Five minutes went by: a black Mercedes-Benz, without license plates and with tinted windows, stopped on the junction, at the Ring. The door opened. Juan Pablo walked over to it, stuck his head in the car, as if saying something to the people inside. Immediately a man got out of the car and Juan Pablo got in. The car started up again, I stepped out of my hiding place as if I were about to jump in a taxi to begin a chase, it was a ridiculous impulse, because I never would have done it, but I couldn't help it. And besides, even if I'd wanted to do it I couldn't have: the man who had gotten out of the car blocked my path, gave me a pair of kisses, pretending he knew me, and took hold of my forearm.

'Let's go get a coffee, Valentina,' he said.

With a movement of his arm he made me go with him, forced me, pushed me, and I was about to shout when another shout materialized from somewhere outside:

'Hey, man, I've been waiting half an hour! Where the fuck you been?'

It was Jimmy, on the other side of one of the streets, Príncipe de Asturias, I think it's called. He started to zigzag through the traffic toward us, while the pressure of the grip on my arm wavered. The guy wasn't sure whether to let me go. He looked around, as if assessing his options. I looked straight at him, at those parts of his face that were uncovered, since most of it was hidden behind a huge pair of dark glasses, the overcoat with the collar up, a scarf tied between his neck and jawbone covering the lower part of his mouth. Dark-skinned. Flattish nose. A thin upper lip, with a cold sore. Finally he decided to let go of me and he said, before Jimmy managed to reach us:

'You have no idea what you're getting yourself into.'

He turned around and hurried away.

'Not gonna stay and say hello, dickhead?' Jimmy shouted after him.

I asked him to shut up. I hugged him, getting a deep waft of the sewer smell coming off his military jacket, off the gunk in his hair, off the pores of his skin, off his foul breath. I thanked him. We saw the guy disappearing into the distance. I suggested to Jimmy that we find someplace quiet to talk, but he said we should go to the Plaza de Sol, we should stick to our routine, we mustn't do anything unusual as that would be to expose ourselves.

'We're safe in the square, girl,' he said. 'You see what happens when you don't tell me what you're going to do, what on earth were you thinking deciding to play detective like that? What were you thinking following your jerk ex-boyfriend? I told you it was dangerous. I told you.'

'And you've been following me, too, Jimmy?' I asked him.

'I live over there,' he said, raising his arm to point toward the other side of the square, where an anarchist flag was hanging from a two-story house that looked like it had been abandoned, or rather, that it had squatters in it.

'So it was just luck you saw me?'

'Of course it was!' he said. 'But that's not what matters, what matters is what I told you yesterday, that your dickhead ex-boyfriend is mixed up in something fucking heavy. I told you. Did you see the car he went off in?'

'A luxury car,' I said.

'A diplomatic car, man!' he said. 'The least you got to do if you're going to play detective is pay attention. The car had diplomatic plates.'

I told him it didn't have any plates. I was sure of that.

'Of course it did,' he said, 'black ones, the same color as the car, that's why you didn't see them, you were looking out for white plates which was why you didn't recognize them. Our eyesight is a total bastard, huh, it's lazy, it gets used to everything and so then it sees nothing.'

We went on arguing for a bit about whether the car did or didn't have a license plate. Him getting more and more certain, even bullying, and me ever more doubtful. Then the conversation moved on to the words the guy who'd gotten out the car had said to me.

'I told you,' Jimmy said, 'I told you you didn't know what you were getting yourself into. You have no idea what these people are capable of, girl, I'm telling you this as an Italian. That's why I stopped working as a lawyer in Milan, the firm where I worked only ever defended real heavy businessmen, ultra-respected people, the kind who show up in the papers or go drink tea with the Pope. Everybody was busy laundering dough, girl, dough from drugs, or arms, or women-trafficking, or oil from African dictators.'

'You're going to think I'm crazy, Jimmy,' I said, 'but if I'm honest, at no point did I feel threatened, I felt the guy was trying to help me, like he was someone I could trust.'

It was true: although I was conscious that it was a dangerous situation, although my brain was telling me I should scream, ask for help, he had barely scared me at all, maybe because there hadn't been time.

'Jesus, man,' said Jimmy, 'that's because the s.o.b. was nicely dressed, you think he wasn't dangerous because he was in designer clothes, thousand-euro Italian shoes, stylish glasses. But they're the worst, man, you got this preconception about criminals being poor people, Africans, gypsies, deep down you're just like the people in this place, girl.'

'Take it easy, Jimmy,' I said, 'I didn't even register what he was wearing, I'm just saying the way he talked to me, even the way he was going to force me to go with him, wasn't violent.'

'You aren't going to tell me you think your jerk ex-boyfriend sent him to help you? Because you did see him, right? You saw he was the one who told that son of a bitch you were following him?'

I said I wasn't sure, it had all happened very quickly, though it was true that after Juan Pablo had said something into the open door of the car, the guy had gotten out and come straight to get me.

'Your jerk ex-boyfriend sent him to threaten you,' he said.

'There's only one way to find out,' I said.

'Do not talk to him, girl,' he said, 'you don't know what you're getting yourself into, you've already seen how dangerous it can be.'

'I'm not going to talk to him, Jimmy.'

'So what, then?'

'This afternoon I'm going to need your help. At five. I'm going to need you to go to the locksmith while I take Alejandra to the park.'

I began this diary haltingly, like a little nineteenth-century miss who was too modest to say what was really happening to her. And just look at me now: these pages are starting to read like a novel. There are mysteries, intrigue, good guys and bad guys, or at least some potential good guys and bad guys.

If somebody reading these pages didn't believe me, I'd say the opposite of those words from Lacan, that fiction is structured like a truth (especially when you're talking about autobiographical literature). But in any case, no one's going to read it, I don't care if nobody believes this is a diary: I don't expect anyone to believe me.

IN NO TIME AT ALL I'M GOING
TO BE EXPENDABLE

Ahmed called me up and said: Oh man, you've got to come with me to the vet, the dog's sick. I was sitting on the train, two stops from the university, I'd planned to spend the day at the library. I looked out the window at the forest sliding past (it was the train sliding along the track that cut through the forest, to be precise) and allowed myself the fantasy of imagining that I was disappearing into the trees to look for branches to scratch myself with and I was getting lost and never coming out again. What's wrong with her? I say. She's bleeding, man, says Ahmed, it's urgent. From her vulva? I say, covering my mouth and the tiny phone with my right hand, so the students hugging their folders as if they were cardboard babies can't hear me. From where? says Ahmed. You don't know what a vulva is, *man*? I say, lowering my voice when I say the word vulva. From her vagina, I say. The girl sitting opposite me looks up from the photocopies she's reading and pretends (very unconvincingly) she isn't looking at me. Then she looks around, as if to check whether anybody else has heard this pervert. Fuck, man, says Ahmed, I like men, I've never been with a girl. And you've never been to school either? I say. That was in Pakistan, man! he says. Can you imagine what sex ed is like in schools in Pakistan? Can't be all that different from sex ed in the schools in Los Altos de Jalisco, I imagine, or the ones in Guadalajara. Actually, now I think about it, I learned what the vulva and clitoris were from late-eighties porn, and I didn't learn it properly, or not completely, owing to the abundance of pubic hair and the poor quality of photos and videos available in those days.

I take my hand away from the tiny phone: The bitch is in heat, I say, there's nothing the matter with her. The girl opposite pretends to return to her photocopies. Oh man, says Ahmed, she's sick, she's always wanting to pee and she's not eating. I'm out on the street all fucking day, he says. And other dogs come over to try and mount her and she won't let them, I say. How did you know? he says. Because the bitch is in heat! I say. You'd better be careful because in a few days if you don't keep an eye on her even the pigeons are going to be mounting her, I say. The girl opposite giggles, staring hard at the underlined passages of her papers. The one next to me gets up to gather her things. And what am I supposed to do, man? says Ahmed. The dog can't end up pregnant, or what am I going to do with the puppies? The students start to straighten up, to put on their jackets and scarves, to retrieve their backpacks and books and folders from the storage compartments above them. There's still one stop before we reach the university. Ahmed won't stop talking: he asks me to call Sketch, he says I've got to help him. Listen, I say, I can't talk now, I'm just arriving at the university. I'll come round to your apartment this evening, around six.

Here, I say to Ahmed when he opens his front door, and I hand him a bag. What is it? he says. *Panties*, I say, for the dog. You're shitting me, he says. Look inside, I say. Can I come through? I say. Ahmed moves to one side and I cross the threshold and take off my coat and scarf and hang them on the coat stand.

Holy fuck, man, he says, looking at the parcel, these are great. Thanks a lot, man, he says. You can buy them at any vet's, I say. They're disposable, you've got to change them. You buy the next set yourself. I walk across the reception hall and sit on the living-room sofa, while Ahmed chases after the dog to put her panties on. Or her bloomers, to be more precise. There are two laptops, both turned on, on the dining-room table. A glass of water, an open packet of cookies, the crumbs on the table and the position of the chair reveal what Ahmed had been doing before I arrived.

Listen, I say, we've got to talk. Ahmed looks up from his place on the floor, where he's crouched wrestling with the dog (the dog thinks the piece of clothing is a toy or food). You screwed up, I say. Keeping the dog, I say. And I'm not saying that just because of all the problems. The lawyer says you can't be trusted, I say. I leave little rhetorical pauses for Ahmed to process the information. He says you're putting the project at risk. You know the dog's owner was Carbonell's brother-in-law, I say, though I still pronounce the name without that Catalan double-l. The dog gets away from Ahmed because what I've said has had an effect. Ahmed gets up. He walks toward me. He's forgotten all about the dog, which is carrying the panties in its mouth and heading into the main bedroom, disappearing under the bed.

Are they going to kill Viridiana? he asks. I nod without saying anything, to make the effect more melodramatic. How do you know? says Ahmed, and he sits down on the little armchair beside mine. Because the lawyer's told me, I say, how else would I know? Ahmed says nothing; if he weren't so dark you might think he'd turned pale, as pale as if he himself had been condemned to death, as pale as a tortured Russian in a Dostoevsky novel, or a Turgenev novel at the very least. For a moment I feel bad for lying to him, for a second the whole meanness of my survival strategy overwhelms me and I'm about to give up entirely. I knew that bastard couldn't be trusted, says Ahmed, rescuing me. Jesus fuck. The bastard's a thug, I'm not used to working like this, man, I totally don't have to put up with this. Me and the dog are getting out of here, man, he says. Where to? I say. I don't know, he says, wherever. You can't go, I say, so like, if you disappear they'll think you've betrayed them and they'll come after you, so like, you won't be able to live a peaceful life. Oh man, I haven't had a peaceful life in ages, he says. Why don't you give her away? I ask, taking a big risk to earn myself some credibility. Why don't you take her to a shelter? The dog's mine, man, he says. The dog's already lost one master. There's no way she could bear another loss, he says. From the bedroom we hear the sound of the dog who seems to be fighting with the panties, perhaps she's wearing them on her head. Why are you telling me this, man? says Ahmed. Don't you get it? I say. I allow the question to have its desired effect, which is to make Ahmed guess that my interest in the dog is selfish, that I'm no good Samaritan or Mexican St Anthony, that the dog's possibilities for salvation are also my own. I even manage to contemplate the sad irony which I alone, with my lies, have constructed: that my life is worth exactly as much as the dog's.

Actually, I say, the same thing's happening to me as to the dog. In no time at all I'm going to be expendable. In no time at all I'm going to be in the way. An asshole who knows too much, I say. The *bastard* who's superfluous in this whole business. I probably am already, I say. They just used me to soften Carbonell up. I stand and walk over to the dining table, I circle it and, before I'm able to see what's on the laptop screens, Ahmed reacts: he almost runs to close them, with two slaps (one for each). I know how we can save the dog, Ahmed, I say. I know how you can keep her. Ahmed flinches, I don't think I'd ever spoken his name out loud. He puts his hands on the back of a chair and looks over to the window, to the curtains that stop him seeing out (and most important of all make it impossible for those outside to see what's happening inside). There are strange noises coming from the bedroom, guttural sounds, the dog must be choking. Ahmed says nothing. What's that? I say. It's the dog, he says, ever since she had her period she doesn't stop talking. She doesn't have her period, I say, she's in heat, the first phase of being in heat, I say, it's called proestrus. Did you have a dog in Mexico? he asks. I say no. How come you know so much about dogs, then? he says. I did some research once for a novel I wanted to write, I say. (An abandoned novel, naturally, like all the novels I've attempted to write to date. To date: because this time I'm going to get to the end and if I do want to finish the novel I've got to save myself, nobody's ever come back from the dead to write the end of a novel.) A novel about dogs? says Ahmed. There was a dog in the novel, I say, or a bitch, to be more exact. Did you use to be a writer? he asks. I say no, not yet, that I studied literature and that, in reality, I was more a professional reader than a writer. And how did you get mixed up in all this? he says. I thought people who read were all good people, who didn't get themselves in trouble. I keep quiet. Thinking about this idea, a kind of wide-reaching one actually, according to which cultured people, and literary people in particular, have a moral superiority, though the truth is that we readers don't look to literature for guidelines for our behavior in reality. Nor do writers, either. All we readers and writers want is to perpetuate a hedonistic system, based on self-indulgence and narcissism. All a true reader ever wants is to read more. And a writer to write more. And we academics are the worst: scavengers who want to extract some bit of existential meaning from all this shit. Hey, says Ahmed, pulling me out of my sudden self-absorption and this digression. I need you to tell me why I should believe you, he says. How am I supposed to trust you if you don't tell me anything? You haven't told me anything either, I say. Who's the lawyer's boss and how you met him and what the work is that you do, for example.

Ahmed looks me in the eye, then casts his gaze over my face, as if he were counting the rashes (there were seven this morning).

What do you suggest? he says at last.

I look over to the door, as if the lawyer or one of his thugs was about to smash it in at any moment. But the door holds firm. It's solid and me and Ahmed are inside.

Talk to Chucky, I say. But first you need to explain how this business works.

The Italian was sitting at the foot of a small statue on one side of the Plaza del Sol. He was playing the recorder and holding up a cardboard cup to beg each time somebody passed close by. Though it was past 8 p.m., the square was kind of quiet. Not many people in the bars. Slightly more in the kebab place. It was Monday. The only people who didn't stay home on Monday nights were the squatters.

Unlike the rest of the squatters on the square, the Italian was alone and he didn't have any dogs. He was alternating swigs from a bottle of beer with swigs from a carton of wine or juice. I sat down with my back to the square (or rather my side, my back half-turned to the square) on the steps outside a Lebanese restaurant. From my overcoat pocket I pulled out the little novel by Jardiel Poncela I'd brought with me, borrowed from the library at the Autónoma, on the recommendation of a fellow doctoral student. I opened it at random: the street-lights made it bright enough on the square for me to pretend to be reading.

From time to time I looked up from the book (from time to time I turned pages, too), and gave a glance of recognition, as though I was waiting for somebody, in order to keep an eye on the Italian, who just sat where he was, twenty meters away, diagonally opposite. Fifteen minutes went by.

Then the Italian gathered up his things, put them in a backpack and started to make his way across the square. I stayed where I was, not moving but not letting him out of my sight. I stood up when the Italian disappeared down Calle Planeta and followed him through the Gràcia alleyways, an erratic route, as far as a desolate-looking corner where he met another person. I watched them from a distance as they walked down Calle Asturias. I saw them from a block away, on the move, out the corner of my eye, a mere second's glance. But I'm sure. The Italian was talking to the Chinaman.

I returned home, thinking about Valentina, about whether the lawyer had perhaps set the plan in motion to get rid of her. About how the Italian wasn't what she thought he was (assuming whatever she thought the Italian was, really *was* whatever I thought she thought he was, and assuming the Italian really was whatever he was). About how I needed to hurry.

When I opened the door of the apartment, as if I'd summoned Valentina with my thoughts, Alejandra shouts at me: Yo, shithead, your girlfriend's just left! I look to Facundo for an explanation. He's standing at the stove regulating the boiling of the water to make pasta. Ále, he says, don't say shithead. And she isn't Juan Pablo's girlfriend anymore. Vale's been here? I say. She's helping me take care of Alejandra, says Facundo. What am I supposed to do, shithead, the kid kind of likes her.

Did anyone see you two come up? Chucky asks the guy who came to meet me at Plaza Lesseps, where I'd agreed to meet Chucky at eleven-thirty and instead I'd been met by a Mafia car, or rather, a mafioso's car, a very expensive car, without license plates and with tinted windows, whose back door opened to invite me in. Where's Chucky? I said, as I leaned inside and saw that Chucky was not there, that the only person in the car was the driver (up front, naturally) and another guy who was very well dressed (in the back) who having told me to get in quickly immediately decided to get out, and when he was out of the car told me to just get in once and for fucking all, and told the driver to drive around and come back down the other side of the square in five minutes. We drove around for five minutes, maybe six, with me sitting in silence, looking out with the impunity of not being seen, with a melodramatic impression that I was seeing things for the last time. Or the penultimate time, if I was lucky. The cars. The buildings, modernist or just plain modern. Those fucking pigeons. The parakeets that amused me so much until I learned they're a plague, totally out of control. Those aseptic streets, with no trash, no begging kids, no hawkers at the lights, no minibuses to attack you, even if today I might still end up, like my cousin, with my head smashed in.

Negative, boss, the guy who had come to meet me at Plaza Lesseps said to Chucky, the same guy who after the five or six minutes had gotten back into the car and said to me as if he'd known me his whole life, as if this wasn't the first time we'd clapped eyes on one another and he knew everything about me: Jesus, she's stubborn, your girlfriend, he said. I mean, your ex-girlfriend. What? I said. Didn't you see her? he said. You didn't see Valentina? She was following you. Again. She's making a bad habit of it, he said. His use of the present continuous brought me some temporary relief, it was a sign the guy hadn't done anything to Valentina, that Valentina was still alive, unlike if he'd used the continuous past and had said she *had been* making a bad habit of it.

On the journey to Pedralbes, a neighborhood I'd never been to before but which I knew existed, the *fanciest* neighborhood in Barcelona, I'd been told, I decided to keep my mouth shut and focus on the conversation I was going to have with Chucky, on the arguments I was going to use to persuade him, I couldn't let myself get distracted by anything right now, not even by Valentina, because my life depended on this conversation and so did hers.

At last we reach our destination, a small building in the Californian style (or that's how it seems, though my ability to identify architectural styles goes all to hell when I'm stressed), a stylish fortress, guarded by private security, we go through the electric gate and park in an underground garage, we get out the car and into an elevator that does justice to its name by *rising upward* (as the enlightened folk of this redundant country like to say).

The elevator doors open and there's no hallway or front door, the elevator doors fold open and I take one step forward onto the wooden floor of an unusually large living room, forty or fifty square meters of nothing but living room. Sit down, says Chucky, gesturing with his chin at the armchair next to where he's seated, on an easy chair that looks like a throne, I can see there's a Tàpies picture on one of the walls, with a sandy texture and a bit of plastic piping stuck onto it, and on the back wall I can see an engraving that could be a Miró or just one of his imitators.

Well? he says, when I sit down, but instead of letting me speak he adds: Is it possible the lawyer's underestimated you? he says, with that distinct northern accent of his, from Monterrey or Saltillo, I'm guessing. He's wearing a perfectly ironed white shirt, his initials embroidered over his left breast: CH. A watch that must be incredibly expensive, but not showy. Gray socks the exact same color as his woolen pants. He looks me up and down when I stand up to take off my overcoat and scarf (the apartment has central heating, it's hot inside), I look around me and put my clothes down on a stool.

You ought to go to the dermatologist, buddy, he says, stroking his chin, as if he had a beard. And then, once again, without giving me the chance to speak: I imagine I don't have to tell you this situation is totally irregular, he says. The lawyer isn't going to like this one bit. You better hope this is real important. Or you better hope I find it interesting. Otherwise you know how this is going to end, he says. Badly, he says. You must have realized by now I don't like jokes. And bad jokes even less, he says, and then finally he falls silent.

I swallow gastritis-flavored saliva and of all the things I've been practicing to say what I actually say is: So like, I say, so, what was I going to say. Let me guess, Chucky interrupts me again. You've already realized that now the project's up and running you're going to be expendable, he says, his tone revealing just how easy it was to come to this conclusion, how obvious the syllogism. That you're just going to be in the way, he says. I nod. You're right, buddy, he says, but let me tell you something: you've been expendable all along, from day one, from the first page of the book, if you prefer, since you like reading so much, he says. You've gotten this far by sheer fucking fluke, buddy, but you must be on like page two hundred by now and this book has two-fifty at the absolute most. Really long stories don't work in this kind of business, he says. I've got a proposition, I say, hurriedly, before he starts talking again. A long-term project, I say. What the fuck, he says, you're already talking like your dickhead cousin and you know how that shit ended. Badly, he says. It's all projects projects projects and the whole shitshow goes up in smoke. You know why people call me Chucky? he asks me. Everyone assumes it's from the movie, the demon doll. But it's because

I Don't Expect Anyone to Believe Me

of the English verb. To chuck, he says. I got the nickname from my classmates at the master's I did in the US. They called me Chucky because of the way I solved the business problems they set us. You got five minutes to explain your fucking project, he says, taking it as read I know what he's talking about (I don't).

So like, how about if the lawyer's the one who's expendable? I say, starting off, starting with my conclusion, skipping over my prefaces and my prologues and the whole speech I'd prepared and can't for the life of me remember. What if it's the lawyer who's in the way? I insist. Chucky smiles like someone's told him a joke he's been told a million times before. He gets up and walks over to a little side table, picks up a glass jug and pours himself a tumbler of water. Half-full. Bring me the omeprazole, he says to the guy who went to meet me at Plaza Lesseps, who's stationed at the entrance to the apartment, like a bouncer at a club. It should be on the nightstand, says Chucky. Or in the bathroom. The guy walks across the living room and disappears into the corridor that leads into the apartment. Chucky remains standing, with the glass in his right hand, looking at me. You're not going to tell me you want me to fuck over the lawyer to save your hide, he says. So like, I say. You've got some balls, buddy, he says. And what if I were to call the lawyer and tell him? So like, I say, my cousin said that you— I start saying, but Chucky interrupts me: Your cousin was being such a dick, he says. You know why they fucked him over? I say nothing, which is the same as saying no. For being a dick, he says, or for being too smart for his own good, which comes to the same thing. According to him he'd been working on a mega-deal and before he knew it he'd lost fourteen million dollars. You know how much money that is, buddy? I keep quiet, respecting the pause in his rhetorical question that attempts, and manages very successfully, to magnify my cousin's monumental stupidity.

The man who'd gone to fetch the omeprazole reappears and hands the capsule over to Chucky, who puts it straight into his mouth. He drinks some water from the glass. He puts it back down on the small table, beside the jug. Did the Italians send you? he asks, and he looks over toward the door, where the one who'd given him the pill is already back at his post, protecting the den. The guy gives a nod as if he's been ordered to be prepared (to eliminate me or, by some miracle, just to escort me back outside). Chucky sits down in the easy chair. I don't know anything about the Italians, I say, so like, I don't understand what the Italians have to do with any of this, and I go on, before Chucky has a chance to interrupt me again: I talked to Ahmed, I say, we've got a project that's much better than the lawyer's one. That's not hard, buddy, says Chucky, the asshole lawyer was so terrified of losing the project that he took on unacceptable levels of risk, he says. All I need to do is wait for the project to blow up. It's a matter of weeks, he says, two months at the most, three max. I haven't got two months, I say. That's a shame, he says. Maybe the project will work out, I say, so like, maybe in the end the lawyer will get away with it. How'd you think it's going to work out, buddy? he says. The project's a joke! There are seven million inhabitants of Cataluña, if we get all that capital circulating, you know what'll happen? You know what Cataluña's GDP is? The project's big mistake is disregarding the existence of Madrid. The national police are going to love the idea of charging in to flatten the party HQ for money laundering, he says. Picture the scene, bud: a poster-boy of Catalan-ness exposed as a rotten criminal, getting into a squad car. That looks great on the TV news, he says. Feeding the Catalan-phobia. The lawyer's going down all on his own, he says, I don't need to lift a damn finger. Then he says to the guy who went to meet me at Plaza Lesseps, who is still unmoving at the entrance: Go on, beat it, make tracks. The guy turns around, presses the button to call the elevator, and waits. Come with me, says Chucky. He gets up, crosses the living room, walks down a corridor with three, four bedrooms off to the sides, which opens into a kitchen, where a woman is sitting dozing on a stool next to the stove, her head resting against the wall.

Good morning, Doña Mariana, says Chucky. The woman wakes with a start. I'm sorry, señor, I just haven't got used to the time change, she says, rubbing her eyes with her knuckles, standing up, smoothing out her apron. Don't worry, says Chucky, just make us some huevos con machaca. We're all out of machaca, says the woman. The guys finished it all up. Ah, what the fuck is it with those starving bastards, says Chucky. Those guys are meant to go down to get their breakfast at the café, Doña Mariana, that's why I pay their expenses. The guys don't have permission to eat my things. Might you like some quesadillas de huitlacoche? says the woman, hoping to find a way out of this trouble. Very well, says Chucky. Make some for this kid, too, see if they get rid of his rashes, if you ask me what he's got is just a bad case of homesickness, what do you reckon, Doña Mariana? The woman puts the skillet on the stove and starts bustling about between the fridge and the cupboard ignoring the question, well aware it's a rhetorical question, an expert in understanding that nothing that happens around her is any of her concern.

Sit down, Chucky says to me, gesturing with his chin toward the four seats at the breakfast table. He sits and rolls up his shirtsleeves once, twice. You're sure the fag's with you? he says, the moment Doña Mariana puts two large cups of black coffee on the table. Be careful, says Chucky, the fag's the only one with a direct line to the big cheese. The lawyer's boss? I ask. Everybody's boss, buddy, he says, but you haven't answered my question. I take a sip of gastritis before responding. So like, yeah, definitely, I say. He looks straight at me, as if trust were something you could find in somebody's eyes, as if he really believed that old bolero that says the eyes are the mirrors of the soul. Totally definitely, I insist, overdoing it, because the truth is I think it's only more or less definite. How do you know? he asks. I told him that the lawyer's going to get the dog killed, I said. I knew it! shouts Chucky, slapping the table delightedly. I knew it, he says again. Instead of asking him what it was he knew I keep quiet waiting for him to volunteer an explanation, he's so pleased there's no way he could bear to keep it to himself. And indeed, it turns out he can't: You know who was meant to get rid of that dog? he asks. I knew it, he says again. For the first time I think I can persuade him, because now one thing I have in my favor is the hypothesis that the alliance with Ahmed was possible thanks to a *stroke of genius* of his. Explain this project to me, buddy, he says, returning from happiness to reality, truly interested, receptive, and he takes a sip of coffee.

The next day, the Chinaman called me up and said: My grandmother can see you today. At eleven. What? I said. It was eight in the morning and I was still in bed, reading, without paying any attention, or only occasionally paying attention, a little book of the aphorisms of Gómez de la Serna I'd bought two days earlier at the Sant Antoni market, on the way to Ahmed's apartment. I talked to my grandmother and she said what you have is an anxiety attack, said the Chinaman. I'll see you at ten to eleven. Outside the Florida metro station. On the red line.

I called Chucky to let him know, to tell him the Chinaman had offered me acupuncture and I thought he was laying a trap for me, an ambush, or some other kind of fatal action with an unhappy ending. We need to know what game the Chinaman's playing at, he answered. The Chinaman's the one big mystery in this story. We need to know if he's the eliminator (*sic*). Or if the lawyer's such an asshole he hasn't realized the Chinaman's working with the Italians. I told him it seemed really risky, so like, my going into the wolf's lair to find out, that surely the lawyer must already have given the Chinaman the order to eliminate me with one of his kung fu blows and that I had no intention of leaving my room. There was a silence at the other end of the line that lasted several seconds. Well? I said. I'm thinking, said Chucky. And then: I'll send Herpes over to watch your back. Who? I said. The one who went to fetch you yesterday, buddy! he said. Didn't you see his mouth?

CALL YOUR MOTHER RIGHT AWAY

Juan, my child, why aren't you answering your phone? Your mother's been dialing you all day long and it seems you've got your cell phone switched off, do your mom a favor and turn on your cell or call her as soon as you finish reading this mail. Doesn't matter what time it is, even if it's early in the morning your mother will be awake anyway with all the worry.

A man's just been here, an extremely rude fellow who claimed you owe him twenty thousand pesos. He told your mother your cousin Lorenzo had promised you were going to pay it for 'a job' he did for the two of you. Your mother has put 'a job' in quotation marks because your mother didn't like the tone this shameless fellow used to say it one little bit. As if it was something illegal. This whoever he was looked familiar to your mother and when your mother asked him if they'd met before the person in question told her he'd been at your cousin's wake, that he was a friend of your cousin's.

Your mother asked him what work he had performed for you both and whether he had an invoice or a receipt, or a contract, and with utter barefaced cheek the man laughed in your mother's face. Best for a lady like you not to know, lady, the rude young man said to your mother.

Naturally your mother refused to pay him a thing and demanded an explanation with a threat to call the police. This whoever he was told your mother that he came in peace, that he'd give your mother a day to talk to you and that tomorrow he'd be back to collect the money. But that that was the last chance, because you hadn't replied to him and because he'd already wasted a lot of time on your father.

The moment he left I called your father in his office and it turns out this whoever he is has spent months trying to extort money from him. That he'd come up to him on the day of the wake, to ask for your address in Barcelona, apparently to send you some things of your cousin's that your cousin wanted you to keep. Your father thought this strange and asked him to send the things here to Guadalajara, that besides you weren't in Barcelona yet, you were in Xalapa finishing up some arrangements. But this whoever he was insisted and started showing up from time to time at the office, first to ask your father for the address, which your father said he never gave him, then to tell him he'd managed to get it now, then to ask if you hadn't perhaps sent him a message, then to see if you'd told him to pay him, and finally, to insist that he give him twenty thousand pesos you apparently owed him.

And all this while your father said nothing about it to your mother! And today your mother's been through this shock because she wasn't forewarned. Truly your mother doesn't know what to do about your father.

As if that wasn't enough your father asked your mother not to say anything to you. That it was just a case of extortion and if he hadn't notified the police it was only to avoid more distress for your aunt and uncle. Of course your father thought about them before your mother or his son! According to him, your aunt and uncle already have enough to bear what with getting over Lorenzo's death to have to discover now that he'd been running with a bad crowd. Your father says they wouldn't be able to bear this, and he's right, because they've done nothing since your cousin's death but idealize him, and they've been going around saying he's a saint and a business genius, all to benefit the foundation. Because who's going to want to donate money to the foundation if they knew what your cousin was really like, a good-for-nothing liar? But your aunt is totally shameless, she's even already managed to get a Maná benefit concert! Your aunt called your mother, all emotional, to tell her they'd written a special song dedicated to your cousin, 'Crossing the Street of Hope', it's called, because according to this song there's a street separating life and death and you have to cross carefully to get to hope. You know your aunt!

But your mother isn't writing to tell you about your aunt's sickly ramblings, your mother's writing to tell you about what's happening and to say call her at home right away. If your father answers you're not to say she told you, say he should pass the phone over to your mother.

Son, your mother really would rather not be put in this position, your father promised your mother that tomorrow he won't be going to the office and that he'll be home when this man shows up, to put a stop to all this. And your father's so naive he thinks he'll listen to him! It wouldn't surprise me if your father's already made friends with this shameless fellow, you know what your father's like, he'd even rather have a word with the ants to ask them to kindly get out of the garden instead of putting down poison.

To be honest, Juan, your mother's starting to worry about your cousin's problems ending up affecting you right now when you've finally got your life on track. Your mother thinks your cousin's perfectly capable of ruining your life from the grave, people are superstitious about speaking ill of the dead but the fact is there are some dead who don't stop being a nuisance just because they've been cremated.

Son, you're not to tell Laia anything, there's no way in the world you're telling her. Merely imagining Laia finding out your cousin's been mixed up in some illegal business or other with disgusting people is enough to make your mother's blood sugar go through the roof. What's Laia going to think of you and your family if they're also constantly showing news on the TV that make Mexicans look like savages?

Call your mother now, Juan, and be ready to tell your mother what's going on, what the meaning is of these alleged letters that your cousin sent you and Valentina and who this shameless man is who has the barefaced cheek to come laugh in your mother's face. Your mother needs a good explanation, and you'd better have one, she's put up with a lot of years of being distraught watching you and your sister throwing your lives away only for you to disappoint her again now. At this point in your life what you need to do is focus on your relationship with Laia, not sort out the tangles your irresponsible cousin has left behind.

Call your mother right away, and don't you believe for a moment your mother's forgotten you haven't sent her the photo of Laia she asked for.

Send your mother the picture and call her right away.

NO NEWS FROM JUAN PABLO

Wednesday, January 12th, 2005

10 a.m. One hour waiting outside Julio Verne. I arrived at nine, when people are leaving for work, just in time to see Facundo hurrying out, dragging and nagging Alejandra. The two of them were running late, him for work and her for school. Then Cristian came out, in sweatpants, with a sports backpack, like he does whenever he goes to play football with his Argentine friends, all of them from La Boca, all of them waiters or cooks or barmen. At ten, Juan Pablo. He stopped on the sidewalk for a moment to double-check the contents of his coat and pants pockets. He took out his keys. His cell phone. A book. Another cell phone (another!). He went down Calle Zaragoza but this time instead of following him I watched him leave, I made sure he'd gone, I kept an eye on him till he had become a little doll two blocks down. I hurried over to the building, to the elevator, to the apartment, to Juan Pablo's bedroom.

The bed made, the window open to the inner courtyard to air the room, books on the nightstand, surrounding the computer, pajamas folded on the bed, clothes in the closet, the laundry in a big garbage bag, condoms under a pile of underpants, hidden, as if his mother was going to come in to check the room, as if he was afraid I'd learn he was sleeping with another woman, because he hadn't needed to wear them with me, because I'm on the pill. Or I was. Under the bed, a pair of slippers. Women's slippers. Laia's.

I turned the computer on. Juan Pablo hadn't changed his password. I started opening files. Notes toward an essay on Albert Cohen and humor in the Holocaust. Transcribed quotes from Jung. Fifteen pages on the history of blow-up dolls and Felisberto Hernández. A thesis project on machista misogynist humor in twentieth-century Latin American literature (?!). It wasn't a project, really, just the title and two introductory paragraphs. I went on looking through the folders, the stories I knew by heart, the fragments of abandoned novels, the essay on Gabriel Orozco with which Juan Pablo had not won the university competition, the thesis on Ibargüengoitia, articles on Ibargüengoitia, transcribed stories and novels by Ibargüengoitia, his articles, his interviews. I don't know what I was expecting to find, maybe I just wanted to rule out the absurd theory that Juan Pablo was also writing a diary. If he was, I'm sure he'd do it on his computer, I've never seen him write by hand.

Of course, Juan Pablo wasn't writing a diary, that minor literary form he held in such contempt, though he'd never said as much to me, so as not to offend me, not to get in the way of my academic interests. But he was writing something else. A novel. An autobiographical novel. He'd already completed six chapters, almost a hundred pages, much more than he'd managed to write on any of his previous attempts. *I Don't Expect Anyone to Believe Me*, that's what the novel was called. Is called. I don't expect anyone to believe me. I emailed myself the document, turned off the computer, quit the room, the apartment, the building, without anybody seeing me. I ran off in no particular direction, down Calle Pàdua. On Calle Balmes I found a call shop and printed out the manuscript.

*

I called Juan Pablo, still trembling, out of fear and also from the adrenalin which my organism, so used to nothing ever happening, doesn't know how to process. His cell was off. I went on calling him, always with the same result.

In the afternoon I picked Alejandra up and took her straight to Julio Verne. I told her it was going to rain (there wasn't a single cloud, but the girl didn't so much as glance up at the sky). She contented herself with my promise to do something fun with her hair.

There was nobody in the apartment but Cristian, who was getting ready to head out to work. I made up some story about urgently needing to talk to Juan Pablo because I couldn't find an important document and needed to know if I'd left it with his things. He said he hadn't seen him, that when he'd arrived, about one, he had already gone out and he hadn't come back since. I started putting Alejandra's hair in little plaits. It turned eight, eight-fifteen, Facundo arrived but no sign of Juan Pablo. As if that wasn't enough, Facundo yelled at me.

'What are you doing, shithead?' he said, when he saw Alejandra's hair. 'If her mother finds out she'll kill me, the shithead thinks makeup and hairdressing are impositions by the patriarchy. I got enough trouble already with the shithead blaming me for the fact Ále likes drawing princesses.'

On my way back home I stopped at a call shop and at a public phone to call Juan Pablo. His cell was still off.

I arrived at the apartment to find the last thing I needed: a party. And worse still, a Brazilian party. There were six or seven Brazilians, besides Andreia and Paulo, plus Gabriele, in camouflage. Andreia scooped me up as I walked through the door, she put a glass of beer in my hand, introduced me to her friends and tried teaching me a few little samba steps. All embellished with that tooth-filled smile. I felt so clumsy, so overwhelmed, so out of place, that the glass slipped out of my hand. I apologized and went into my room. Then Gabriele came knocking at the door: Hey, princess, he said, you could at least have cleaned it up.

Thursday, January 13th

All morning going to the call shop to phone Juan Pablo. The cell phone off. Noon I called the landline in the apartment, Cristian answered. He said Juan Pablo wasn't in and he hadn't spent the night there. I got over the shame and asked him if he thought he was with Laia. He said he didn't know, but it tended to be Laia who came to sleep at the apartment, occasionally, only very occasionally, he said, as if they really didn't sleep together very much or as if he felt sorry for me. I went back to the apartment to get Laia's number. Laia the Mossos d'Esquadra officer, of course, not Laia Juan Pablo's girlfriend. Girlfriend or, well, whatever she was.

At five I fetched Alejandra and took her to a different playground from the one I'm meant to, the one Laia said when I called her to ask for help. This playground was right next to the Ring, beside some drainage works, this city does love being gutted. Alejandra hasn't stopped complaining, though not about the noise, but about the fact I'm not taking her to the usual square, the one we go to every day, she said, where her schoolmates go. Fortunately there was a sandbox and Alejandra set about scratching around and transporting sand over to the slide together with a smaller boy she used as a little laborer.

Laia arrived at the promised time, five-fifteen, in plain clothes. She had told me that today was her 'free day', that she wasn't on duty, but that if I said it was urgent and confidential (that's what I'd said) it was no problem for us to meet.

Better this way: seen from outside it looked like just a regular everyday meeting between a couple of friends. Of course, Laia's presence, which is so striking, she had her red mane loose and her hair really is beautiful, wouldn't go unnoticed by anyone who knew her.

When I greeted her, she gave me a pair of kisses and squeezed my forearms, a greeting between friends, indeed, and I told her she looked amazing, and she answered that later she'd be going to see a movie with her girlfriend. She gave a happy laugh, as though being a lesbian was very amusing or as if she thought it was funny to be telling me.

We sat down on a bench beside the sandbox, from where I could keep an eye on Alejandra's activities, and I started reading her a few excerpts from Juan Pablo's novel, the passages I'd underlined, the ones that contained information that had disturbed me and which had led me to believe something had happened to Juan Pablo. (I'd removed a number of pages in which Juan Pablo had, indirectly, confessed to committing a murder. I had left those pages hidden in my room. Maybe I shouldn't even be writing about that here.) The noise gave us a fair amount of freedom to talk without anybody bothering us.

Laia listened very carefully, interrupting from time to time so I could pass her the pages to reread some part or to read beyond whatever I'd underlined. She wanted to know how I'd gotten hold of the manuscript and I got tangled up in a meaningless explanation to avoid confessing, as if I had to protect my sources, when in reality I was just too ashamed to tell her what I'd done.

'So listen,' she said, after a lot of thought, 'man, don't get offended, but I think you're tripping, this looks like a novel.'

I told her it was a novel, an autobiographical novel, that even though it was a text that used the mechanisms of fiction, everything it described was truthful, everything had truly happened.

'How do you know?' she said. 'You weren't there when they allegedly killed your boyfriend's cousin, sorry, your ex-boyfriend's cousin, and he didn't tell you anything about it, or did he?'

'But from that point Juan Pablo started acting real weird,' I said, 'I do know that, and he did try to stop me coming to Barcelona, like it says in the novel, he dumped me, then he changed his mind, though now I know he didn't change his mind, he was obeying orders.'

'Man,' she said, 'you've got to admit, the idea some criminal organization ordered him to get back together with you is kind of ridiculous.'

'Because that was part of a plan,' I said. 'Everything he says in here that has anything to do with me is true. Other things I witnessed, too. I saw Juan Pablo get into a black Mercedes-Benz, without plates, on Plaza Lesseps. And I saw him leave, yesterday, apparently to get some acupuncture done, and he hasn't been back since.'

'Were you following him?' she asked.

'It was a coincidence,' I said.

'Well, actually two coincidences, right?' she said, and she was about to say something else, but stopped herself.

I got up to tell Alejandro not to put sand in the little boy's pants, which is what she was doing while the poor innocent's mother wasn't paying attention. I returned to the bench, where Laia was still looking over the manuscript.

'You don't believe me, do you?' I said. 'I don't blame you, I don't expect you to believe me, all I'm asking is for you to help me investigate it.'

'Oh man, I don't know,' she said, 'it's too twisted, too implausible. Besides, there's nothing in here that's any use. Who would we investigate? The "lawyer"? This "Chucky" guy? Or "The Chinaman"?' she said, looking through the pages for the blue-ink circles I'd used to mark the characters. 'The "guy who had come to meet me at Plaza Lesseps"? The "big cheese"? Ahmed? Man, these Pakistanis are all called Ahmed, it's like a Catalan being called Jordi. There aren't any people here, man, there are only characters.'

'I'm there,' I said, 'I exist, though to tell the truth, Juan Pablo doesn't talk about me much, I'm like a supporting character in the novel. Laia's there, I know her, I met her, I've been with her, more than I'd have liked. Her father Oriol Carbonell's there, you know him?'

'Of course I know him, everyone knows him, he's a big shot, he's a public figure,' she said, in a tone that emphasized the word 'public'.

'And the bit about Jimmy's also there,' I went on, 'the Italian, Giuseppe, you met him too. To tell the truth, I decided to call you when I realized I'm not sure I can trust him either.'

'So why do you trust me, if you're so paranoid?'

'Because you were kind to me,' I said. 'You were concerned for me. You inspired confidence. You still do.'

'Man, I don't know,' she said, 'to be totally honest, it looks like what we've got here is a mixture of truths and lies. I don't know much about literature, or the theory about literature, but I'd have thought that's how you make novels, isn't it? Don't authors use their own lives and experiences to transform into fiction? As far as I know, that's what novels are: fiction. You can't expect me to believe Juan Pablo just because he says it's all true. You don't think if he wanted to leave a record he would have written a diary? Or letters to a friend? And anyway, to me the key to the whole thing is the way the pages are written. I don't believe that if Juan Pablo was so worried, if he feared for his life, he'd be writing like this, like with style, I don't know if I'm making myself clear. Sometimes he even tries to be amusing. And with this whole shtick he has about humor and laughter.'

'You don't know the people I know,' I said, 'literature's an illness for these people. I get what you mean about style, it's the only way Juan Pablo ever writes, it comes out naturally for him because it's the same style he's used in the past in various short stories, in various novels he gave up on without finishing. He's internalized it so much he no longer even notices. He used to tell me sometimes that he'd written something different and it turned out it was exactly the same as everything he'd written before. He's always written with the same narrator, the same tone, the same tricks, have you noticed the way his protagonist always uses "so like" all the time? Those filler words are a bad habit all us Mexicans have, when we don't know what to say or when we want to buy some time to see what we can come up with we start saying "so like, so like" over and over like imbeciles. Juan Pablo thought it would be funny to put it in his dialogue, he'd already started using it in another novel he was writing last year.'

'Another autobiographical novel?'

'Yes, but he couldn't carry on with it because nothing happened to him, his life wasn't enough for a novel, we had a kind of boring life in Mexico, kind of happy, kind of dumb. We read, we studied, we tried to write, we had a writing workshop, a reading group, we did translations for fun.'

The mother of Alejandra's little slave-boy finally noticed what the kid was doing to her son. I had to get up to apologize, to scold Alejandra, threaten her with punishment, help the mother get the sand out of her little boy's underpants. I went back to the bench, where Laia was waiting for me with a pitying expression, but a misplaced pity: she didn't feel pity because she believed Juan Pablo had disappeared and I was in danger, she felt pity for what we'd lost by moving to Barcelona, that insipid life we'd lived in Xalapa.

'You've got to help me,' I said, trying to take advantage of her condescension. 'Please, I've got this feeling something bad's happened to Juan Pablo.'

She shook the sheaf of pages and straightened them out, before handing them back to me. She looked me in the eye to try to work out how scared I was.

'Look,' she said, 'to be totally honest,' she said, repeating the same polite expression, 'to be totally honest I think Juan Pablo's off someplace with his girlfriend and when he shows up you're going to feel like shit. It's not really for me to say, but honestly, girl, I think you should get over him. Enjoy the city for the rest of the time you've got and go back to your country and start a new life.'

'Why don't we call Laia?' I said. 'You can get her number, right?'

She hesitated a moment.

'It's only going to cause you more pain,' she said.

'I need to know Juan Pablo's OK,' I said.

She hesitated again.

'Wait,' she said, and she moved away to make a phone call.

She returned two or three minutes later.

'I had to explain a bit more than I would have liked,' she said.

She dialed the number on her cell.

'Here,' she said, handing me the phone. 'You call.'

I waited for Laia to answer.

'Hello?' said Laia.

I was struck momentarily dumb.

'Hello?' she said again. 'Who's this?' she said, in Catalan.

I explained who I was and without giving her a chance to react I said Juan Pablo's mother had called me to say they hadn't been able to track him down since yesterday. That they'd been calling him but his cell phone was off. That his mom had called the landline of his apartment and one of the Argentinians had told her Juan Pablo hadn't come home to sleep. That they were very worried.

'Oh Jeez,' said Laia, without the -us, she didn't say Jesus, only Jeez.

'Is he with you?' I asked.

'We were meant to meet up last night,' she said, 'I sent him a message to arrange to meet, but he didn't answer. And it's true, his phone was turned off.'

'When was the last time you saw him?' I asked, like the dialogue in a movie, a police interrogation in a crime novel.

'I saw him briefly on Monday morning at the university,' she said, 'we got a coffee together. Tuesday I didn't see him, but I did talk to him and we exchanged messages.'

I thanked her and I was about to hang up. She stopped me.

'Hey, listen,' she said, in Catalan. 'Could you tell me if you find him?' she asked, switching back to Spanish now. 'I'll try and find him too. Is this your cell number?'

I was about to say no, that I didn't have a cell phone, that I couldn't afford a cell phone, but I realized just in time that if I told her I didn't have a cell phone I wouldn't be able to explain how Juan Pablo's mother had apparently tracked me down.

'Yes,' I said, 'call this number anytime.'

I was about to hang up again, and again she stopped me.

'Hey, listen,' she said, in Catalan. 'How'd you get my number?'

I hesitated a fraction of a second.

'You gave it to me,' I said. 'Don't you remember?'

I hung up. I gave the phone to Laia, the other Laia, along with an explanation.

'I don't know, man, I don't know,' she said again. 'You got to understand that for someone to be considered a missing person they need to have disappeared for forty-eight hours.'

I took out a folded sheet of paper I'd been keeping separately in one of my coat pockets, I unfolded it and handed it over.

'Look at this,' I said.

The underlined passage began: 'Riquer called me up and said: Come to my office first thing tomorrow morning. We agreed to meet at eight at his office on the Paseo de San Juan. When I arrived, I found him on his own: it wasn't the station of the Mossos d'Esquadra, it was the off-ice where they finish off (*sic*) private matters, he explained.'

'Jesus fuck,' said Laia, turning pale.

'Is your partner trustworthy?' I asked her. 'The officer who was with you when you came to pick up Jimmy?'

'That's my boss,' she said. 'Oh shit. Oh shit.'

'There's more,' I said.

I took Lorenzo's letter out of my other coat pocket.

'This is Juan Pablo's cousin. This is where it all started. When I received this, I started to get suspicious and that's why I went to check things out. Actually, now I think about it, the whole thing's your fault, you're the one who told me to go to the consulate and that's where they gave me the letter.'

She unfolded the sheets of paper and started to read.

'There's not a lot of detail,' I said. 'Almost nothing, really. But I didn't even know him. What's weird is that he wrote to me at all. Do you have any idea what it's like getting a letter from a dead guy?'

Laia was still focused on her reading. She gave up after a couple of pages.

'This guy was kind of retarded, right?' she said.

'That's why I didn't show it to you right away, because you'd think I was crackers.'

'You're what?'

'Crackers, crazy.'

'Oh, a wack job.'

She stared out into space for a moment, the space that was located precisely at the endless line of cars that were jammed up on the Ring, it was almost 6 p.m., home-time for the schools, the end of the working day. She shifted out of her immobility to pull her cell phone out of her pocket.

'Cari,' she said into the phone, having dialed and waited for the other person to pick up. 'Something's come up, I'm so so sorry. Can we leave it for another day? Yeah, I know. I'll make it up to you, OK? I promise.'

She put the phone back in her pocket and looked at me very seriously.

'Oh man,' she said, 'if even half of what I'm imagining is true, this is dynamite. What are we talking about here? A conspiracy between Mexican narcos and the Italian Mafia to launder money in Cataluña? Using Oriol Carbonell? The party? And under the protection of the head of the Mossos d'Esquadra! Jesus, man, this is some heavy shit.'

'You think they're narcos?' I asked.

'I don't know, who else could it be, I'm just thinking aloud.'

'So you think it's true,' I said.

'There's a talking dog . . . '

'OK,' I answered. 'That bit's definitely fiction.'

'Or the Pakistani guy's a bigger wack job than Bin Laden,' she said. 'Till what time do you have to look after Alejandra?'

'Eight. Eight-thirty.'

'Give me the girl's address, I'll pick you up there at eight-thirty. In the meantime I'm going to make some calls, and I'm taking the papers with me, I want to take a look at them more calmly.'

'Guess,' I said. 'Number 2, Julio Verne, sound familiar?'

'No shit! That's how you got it?'

She got up to leave. I asked if she thought Juan Pablo was in danger.

'I'd rather not confirm that,' she said. 'Or, yeah, that's exactly what I want to confirm. I'd rather not hazard a guess, that's what I meant, ah, I've gotten myself in such a tangle.'

'You can also tell me you don't believe me,' I said, 'that I'm being paranoid, you can go see a movie with your girlfriend and forget me. Are you sure you want to get involved in this?'

She put her hand on my shoulder, like last time, except now it didn't feel like an insulting gesture of condescension.

'Someone's got to be the good guy in this novel,' she said, 'don't you think?'

'The good girl,' I said.

'The good girl,' she repeated. 'But the good girl's not an idiot. Tonight you're going to give me the missing pages, don't think I haven't noticed.'

She walked over to the edge of the sandbox and said good-bye to Alejandra.

'Bye, Ále,' she said, in Catalan. 'You behave, OK? Don't be a hooligan.'

'Your hair's frosted by the fire!' Alejandra shouted back.

I saw the confusion on Laia's face.

'One of those things her mother says,' I said, to reassure her.

I left Julio Verne at eight forty-five, fifteen minutes late, but Laia was still waiting for me, on the corner, leaning against the wall of the stationery store. She asked if I'd had any news from Juan Pablo and I said no, and that in fact Facundo and Cristian were alarmed now too, that they'd told me Juan Pablo had never stayed away so long before.

'I've spent this whole time at Plaza del Sol,' she said. 'Looking for the Italian. If what Juan Pablo wrote in the novel is true, the Italian can lead us to the Chinaman and the Chinaman to Juan Pablo. But the Italian wasn't there, they told me he hasn't shown up at the square all day. He wasn't at his home either, at least not the address we have on file for him.'

'The squatter house in Plaza Lesseps?'

'Right. I talked to a couple kids who insisted he doesn't live there. They were so high I'm not sure they even knew who I was talking about. I asked a colleague of mine to help me track him down. We can't just sit in the square and wait to see if he shows up.'

'We've got to talk to Laia's dad,' I said.

'Man, are you crazy?' she answered at once, not giving me a chance to explain my reasoning. 'If what Juan Pablo's novel says is true,' she said again, 'if half of what's there in the manuscript is correct, Laia's father is in it up to his neck. All we'd achieve would be to put him on the alert and position ourselves right in his sights. They suspect you already, girl, we've got to be real careful. You don't know this country you've gotten yourself mixed up in, these people are untouchable, I'd be out of this job for so much as knocking at his door without a court order.'

'Well, what then?' I asked.

'There's another thread we might start trying to pull,' she said.

I knew what she was about to say, but I didn't interrupt her, I didn't want to disrupt her analysis, maybe she'd spotted some detail that had escaped me.

'Laia,' she said, just as I'd expected. She'd be able to identify the dog, her uncle used to ask her to look after it when he was traveling. 'His name, Laia's uncle's, really is Pere Lleonart.'

She paused to see whether I said anything. I noticed the carefulness with which she hadn't said 'his name was', and I realized this was what made me trust her, her precise politeness, not hypocritical or exaggerated, just right.

'I already know what the pages you kept say,' she said, 'it wasn't that hard to work it out.'

I said nothing.

'Did they force him to do it?' she asked, not specifying who or what.

I broke down. I started crying. Laia waited for me to calm down. She didn't put her hand on my shoulder, she didn't even touch me, she was clearly confused about how she should behave, and finally chose to remain still.

'Come on, we'll have to hurry,' she said, when I'd stopped crying, while I blew my nose.

'Where are we going?' I asked.

'To fetch Viridiana, it's just the time for taking the dog out to pee before going to sleep. It's a very narrow little thread, but we've got to start somewhere.'

'And if we find the dog, are we planning on questioning her?' I said, wiping my eyes.

She laughed to help me finish calming down.

'And if she refuses to cooperate we can question whoever's holding the leash,' she said.

Getting myself back together, I shook my head to clear the daze into which the drama had plunged me.

'Come,' said Laia, 'I've agreed to meet Laia.'

We'd been going up and down the Rambla del Raval when I spotted Laia standing next to the statue of an obese cat, Botero's cat. In spite of the cold, it was Thursday and the Rambla was full of students who were going partying, Pakistanis selling beer, people out drinking and locals taking their dogs out for the last time.

'That's her,' I said to the other Laia.

She was wearing a long overcoat, in bottle-green, buttoned up to her neck, denim pants and boots, her face washed clean without a speck of makeup. She was impatient, an impatience that predated this encounter, inherited, or genetic, as if being impatient was a personality trait and not a lapse in behavior. She interrupted the other Laia before she'd finished introducing herself and explaining that she was the Mossos d'Esquadra officer who'd called her to arrange a meeting.

'Why aren't you in uniform?' asked Laia.

The other Laia explained that she had a free day and to head off her suspicions she showed her ID that confirmed that she was a Mossos officer.

'And you work on your day off,' said Laia.

The other Laia glanced over at me and answered that she was helping me look for Juan Pablo because we were friends.

'I've spoken to my dad,' said Laia, without looking at me. 'My uncle isn't missing, my father knows where he is, he didn't want to tell me, but I pressured him and he finally told me.'

She paused, and ran her tongue over her crooked teeth. I hadn't remembered she had reddish hair, or that it was cut so short, maybe she went to a beauty parlor before going to parties.

'So where is he?' said the other Laia.

'In Sitges,' said Laia. 'My father still thinks I'm five years old and that he can't tell me my uncle's gay and that he's shut away in an orgy.'

'That's a lie,' I said, without even realizing it, but the other Laia grabbed hold of my forearm to shut me up before I said what I was thinking: that it was her fault, or her father's, or both of theirs, that Juan Pablo hadn't shown up and I had to put up with all this crap.

I kept quiet as she wanted, and she hesitated a moment, working out how far she could go, what it would or wouldn't be a good idea to reveal.

'Your father told you that because he's also mixed up in it,' she said.

'And what the fuck are my father and uncle supposed to have to do with Juan Pablo?' she asked, in Catalan.

'Speak Spanish, please,' said the other Laia, in Catalan.

Laia turned to face me for the first time. She made sure her expression conveyed no hidden motives, or hidden feelings.

'You understand me, don't you?' she asked me, in Catalan.

I had understood her, but just to annoy her I said no. She repeated what she'd just said in Spanish. We both looked at the other Laia, who was taking the most minute care over her choice of words.

'The link is Juan Pablo's godfather,' she said at last.

She paused, rhetorically, as Juan Pablo would put it, to allow Laia to remember.

'Apparently,' she said, then 'allegedly', she corrected herself, 'allegedly', she repeated, 'Juan Pablo's godfather, who isn't really his godfather, made your father a business proposition and your uncle got in the way.'

'A business proposition?' said Laia. 'What business proposition?'

'Money laundering,' said the other Laia. 'He wanted to use your father's political connections.'

'Money laundering?' said Laia. 'You're nuts! This guy was so totally charming, polite, cultured – we talked about Rosa Luxemburg, about Berlin, which he knew better than me even though I lived there for six months. He spoke Catalan, he'd done a master's in Barcelona, it turned out my father had even taught him!'

'Too much of a coincidence, don't you think?' said the other Laia.

'You're both crazy,' said Laia again, in Catalan, but as she spoke these words she suddenly froze. 'Oh fuck,' she said, 'Oh fuck.'

'Don't shou –' was as much as the other Laia managed to say before Laia shouted:

'Petanca!'

The dog came running over to Laia's feet, dragging a blue and red leash behind her, or rather, a blue and scarlet leash. The guy walking her took off in the opposite direction, up the Rambla, and the other Laia raced after him. Halfway up the Rambla somebody dropped a green plastic bag. I went over to confirm what I knew would be inside: six red tins of beer, unchilled. I took them back with me to the Botero statue of the cat at whose feet the dog had started to pee.

'Fucking hell, girl,' said Laia, crying, 'Jesus, you've got to fucking tell me what's going on.'

She'd crouched down to pet the dog, running her hand over her head, her back, under her chin, whispering to her, in Catalan:

'Where's Uncle Pere, sweetie? Where's el tiet?'

The other Laia hadn't returned. We walked the dog up and down the Rambla, never straying too far from Botero's cat. All the other dogs came over toward Petanca to try to mount her, but she and we didn't let them.

'How did you know the dog would be here?' Laia asked me, with the effortful awkwardness with which one asks for a favor or admits a mistake.

I told her we'd been following a lead to track down Juan Pablo, that it was hard to explain, it would be better if Laia told her. She didn't insist, she just accepted it, presumably concluding, as I did, that Laia's mediation was essential if we were to remain level-headed.

We stopped in a store to buy kibble. We went on walking the dog, in silence. Then something truly unusual happened: I started to get turned on. It was probably a weird reaction to the stress, combined with the sad statistic that I hadn't screwed anyone since Christmas and I hadn't masturbated since the New Year. It also, and I'm not going to deny it, had to have something to do with Laia's presence. I'd told myself

I wasn't going to think about what had happened, not to remember it, to allow it to disappear into the dark woods of memory, which wasn't that complicated, since the effect of the pill meant I barely remembered it anyway. If I tried hard I could retrieve a few images, a few sensations, the general impression of a pleasure better suited to an erotic dream than to any real sexual relations. As Juan Pablo would have said: I'm sure you could explain it with Bataille. Finally the other Laia reappeared.

'I lost him,' she said, when she was back with us, still panting from the exertion.

'He looked Pakistani,' said Laia.

'Did you notice he didn't have a moustache?' the other Laia said to me.

'The dog's not called Viridiana,' I whispered, without Laia noticing.

'Do you guys know that Pakistani?' Laia asked us.

The other Laia ignored the question and squatted down to pet Petanca.

'So cute,' she said.

'She's on her period,' said Laia.

'Dogs don't get periods,' the two of us said in unison.

We went into the first place that allowed us in with Petanca, a kebab place on Calle Joaquín Costa. The TV was tuned to a channel showing music videos from India, from Pakistan, at incredibly high volume. As if that wasn't bad enough, the music was playing over the usual racket you always get in the city's restaurants and bars, that unbearable dull roar peppered with shrieks and peals of laughter. It was the perfect setting for us to go unnoticed. The waiter came to take our order and gave us a compliment that, oddly, I'd heard many times before in Mexico.

'Well, here's a three-of-a-kind that's worth more than a poker of aces,' he said.

'There are four of us,' said the Laia from the Mossos d'Esquadra, gesturing toward the dog.

'Didn't they teach you what harassment is in Pakistan?' said the other Laia.

'Take it easy, man,' said the waiter, 'I'm from Bangladesh, in Bangladesh we like beautiful women like you, in Pakistan they're all fags.'

I ordered some food before Laia had a chance to start telling the poor waiter about Judith Butler. I was starving, not having noticed that the only thing I'd eaten since breakfast had been half of Alejandra's afternoon snack. The dog sprawled under the table and I saw she'd left a smear of blood on the white mosaic.

Laia's natural impatience was a terrible combination with fear and a sense of urgency. She behaved rudely, hurried and hysterical, demanding explanations as though she was the victim of all this, the only victim.

'Listen, princess,' the other Laia interrupted her, 'you got to calm down. And you too,' she said to me, totally unjustified.

As for me, the reason I was struggling to control myself at that moment was entirely down to my lack of energy, I'd used up the last of my strength repressing the episode of involuntary arousal and I felt I was completely empty of adrenaline and about to faint.

'If we all become hysterical we're going to get nowhere,' she added, as a threat.

Then she started to tell Laia one possible version of what we knew up till that point. She did it with pauses, thoughtfully, as if instead of telling the story she too was hearing it for the first time, as if she was arranging the plot as she went along, repeating names to avoid confusion, avoiding ellipses, choosing the same words Juan Pablo had used in his novel and replacing the murder of her uncle with a hypothetical, unconfirmed, kidnapping.

'Man, what the hell are you saying?' said Laia when the other Laia had finished giving a synopsis of the novel, shifting around in her chair as if something were pricking her butt. 'Do you realize what you're saying? Can you hear what you're saying? Can you hear what it sounds like? Man, you've gone totally batshit.'

'And how do you explain about the dog?' the other Laia asked her. 'We knew the guy who'd kept the dog, Ahmed, usually walked her on the Rambla del Raval.'

'He could be a friend of my uncle's who asked him to look after her,' said Laia, 'we didn't give him a chance to explain, you threw yourself at him.'

'And he just started running away just because?' said the other Laia.

'Probably he hasn't got any papers,' said Laia, 'or out of habit, didn't you see how he ran away? The guy's gay, he's probably used to running away to avoid getting beaten up, you guys have no idea about the discrimination these poor people suffer in their countries.'

'We also know,' I said, to stop Laia continuing to assemble a coherent speech that might ultimately allow her to escape us (there's no worse enemy to truth than narrative logic) – 'we also know', I repeated, 'that you've been deceiving Juan Pablo, that your supposed conversion to heterosexuality is all just part of your doctoral thesis, you're doing this whole thing as if it was some kind of performance piece.'

I'm sure it must have seemed I was motivated by jealousy, but the truth is that I'd been thinking we needed to give Laia information for her to corroborate. Laia made as if to stand up, she flinched backward and tugged on the dog's leash, but a dish of chickpea croquettes and the arm of the Bangladeshi waiter putting it down in front of her made this impossible.

'As if it were some kind of performance piece?' she said. 'Man, what the fuck are you talking about?'

'That's what a friend of yours told Juan Pablo,' I said. 'A *very very very* good friend of yours. Some girl called Mireia,' I said, and I took a bite of the kebab I'd just been served.

'How do you know?'

I looked to the other Laia for help, I'd asked her not to say anything about the manuscript and she'd said we had to tell her.

'He told me,' I lied, before Laia beat me to it.

'To hell with Mireia,' said Laia. 'To hell with all my bitch friends. Mireia's jealous, man, Mireia can't accept I dumped her. Hey, just like you, you're both capable of making up any ridiculous bullshit just so long as you don't have to deal with reality.'

'You met Juan Pablo's cousin who was murdered,' said the other Laia, who'd understood the point of my strategy. 'You met him on the Caribbean coast, that's where it all started.'

She put her fork loaded with salad into her mouth, enjoying the effect of her words, or so that her words could have their effect. I kept my kebab suspended in front of my mouth, my lips smeared with yogurt sauce, because this was a detail I'd missed. The expression on Laia's face now told us she really didn't understand a thing. She fixed her olive eyes on the other Laia so she would go on.

'In Cancún. A guy who recommended places for you to visit, you and your girlfriend. You gave him your details in case he ever came to Barcelona.'

Laia opened her mouth to say something but thought better of it, her folded-back upper lip leaving her teeth exposed. She was finally accepting that we were telling the truth, or at least that there was some truth in all this, and that, the truth, had the effect of stripping away her mask of arrogance, leaving her totally vulnerable. Then I remembered something: I had sucked this girl's teeth. The sensation hit me all at once in my groin, running my tongue over her four upper incisors, slightly raised above the arch of the molars and canines.

'Call Juan Pablo's apartment,' the other Laia said, yanking me out of my daze and handing me her cell phone. 'Say we'll be there in half an hour. We've got to search Juan Pablo's room.'

I told her I'd done that already and I hadn't found *anything*.

'We've got to look again,' she said, 'don't take it the wrong way, but you might not have looked properly. And you should eat,' she added, as though giving us an order, 'with all this emotion you're going to crash.'

'Listen, shithead,' said Facundo's voice in the intercom, 'what's this about Alejandra having been playing in the sandbox if there isn't a sandbox in the Plaza de la Revolución?'

'Can we come up?' I asked.

'Who else is there with you?' he said.

'Laia,' I answered, 'and another friend.'

'Laia?' he said, 'and what are you all going to do, another threesome?'

'Will you open up?' I said, touching the key in my coat pocket that I could be using to open the door myself.

We heard the electric buzz that opened the door, I gave it a push and we crossed the entrance hall toward the elevator. Laia said she'd take the stairs, that the dog was terrified of elevators. The three of us looked at the dog, who really had sat down two meters away from the elevator and was recoiling. The other Laia said she'd go with her, that it would do her good to take the stairs, that climbing stairs is good for logic, that it's the sort of exercise that helps you think.

I guess she was afraid Laia would have a change of heart on the way and decide to go home. I went into the elevator and waited on the landing of the sixth floor, I didn't feel I had the energy to put up with Facundo's coked-up verbal diarrhea on my own.

The three of them arrived breathing totally calmly, with no sign of having made any effort, I was envious of the lung capacity they demonstrated, even in circumstances like these. Once, right near the start of my time living there, the elevator had been undergoing maintenance for a day and when I'd taken the stairs I'd had to sit down for a bit on the fourth floor so as to recover and then make it up to the sixth.

Facundo opened the door and immediately resumed the rant from the intercom.

'Which park did you take Ále to today, shithead?'

I said it was the one round the back of the building, on the Ring. The two Laias tried to say something, I'm guessing good evening, hello, but Facundo didn't stop.

'On the Ring? Are you crazy? There's a hell of a wind blowing. And you let her play in the sand?'

I kept quiet.

'Stop screwing around, Vale,' he said, 'don't you know the sand's freezing? Your little brain's not up to it? The kid's got a fever, shithead, and tomorrow I got to go see a client in Manresa. If Ále can't go to school, you're the one looking after her. And don't think for a second I'm going to pay you, it's your responsibility, for being a shithead, shithead.'

'Man,' Laia broke in, 'why'd you let him talk to you like that?'

And then she said to Facundo:

'Could you not be such a dick, *shithead*?'

'Jesus, I've had it up to here with all these women,' said Facundo, 'they wanted their fucking women's lib just so they

Juan Pablo Villalobos

could act irresponsible, Alejandra's shithead mother just
clears off and abandons me with the girl, and I can't do everything.'

'Is she sleeping?' I asked, before the two Laias could join
forces to kill him.

'I gave her Apiretal ten minutes ago,' he said, 'she seems
to have calmed down a bit.'

'I'll go look in on her,' I said.

'Go,' he said, 'and keep an eye on her to see if she wakes
up. I'll take a shower meantime.'

'I'm going through to Juan Pablo's room, OK?' said the Laia
from the Mossos d'Esquadra.

The two Laias headed for Juan Pablo's bedroom and I went
into Facundo's, where Alejandra was sleeping uneasily in her
cot. I walked around Facundo's bed and touched her forehead:
she was still burning. In her dreams, in the middle of a nightmare, the girl was delirious.

I looked into Juan Pablo's room: the two Laias had lifted up
the mattress and were rummaging around inside his socks.
I saw that Laia had put her slippers on the table, on top of a
pile of books. I helped them look. We didn't find anything.
We went into the living room, with one of the Laias carrying
her slippers, the other with Juan Pablo's laptop, which she
said she was going to take with her to search.

'I'd better go,' said the Laia with the laptop, looking at her
wristwatch, it was twelve-thirty. 'I've got a really early start
tomorrow,' she added.

'So now what?' I said.

'One of you should stay here,' she said to us both. And
then to me:

'If I manage to track down the Italian, I'll let you know,
buy yourself a cell phone first thing tomorrow and call me so
I've got the number.'

I said yes without telling her I didn't have any money, but something in my attitude gave me away.

'Here,' she said, giving me a fifty-euro note. 'A prepaid cell phone.'

She said goodbye to us both with a pair of kisses apiece.

'Keep your spirits up,' she said, from the door. 'I'll talk to some of my colleagues tomorrow and we'll find him, just see if we don't.'

She crouched down to say another goodbye to the dog, who had approached the door, thinking that the other Laia was also leaving, but the other Laia shut the door, from the inside, and said:

'I think we should talk.'

I walked back to the living room and Laia and the dog followed me. Facundo appeared with a towel tied around his waist, bare-chested, droplets of water trickling from his hair down his neck.

'Has the redhead gone?' he asked. 'So stunning, that redhead, Jesus, that's a nice piece of ass. But there's still enough to work with, how's about a threesome?'

'Seriously, man, you're such a moron,' said Laia.

'That was a joke, Laia,' Facundo replied, 'no sense of humor, these Catalans are so serious. Don't worry, girls, you'll see that shithead Juan Pablo will be back any moment, couldn't he have gone to Tarragona? Didn't he have a friend in Tarragona? Iván, I think his name was, he came here to the apartment one time.'

'He's not with him,' said Laia, 'I've called the other doctoral students already.'

I told Facundo I wanted to stay to sleep there, that I was going to stay, that someone had to be in the apartment in case Juan Pablo came back.

'Besides,' I said, 'Alejandra's still got a fever, she won't be able to go to school tomorrow, I'll stay with her.'

He said goodbye and headed for his room but came straight back.

'Vale, what are those stains in the hallway, shithead?'

I went with him to have a look.

'It was the dog,' I said, once I'd confirmed what I had suspected.

'Is the dog on her period?' he said.

'Dogs don't have periods,' I said, 'it's called proestrus, the dog's going into heat.'

'All the same to me,' he said, 'you're cleaning it up. And make sure the dog doesn't lie on the rug.'

I went back to the living room and saw Petanca sprawled on the rug under the center table. Laia had sat down on the sofa. I threw myself down next to her.

'You really believe I'm deceiving him?' she asked.

I said I didn't know, that to tell the truth, I didn't know anything anymore, and I closed my eyes and took in the first calm moment of the day. If Laia hadn't gone on jabbering away I'd have fallen asleep. She justified herself, arguing that she'd done it out of curiosity, saying Juan Pablo had been really insistent, that now she thought about it that insistence could actually be suspicious, but there's no way she could have suspected earlier, the idea that somebody wanted to pick her up because they'd been coerced by a criminal organization was frankly ludicrous. I allowed myself to be distracted thinking about the precision of that verb, coerced, which I'd never used in regular conversation, nor ever heard anybody else use, and I reflected on the way Spaniards use language, how that manner that so often offended me and which I felt was packed full of aggressions was based on an idea of precision that we Mexicans, and maybe Latin Americans in general, just don't know how to handle. When I returned from my metalinguistic reverie to Laia's chatter, she was accusing her friends of bearing part of the blame, for having judged her so unfairly, for having concluded that her behavior was a reaction to the pressure from her family, her father in particular. She said they acted so sophisticated but deep down they were total fucking behaviorists and that they were so annoying that she'd ended up giving Juan Pablo a chance.

'Don't I have a right to be curious?' she asked me, though it was a rhetorical question, as Juan Pablo would put it. 'You have no idea what a pain in the ass it is, man,' she went on, 'friendship ends up turning into this kind of repressive militancy, y'know? People don't want you to change, people just can't accept you turning into a different person from the one they imagined, even my uncle, the only person who protected me, turned against me, suddenly turned into this kind of commissar enforcer of homoerotic Stalinism.'

She fell silent a moment.

'Do you know what happened to my uncle?' she asked.

Without opening my eyes, I shook my head, side to side, to answer no. She returned to her subject of the difficulty of people not accepting her as she was, how hard it is to resist when everyone wants you to fulfill their expectations, how tired she was of all her acquaintances and relations and lovers, of friendship, professionals, they operated under the dialectics of conflict, and all of a sudden, for no particular reason, or without my understanding what the reason was, she started to talk about her teeth. I opened my eyes wide in shock.

'Yeah, man, don't pretend,' she said when she noticed my surprise, 'everyone says I should sort out my teeth, nobody understands why I didn't sort them out when it was the right time, in my adolescence, but I didn't want braces because they bothered me, it wasn't just the pain or the discomfort, but the very idea of having all that in my mouth, the wires and the plastic bands, making my breath rotten, I was a pretty badly behaved little girl, and my parents wanted to make me do it, they insisted so much that I turned it into a fetish for my rebellion, I built my whole identity around that rebellion. If that makes sense?'

'I guess,' I said, looking at her teeth, now she'd given me the perfect pretext to look at them blatantly.

I closed my eyes again to pull myself together. We stayed silent a little while, I could almost feel the heat of Laia's body on the sofa, I opened my left eye and saw she was looking at her cell phone. From that rug came the guttural sounds that Petanca made in her dreams, a kind of snoring. All we needed now was for the dog to have sleep apnea. Laia laughed.

'What's up?' I asked, thinking she had read something on her cell phone.

'The dog,' she said, 'my uncle says she talks.'

I opened my eyes, gave a stretch then leaned in closer to the dog to listen.

'That is what it sounds like,' I said, 'what do you figure she's saying?'

'Aydonbilivit,' said Laia.

'What?' I said.

'That's what my uncle says the dog's always saying, listen: *Aydonbilivit*. Ay-don-bili-vit. Do you get it?'

I looked at her like she was crazy.

'I'm joking, man,' she said 'It's a line my uncle always used to say to me and my sisters when we were little and we told him about some prank of ours: I don't believe it. I don't believe it, that's what my uncle used to say when he was acting surprised, to make our exploits seem bigger. My uncle has always been so affectionate with us.'

'How many sisters do you have?'

'Four.'

'Four? I thought you had more.'

'More? How many?'

'I don't know, like eleven. Weren't your parents Opus Dei?'

'Yeah, but my mother's polycystic. Luckily.'

I started thinking about the inconsistencies in Juan Pablo's novel that I'd discovered so far, how the dog's name was different, what the Pakistani looked like, how many sisters Laia had, those were three details that revealed that there was some novelistic intent to those pages, that Juan Pablo was acting with an awareness of the mechanisms of auto-fiction. The fact that Laia had eleven sisters in the novel, for example, seemed like a comic element to be exploited, very much in the style of the comedies of intrigue Juan Pablo liked so much, something he hadn't yet had the time to develop. Identifying the fictional side of the manuscript had the effect of calming me down, as if the fact of the novel being unfinished, left halfway, gave me some kind of guarantee that the author would be coming back to finish it. The dog woke up, disturbed by her own snoring.

'I better go,' said Laia.

'What are you going to tell your folks?' I asked her. 'About the dog, I mean, how are you going to explain that you found her?'

'They're the ones who're going to have to explain things to me,' she answered.

We got up and it looked like we were going to hug, but we stayed apart.

'Try to get some rest,' she said. 'Call me tomorrow so I've got your number and we can be in touch. I'll tell you what my dad said.'

'Wait,' I said, remembering that her number was in the other Laia's cell phone.

I went over to the coat stand where I'd hung my handbag and took out my notebook.

'Write your number in here,' I said.

I opened the notebook and found an empty page, under Laia's careful gaze.

'Is that a diary?'

'In theory,' I said, 'though actually it's got so much plot it's started looking more like a novel.'

She leaned on the dining-room table to jot down her number.

'Let's hope it has a happy ending,' she said.

'It will,' I replied. 'You'll see.'

EPILOGUE

My dear son, you must forgive your mother for not having written you in so long, your mother didn't forget she promised to write you every day, or at least once a week, but your mother hasn't had the heart to keep her promise. You know what they say, Juan, that life goes on, and your mother's had to pull through, make out like life goes on, your mother has had enough trouble with your father ever since he decided to retire and now he does nothing all day but stare out the window, as if that might bring you back.

Although your mother stopped writing you, son, you must know your mother hasn't lost hope that one day you'll read her messages, or that you have read them already, but that, for some reason your mother cannot understand, you can't or don't want to answer. But your mother isn't writing to make excuses, or to ask you for explanations, you know perfectly well your mother isn't that kind of mother, your mother's writing to tell you she's in Barcelona, your mother's come to Barcelona as the guest of a foundation to take part in a congress on missing persons.

If your mother must be honest with you, Juan, your mother must confess that accepting the invitation wasn't a good idea, your mother was tricked into coming. The people from the foundation never informed your mother that Valentina's family would be coming too, and your mother suffered the misfortune of being taken by surprise meeting them at the hotel. They all came, the father, the mother, the two brothers, taking advantage of the foundation to see Europe, you know those sorts of people would never get the chance to travel outside Mexico otherwise. They were moved, even happy, telling the reporters that the important thing was that nobody should forget Valentina, that her memory must be kept alive, and when your mother said that the only thing that mattered was you and Valentina reappearing nobody paid any attention. That's the sort of thing your mother has to put up with, son, the foolishness of people who think a lovely memory is the same thing as getting your child back. Your sister warned your mother, when she decided to turn down the invitation, that your mother shouldn't come to Barcelona if she wasn't ready to deal with things, your father wanted to come but his cardiologist forbade it, he said your father's health isn't up to strong emotions. Your mother felt she had to come because she thought that if she came, it would help to make you show up again, somehow, but now your mother knows it won't do any good. When your mother realized she had gotten herself into a conference about mass graves in Andalucía, listening to people asking for their relatives who died in the Spanish Civil War to be identified, you'll be wondering what this has to do with you and your mother. Nothing, son, not a thing. And your mother was also really troubled by the way they wanted to present your case, first of all doing it together with Valentina's and the story of a little Argentine girl who'd disappeared along with Valentina, they wanted to present you all as victims of transnational criminal networks operating under government protection, son, your mother might not understand much about politics and even less about the criminal world, but what your mother does know is that you can't say somebody's dead if you haven't found their lifeless body. Naturally, your mother refused to take part and escaped from the congress, your mother wasn't about to be part of such a spectacle, your mother would rather spend her time wandering the city, the streets where you walked, the Paseo de Gràcia which really is so gorgeous, the Ramblas which are so delightful, so picturesque, where your mother drank a sangria to your health, the Sagrada Familia, the Gaudí houses, all those winding little streets in the Barrio Gótico your mother wandered down and couldn't find her way out of again. Your mother also wanted to visit your apartment on Julio Verne, where there's now a German couple living who are very mistrusting and told your mother they'd never met you and didn't want to open the door.

At least your mother was able to meet Laia, your mother and Laia had a coffee in a very smart patisserie she chose, a charming, discreet little place, with proper china and long tablecloths, you can really tell Laia knows how to take care of your mother. So beautiful, that Laia, son, so lovely, your mother completely sees why you fell in love with her, though it wouldn't hurt for her to go to the dentist to get some braces put in. And so classy, that Laia, son, so polite, the first thing she did with your mother was apologize for her parents not having come, her mother was in New York for a medical checkup and her father hasn't had time for anything since he's become a government 'consejero', Laia explained to your mother that that's like being a minister. But Laia didn't come alone, son, she had one of her father's lawyers with her, a very discreet gentleman who sat at the next table to drink some tea and didn't interfere at all, and he brought a dog with him, the cutest, best-behaved little thing, she just went to sleep under the table and didn't make a fuss at all. Laia also apologized for the presence of the lawyer, and oh the way she apologized, son, without bowing her head, such a show of elegance, and your mother of course said don't worry, your mother understood perfectly that people of her class have to take care because there are a lot of opportunistic people about. A uniformed waiter, like something out of the nineteenth century, came over to take our order and your mother asked for a coffee with milk and a fruit tart that was so lovely I was sorry to eat it. Laia just asked them to bring her a glass of water – a glass of water! – there were so many delicious things on the menu and all she wanted was a glass of water, oh, my child, your mother still has so much to learn about European etiquette, your mother ended up feeling ashamed when they brought her coffee and dessert like she was some poor starveling who'd just come down from the Chiapas mountains, which is why your mother didn't even touch them, she left them untouched on the table so Laia would realize she wasn't that kind of person.

Oh, son, your mother knows you're going to show up again, you've got to, Juan, you've got to show up again and marry Laia and give your mother some European grandchildren. That's what your mother told Laia, your mother behaved with such dignity, so optimistically, so positively with her, your mother knows perfectly well that people like Laia shouldn't be troubled with squalid things, you should be so proud of your mother. Juan Pablo will show up, child, that's what your mother said to Laia, you'll see he'll show up and you'll marry him and you'll be happy together. She started crying, the poor little thing, heartbroken, you can see how much she misses you, you needn't worry, she'll be waiting for you when you come back.

A real ray of sunlight, that Laia, my child, she made it worthwhile your mother dealing with the foundation kicking up a fuss about her not having taken part in the meetings, as if it had been their way of making me pay for my plane ticket, and because your mother refused to sign a letter demanding that the Catalan and Spanish governments take responsibility for your disappearance and Valentina's. So rude, those people, it came as quite an unpleasant surprise to your mother discovering that even in Europe there are people with quite so little class, people who are common, coarse, uncultured. They took Valentina's family's side and really insisted your mother should sign the letter, they threatened to not pay your mother's hotel bill, but your mother stood firm. How's your mother supposed to sign a letter against the Catalan government now your father-in-law's a minister? They thought your mother had no principles, that she'd rather side with some riffraff.

But your mother was more put out than ever this morning, when she was having breakfast at the hotel and a lady came up to your mother and asked if she might sit down. Your mother didn't get a chance to say no because this whoever she was sat down without waiting for your mother to answer and she introduced herself saying she was the person who'd tried to talk to your mother several times on the phone, but your mother had refused, that she'd talked to your father when he came to Barcelona to look for you and he must have told your mother about her, that her name was Laia and she used to be a police officer, and she'd met Valentina and helped her to look for you when you disappeared. Of course your mother knew who she was, she was the person who'd filled your father's head with all kinds of nonsense, who came out with the story about how your disappearance was connected to your cousin Lorenzo's death, that apparently your cousin had gotten you involved with some criminals who laundered narco-trafficking money, ridiculous as you may think this is. That's what ended up embittering your father's character, son, you can't imagine what he was like when he came back from Barcelona, like a madman, he argued with your uncle

and aunt, he played along with that rude young man who
said you owed him twenty thousand pesos and just ended
up getting another hundred thousand taken off him, and he
even went to the prison to visit the driver who ran over your
cousin. Your mother doesn't mean to worry you, and she's
not blaming you for anything, son, but your father's not the
same anymore, your father's always been a difficult man but
now he's become impossible, locked away in his persecution
mania and in the conspiracy theories this woman put into his
head. Your mother requested that she please leave, that she
wasn't prepared to put up with these fantasies she was telling
everybody, this story about how Valentina was a heroine who
disappeared because she tried to save you. Your mother asked
her to leave politely, but these people have no manners, the
woman ignored your mother and started lecturing her, saying
she wasn't judging your mother for not wanting to face up
to the truth about what had happened, that she knew your
mother deep down was a good person who was in denial about
reality because she couldn't bear the pain of having lost you,
that your mother had the right to protect your memory and
the family's honor, but that your mother mustn't be selfish,
that your mother mustn't think only about you and your
family, your mother should also think about Valentina and the
little Argentinian girl, that if your mother went on refusing to
cooperate then those responsible would never be punished,
that this went beyond just you and your cousin Lorenzo, that
after all they'd been victims too. And the saddest part was the
little Argentinian girl, this woman dared to say this to your
mother as if the life of a girl just because she was small was
worth more than yours, and how the girl's only sin, she said,
had been that it was Valentina taking care of her, that Valentina
had been her babysitter. Honestly, who did this person think
she was to speak to your mother like this?! And she said it all

with such violent vehemence, Juan, your mother needed to use a positively superhuman effort not to throw the yogurt she was eating in her face, your mother really can't understand how your father believed anything she said, the woman's crazy, and it's not enough for your father to know she was even thrown off the police force, that the police had psychiatric tests done and it turned out she had fits of psychosis, of paranoia, or megalomania and who knows what else, that this so-called proof she had, a novel you had apparently been writing and where you described everything that happened, well, she'd never actually shown it to them, she said it'd been stolen. That's what your mother was told by the Catalan chief of police, your father got so insistent, he was bothering the embassy and the consulate so much that the chief of police called up your mother in person to tell her this woman was unbalanced, that he understood and respected the fact we were desperate, but that the worst thing we could possibly do would be to place our trust in a person who just wanted to take advantage of our pain. And he explained to your mother that there wasn't even enough in this woman's accusations for them to launch an investigation, that this woman had said they had to find a Chinese man, and she didn't even know what this Chinese was called, can you imagine, a Chinese man when there are billions of Chinese in the world, all just identical, and that the whole thing was like that, that she had no details about anything, that it was all the vaguest accusations, and that the only person she'd been able to identify had been an Italian tramp who'd died of a heroin overdose before you and Valentina disappeared. The chief of police said there's currently an ongoing investigation into your disappearance anyway, that the Catalan police would do everything they could to find you, though there are a lot of people who never reappear and that also doesn't mean they've died, people are strange, the chief of police said to your mother, we'll never understand why there are people who say they're going out to buy cigarettes, or to walk the dog, and never come back. Your mother found him a very sensible man, and your father just keeps on insulting him, accusing him of covering up some fantasy or other, and even Laia's father!, just as well Laia's father is a very understanding man, otherwise he would have reported your father for defamation and for all the slanders he tells any journalist he can get his hands on.

Your mother asked this woman to stop, she explained that your mother was well aware of her ravings, that the chief of police had been kind enough to warn her. This woman grabbed hold of your mother's hands, son, totally deranged, and asked her please to believe her, she confessed that she felt guilty for not having paid attention to Valentina, for not having realized in time that she really was in danger. Your mother thought enough was enough, this woman was really going too far now, and she got up and went to her room without making a scene, your mother didn't want to give her the satisfaction of seeing your mother lose her composure.

I'm sorry, my child, that your mother is telling you these awful things, your mother wanted to write to tell you that in spite of everything it's been lovely coming to Barcelona, to tell you that your mother knows you're going to show up, that your mother has never lost hope, that your mother knows stories are never finished till you get to the end, that you still have a lot to live for, you can't abandon your story halfway, son, these things need an ending, a happy ending, or an unhappy one, but an ending. And you can't abandon your story halfway. And if you never do come back, son, if your mother never sees you again, Juan Pablo, at least your mother will be left with the consolation of knowing you spent your last days in a city as beautiful as this one.

To Andreia, Cristina, Maricarmen, La Flaca, Marifer, Iván, Chico, Jorge and Manuel (at the Universidad Autónoma in Barcelona), to Mousie, Cristian, Fito and Manolo (in Julio Verne), to Paula, Tere, Ana, María and Topi (at the Universidad Veracruzana), to Manuel and Javier (in Guadalajara) and to Rolando and the Villalobos Alva family (in Lagos de Moreno). They alone know how much truth these pages contain. I don't expect anyone to believe me.

Valentina's diary quotes passages from Sergio Pitol's 'Diary from Escudillers', which appears in The Art of Flight. *Some of the lines spoken by Alejandra are taken from poetry by Alejandra Pizarnik and Oliverio Girondo.*

Apologies in advance to my mother in case any misguided reader finds themselves thinking that Juan Pablo Villalobos's mother in this novel bears any resemblance to her. I'm sorry, Mamá.

This novel wouldn't exist were it not for a conversation I had with Jordi Soler on the corner of Calle Bailén and Calle Consell de Cent, one autumn afternoon. I owe you a novel, Jordi.

A million thanks to Andreia Moroni, Cristina Bartolomé, Teresa García Díaz, Paula Casasa, Javier Villa, Iván Díaz Sancho and Aníbal Crístobo, whose assessments of the manuscript of this novel helped to make it significantly better.

WARNING: CONTAINS LANGUAGE

A TRANSLATOR'S AFTERWORD

This novel is tricky.

Good and interesting novels usually are, of course. But in normal circumstances we translators are expected to keep our problems to ourselves; whereas here I have a chance to grumble about a writer, *in public*. What a treat! So, what specifically made this book troublesome for its translator?

Well, the big things were obvious even in my quick first draft.

As you will have discovered, the novel is told in four voices, each quite distinct. And each new voice poses different problems for a translator, rather the way each new writer does.

Juan Pablo's cousin Lorenzo is wilder in his speech (and more untethered in his thoughts) than the others. His voice is vulgar and repetitive, sometimes grammatically 'non-standard' – a high-risk voice that threatens to become slightly wearing but should be energetic enough to carry you through his three sections. Valentina is mostly measured, mostly quite correct, initially poised, and cool. (I've even let her have a 'whom' and a semicolon at one point; cousin Lorenzo would *never* get a semicolon.) Juan Pablo's mother is relatively well-spoken (strictly no expletives), but his mother is idiosyncratic, too, a voice that seems to run on and on, as his mother can't seem to stop 'talking'. I deleted a lot of his mother's commas to help keep this moving. It's easy to 'hear' his mother as you read, I think.

Those parts of the story told by Juan Pablo himself, meanwhile, are the most variable, not only because his own voice varies (from academic explanatory smugness to different degrees of life-threatening panicky anxiety), but also because his story is populated by so many other very lively voices – Facundo, Chucky, Ahmed, the lawyer, Laia, the Chinaman, Sketch, Babe, and so on. Voice is so much of this book; not least because the characters draw attention to their language use so conspicuously – they explicitly compare the precision with which different people deploy language, and Valentina herself jokes disparagingly about the author's narrative voice. (You know you're in trouble when your characters turn on you and start doing lit crit on your work.)

Within these different personalized voices, we have a book of fundamentally different Spanishes, too. Juan Pablo, his family and Valentina are Mexican; he's living in Spain; his flatmates are from Argentina. The author also draws attention regularly to Spanish/Catalan switches, we have characters using US and UK 'English', a Brazilian speaking an English-Spanish hybrid, Jimmy with a Spanish that's Italian-leaning, and so on. So what the hell sort of English language will they be speaking in the translation?

The first part of an answer to that question is to say that the baseline I've used is US English, rather than my own UK. Spellings, vocabulary, idioms, all lean towards the American. (That inflection is my habit when translating Latin Americans: very broadly, I tend to imagine notional Anglophone Spaniards using mobiles, notional Anglophone Mexicans using cell phones.) That's not to say the characters are meant to fool you into thinking they are themselves Americans, but at least an American reader mustn't find herself wondering mid-novel why everybody is suddenly

Bertie Wooster.* (My friend Sean read the final manuscript and kindly rescued me from many particularly aggressive Anglo-Anglicisms that had taken root when I wasn't paying attention.) But within this general broad-brush American-ish inclination, I needed marked distinctions in the way characters talk – distinctions to which the characters themselves so often draw attention.

I couldn't reasonably use different specific Englishes to represent the assorted Spanishes – making Juan Pablo an Australian in New York with Glaswegian flatmates, say, would be intolerable to any reader – so what we have instead are tiny markers, linguistic idiosyncrasies used only by certain groups and not others. This is most noticeable with the swearing, which I'll come to later, but all manner of identifying verbal tics fulfil this function. Some tics are personal (Babe calls everyone *babe*, obviously), but many are geographical. For one example, the word *man* punctuates a lot of dialogue, but only the dialogue of the Spaniards/Catalans (or other long-term Barcelona residents) – roughly equivalent to the original book's *tio/tia*, it serves to unite all those characters as a group, excluding others, who occasionally mock it. We think the *So like* punctuating Juan Pablo's speech is an individual fingerprint, but turns out it's pan-Mexican. Either way, it must be made to sound both odd and natural.

Much of the narrative and almost all the dialogue is quite casual, but this too raises the problem of how to make characters sound demotic without locating them anywhere too specific. There's quite a lot of contraction and lazy dropped syllables, and things like *you got to* for *you've got to*, which is recognizably natural speech without sounding *specifically* like

---

* I am now contemplating the pleasing possibilities of a novel in which one character greets another with a jaunty 'What ho, motherfucker!', but sadly it is not to be this novel.

it's from Dublin or Cape Town or Baltimore. (The characters may be speaking with English words here, but only in the sleight-of-hand way a translation requires you to pretend not to notice – they are *really* speaking Spanish, in Spain, to other Spanish speakers; you only *think* you've been hearing them talk English. Don't be fooled.)

Juan Pablo and Valentina know to say 'Ahmed and I went' correctly (and she doesn't split her infinitives), but they lapse occasionally (Juan Pablo has a 'me and Ahmed went' at a moment of great crisis). Lorenzo's syntax is sometimes eccentric, but again, not in a way that positions him anywhere you could pin down geographically. The translator Anthea Bell used the phrase 'non-specific demotic' to describe what we are constantly trying to create for the voices of our translated characters. Casual speech is so place-based, especially for a language like English with so much regional variation, that the *non-specific* isn't always easy to come by.

But that wasn't the half of it. Even at the first-draft stage, the book posed plenty of other problems, too, requiring some across-the-board solutions.

The dialogue is mostly unmarked, yet it must somehow be quite clear which character is speaking at any time. When a reader like you sees *Why? What do you mean?*, they need to know instantly whether this is two questions by one speaker, or one question responding to another question. Once the first typeset proofs arrived, I found myself occasionally adding or removing a word or two just to nudge a sentence over a line so it would break at a point that would make this as clear as possible. Ridiculous, I know. I don't expect anyone to believe me.

Even the general tense of the narrative is harder to handle than you might think. The book shifts between the narrative past tense and the present, and it's not always clear why the change happens. It's something you'll find in Spanish-language writing not infrequently, but where many translations standardize this sort of thing (assuming it's not especially purposeful, so should just be tidied up), I decided to preserve some version of it – it suits a certain storytelling mode, I think. Look, for example, at the sharp shift at the end of page 135. (Did it trouble you when you were reading? I'm guessing/hoping not.) I was led by the new English voices telling the story, and hope it worked.

Given all the troubles it had threatened to cause, my first draft of this book came quite fast, actually. It was bad, certainly, but at least fast. That rather surprised me! So anyway, I get that first draft done, and I'm busily working on my edits when this guy comes up to me and says 'Whoa, you've just changed tenses right in the middle of a paragraph!' 'Yeah,' I say presently, 'it happens a lot.'

Anyway, where was I . . .

Yeah, so like . . . – as Juan Pablo would say – so I then edited my draft in detail as always, but unusually in this case working voice by voice – editing all of Lorenzo's chapters together, all the mother's chapters together, etc. – to get as much coherence as I could. I started being able to hear them quite clearly at that stage. But there were still problems, so that was the point I brought the author in, and we had a Skype chat, an hour and a half or thereabouts, talking mostly about the swearing (I *will* get to that), but about other things, too. Villalobos' generously helped me understand certain things I'd found difficult; he sympathized over the book's particular translational challenges; and he revealed which of the many cultural references he had simply invented so there was really no point my spending any

---

* For the purposes of this afterword, I'm calling the author 'Villalobos' rather than 'Juan Pablo' so as to avoid any confusion with the character. They are not, of course, the same person. (Oh no, not at all.)

more time trying to trawl around to find that Harrison Ford movie quote because it *doesn't really exist.*

Plenty of the book's cultural references *are* real things, of course; but these were mostly easy to preserve by smuggling in a little extra info – a standard translator's trick. Villalobos's 'We met at Gandhi' becomes my 'We met at the Gandhi bookstore' – every Mexican reader would know it's a bookstore chain, too many English readers would unhelpfully picture not a Mexican bookshop but an Indian man in a dhoti. (Unless they are from Sandy in Bedfordshire, where my friends and I have often *met at the Gandhi*, a local Indian restaurant. Yep, *the Sandy Gandhi*. I don't expect etc.)

Most other cultural specifics, I decided, a reader can guess from context without too much help from me. Look, for example, at page 17 – most Anglophones today know what *tacos* are, they can guess from context that *Sinaloa* is a place, that *pescado zarandeado* is a food. Villalobos's *palapa* has become my *palapa hut*, just in case you don't know that one. (Also note on the page in question my insistent lack of italics for any of these 'foreign' words. That's one of the reasons for the unconventional-but-deliberate accent on the word máte, on page 32, but I won't go into that here. Even I have my limits.) There are dozens of mostly Hispanophone writers referenced all over this book, who likewise remain unaltered, and unglossed – you either know them or you don't, and frankly I don't much care either way. (Though by the way, for the two months I was working on this book, my Word software had an 'Ibargüengoitia' shortcut so I wouldn't have to relearn where to put that umlaut three times a day. It also had some quite lively language added to its dictionary, more of which anon.)

Translators are, I've always believed, naturally attracted to difficulty. The translation challenges in Villalobos's delightful work are themselves delightful – I don't expect anyone to feel sorry for me – but challenges they are, all the same. I've always been a fan of Rosalind Harvey's (she's Villalobos's usual translator) but my admiration only increased as I made my own attempts to translate this book and keep it alive and sparkling.

In my first draft I'd skipped over any particularly thorny problems, so those had to be filled in now, too; sometimes with the author's help, occasionally with recourse to the translator hive mind. There was wordplay to resolve (the Ed Krusher Foundation, pesky bed-buggers, etc.), and a lot of it, some very funny; and there were countless little bits of playful linguistic cleverness, which I fully accept may have been trivial, incidental, but every one of which I stubbornly wanted to preserve if at all possible.

Then there was that one nifty little moment of deliberate language-play that the author said was clearly *impossible* to translate and just not to bother trying to find an equivalent, which of course made me all the more determined to find a solution. (Did he say that on purpose, I wonder? He's a translator himself so he knows how our minds work.) This head-scratcher was indeed resolved rather cleverly thanks to a conversation with my friend Victor. In truth it's the tiniest little thing in the original, and just as subtle in the translation (it's on page 243; and you almost certainly didn't even notice it, and probably can't identify it even now), but I feel quite smug that it's there.

Finally – yes – the swearing. Oh yes, the fucking, fucking swearing. This was a problem. Well, dozens, hundreds of problems.

The language used by the characters of *No voy a pedirle a nadie que me crea* is rich and colourful. Like so much colourful language it is simultaneously relaxed, light-hearted, trivial on the one hand and also really quite offensive if you stop to worry about it – casually misogynist, homophobic, ableist and racist by turns. But translators, like writers, cannot be precious about language – for all the discomfort, we need to be able to use it however it's needed to allow us to be truthful about how our characters talk. As this transnational range of characters demonstrates, swearing varies from place to place (every character swears slightly differently to every other); our sensitivities to this language are culturally specific, too. A word like *cunt* is as strong as they come, but even that is only taboo to different degrees depending where you're reading from.

At the risk of generalizing, Mexicans swear ever so well. There are expletives that exist only in Mexican, some of them marvellously versatile. English swearing doesn't map neatly onto it, and besides, we are stuck in this book with that extra problem of Mexican swearing rubbing up against Argentine swearing, Spanish swearing, etc., each one sharp and distinct. But if I want the *effect* of the swearing in my text to be just the same as in Villalobos's original, WT actual F do I do?

The first step, as so often with translation, was to recognize and accept the lack of equivalence. There are some cases where I could be consistent – *gilipollas* in the original almost always becomes *jerk* in mine, say, and *pendejo* is usually *asshole*. But most required flexibility.

Fuck was always going to be a big part of any solution, as the most versatile of English words. A noun, a verb, part of all kinds of compounds, an exclamation. A useful word to a translator? Oh, fuck yeah. Abso-fucking-*lutely*. Mexican Spanish uses countless variations on *chingada*; my variations of *fuck* would serve many of those purposes well. Though in the English, additional variety in the swearing often came not from the expletives themselves but from the intensifiers – what if the character isn't just a motherfucker, but a titanic, *world-class* motherfucker? Seriously, man, what a genuine, gold-plated, class-A, 360-degree, industrial-strength, mega-weapons-grade *fuck!*

Ah, so many beautiful possibilities. Oh, and occasionally *What the fuck?* becomes *What the ungodly fuck?* Or *the unholy fuck?* And I mean, honestly, *Jesus fucking whatever!* – because there's a religious note to some of the Spanish swearing, so it's worth nodding to a bit of that.

Fuck and variants thereof appear a glorious 269 times in my translation.* Also, since you asked: *dick/dickhead* 63 times (though 7 of the *dickheads* are in one sentence). I've allowed myself just one usage of *cunt* (following a late cull – even at final proof stage there were 32), but the book does boast an impressive 100 *assholes*. (Oh, also *dipshit* just a couple of times, because it's a word I love.) But these instances are not like for like – my swearing isn't always in the same place as the swearing in the original, and sometimes my more colourful language replaces something quite tame from Villalobos, or vice versa. Again, this is about making the voice work line by line, and a lot changed in my last edit, when I felt a sentence just needed an extra emphatic beat, or a bit of weight with a good Anglo-Saxon syllable to land on at the end. As I said, it's the cumulative effect I'm trying to preserve, and the effect of swearing on the balance of a sentence is often about rhythm as much as anything else, so yeah. Fuck. The swearing is often a vector for the humour – humour itself being similarly dependent on hitting just the right number of syllables.

The hive-mind helped here, too. At a meeting at this year's London Book Fair, I was describing my expletive challenge – how to make lively swearing for characters who each have

---

* This may seem like a lot, but I have recently been impressed by Sophie Hughes's remarkable translation of Fernanda Melchor's *Hurricane Season*, which has a far higher tally of fucks per thousand words. Or a higher 'f/k', as we in the trade will henceforth call it.

quite distinctive language but which the reader mustn't be able to identify as attached to particular Anglophone localities – to an eminent member of the British book world. He said, 'Oh, I learned the word *everycunt* yesterday, isn't it great?' Yes, *everycunt* was indeed just what I was looking for – obviously offensive but also obviously casual, easily understood yet hard to locate anywhere in particular. So several variations on that word (*anyfucker, everyfucker*, etc.) appear in this book. (I also passed that word on to another grateful friend similarly working on a contemporary Mexican novel who I hope might use it, too. We translators compare notes about this sort of thing a lot. It's a strange job.) I did, incidentally, allow myself to leave just one instance of just one Spanish insult – there's a lone *pendejo* on page 102, a sort of trace tribute to the swearing of the original – but everything else had to go.

About a week before my deadline, I had a full manuscript with only the swearing left to weave into it. A few days later, that was also done – with just two exceptions. My two final problems were tiny but annoyingly recurring ones, and they came from the voices of two characters: Facundo and Lorenzo, serial troublemakers both.

Facundo's go-to word is 'shithead'; no one else in the book uses it, but he does and so often that I imagine it annoyed you as you were reading? (Good.) It stands in for the Argentine *boludo/boluda*, which is so hard-working in Argentine Spanish – it's used both as a casual vocative (as lightly as you might call somebody 'dude') and as an actual insult. Hence *Hey, boludo, don't be such a boludo, boludo.* It's overused sufficiently by this particular character that others – Valentina especially – mock him for it. Upon extensive consultation (friends, editors, particularly profuse swearers, Argentinians, etc.), I felt *shithead* would do everything that's needed; but it's clearly a weightier, more conspicuous word than *boludo*, so I've used it just a touch more sparingly. (The exchange rate, as calculated with Villalobos on our Skype call, currently stands at: 98 *boludos* = 84 *shitheads*.)

Lorenzo refers to Juan Pablo as his *pinche primo* – *primo* being cousin, *pinche* being, well . . . In other parts of the book *pinche* is just a *damn* or a *fucking* to colour a noun. (*Pinche idiota. Pinche perro. Pinche something-else*.) In this case, Villalobos explained he wanted Lorenzo to be patronizing to his cousin, but also kind of affectionate. He doesn't dislike him, just thinks he's a kind of stupid naive kid. So *pinche primo* became *my dumbass little cuz* in the first instances, shortening to *little cuz* for most instances (because *my dumbass little cuz* is just so much wordier, heavier than *pinche primo*) with an occasional 'dumbass' dropped back in every once in a while to remind the reader of the tone in which it's to be read.

As Juan Pablo's mother would say, ah look, my reader, I do seem to have written an afterword that is far too long, you must forgive me, I don't want you to go thinking your translator is just complaining because you know that's not the kind of translator he is, your translator loves the book really even if it makes him worry and sends his blood sugar through the roof. It's just that, well, some people just don't appreciate that translation is never simple, even when it looks it. Least of all in a book that's frankly so insistent on causing linguistic trouble like the ones by that tricky Juan Pablo Villalobos.

Honestly, *pinche* novelists . . .

DANIEL HAHN
LEWES, SEPTEMBER 2019

Dear readers,

As well as relying on bookshop sales, And Other Stories relies on subscriptions from people like you for many of our books, whose stories other publishers often consider too risky to take on.

Our subscribers don't just make the books physically happen. They also help us approach booksellers, because we can demonstrate that our books already have readers and fans. And they give us the security to publish in line with our values, which are collaborative, imaginative and 'shamelessly literary'.

All of our subscribers:

- receive a first-edition copy of each of the books they subscribe to
- are thanked by name at the end of our subscriber-supported books
- receive little extras from us by way of thank you, for example: postcards created by our authors

BECOME A SUBSCRIBER, OR GIVE A SUBSCRIPTION TO A FRIEND

Visit andotherstories.org/subscriptions to help make our books happen. You can subscribe to books we're in the process of making. To purchase books we have already published, we urge you to support your local or favourite bookshop and order directly from them – the often unsung heroes of publishing.

OTHER WAYS TO GET INVOLVED

If you'd like to know about upcoming events and reading groups (our foreign-language reading groups help us choose books to publish, for example) you can:

- join our mailing list at: andotherstories.org
- follow us on Twitter: @andothertweets
- join us on Facebook: facebook.com/AndOtherStoriesBooks
- admire our books on Instagram: @andotherpics
- follow our blog: andotherstories.org/ampersand

CURRENT & UPCOMING BOOKS

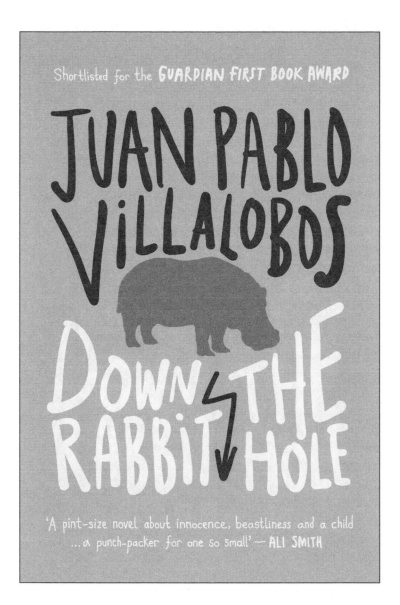

JUAN PABLO VILLALOBOS

DOWN THE RABBIT HOLE

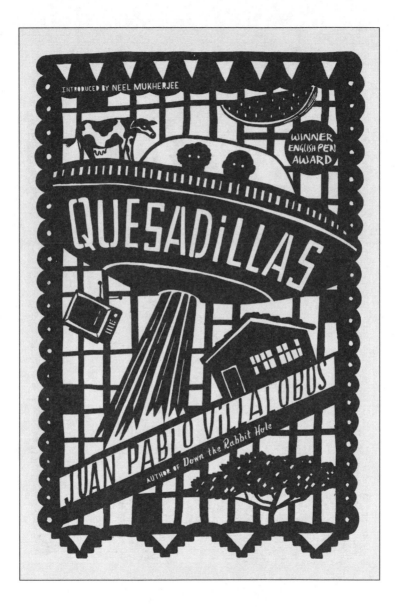

INTRODUCED BY NEEL MUKHERJEE

WINNER
ENGLISH PEN
AWARD

QUESADILLAS

JUAN PABLO VILLALOBOS
AUTHOR OF *Down the Rabbit Hole*

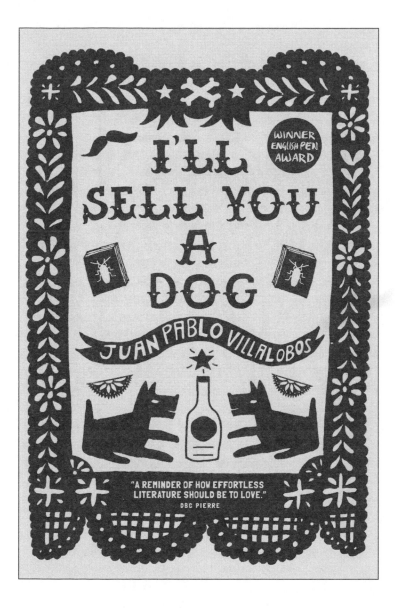

WINNER
ENGLISH PEN
AWARD

I'LL
SELL YOU
A
DOG

JUAN PABLO VILLALOBOS

"A REMINDER OF HOW EFFORTLESS
LITERATURE SHOULD BE TO LOVE."
DBC PIERRE